The
SEASON

The
SEASON

Jonah Lisa Dyer & Stephen Dyer

Viking

Viking

An imprint of Penguin Random House LLC

375 Hudson Street

New York, New York 10014

First published in the United States of America by Viking,

an imprint of Penguin Random House LLC, 2016

LIBRARY OF CONGRESS CATALOGING-IN-PUBLICATION DATA IS AVAILABLE.

ISBN: 978-0-451-47634-0

Printed in the U.S.A.   Book design by Nancy Brennan   Set in Granjon

1 3 5 7 9 10 8 6 4 2

Visit us at www.penguin.com

For our dads, who kept the lights on for a long time.

One

In Which Megan Learns Why It's Called a Sucker Punch

DOWN A GOAL IN INJURY TIME LACHELLE BEGAN A buildup inside midfield, passing it down to Mariah, who fed Lindsay in the right corner. Lindsay beat her girl to the end line, then fired a low cross toward the goal mouth. Cat streaked in, carried her defender and the goalie's attention, and then dummied it—let the ball go through her legs untouched. It was beautifully done, a play we had worked on endlessly. I was now just eight yards out; the wide-open net yawned. All I had to do was ease it home. But overeager, with visions of my highlight reel playing in my head, I hammered it. The extra oomph lifted the ball—and it caromed off the crossbar and out of bounds.

The crowd groaned and I stood there—gutted. I had just missed a gimme that would have tied our first conference game. *Well done, Megan*, I thought. *Well done.* A minute later the whistle blew. University of Oklahoma 2, Southern Methodist University 1.

I kicked over the watercooler, and was working my way through the sideline chairs when Coach Nash found me.

"Hey, stop that!" she yelled. She frowned, and her disappointment washed over me. "What's the lesson?"

"Don't be a freaking moron?" I asked.

"Composure," she said to me for the nine hundredth time in the past year. "No matter the moment, you have to keep your head, execute under pressure. Consistently good is far better than occasionally brilliant."

"I'm sorry," I said.

"I'm not interested in your apology." Ouch.

"I let everybody down," I said, hanging my head.

"Yes. You did." Ouch again. But now she lifted my head and looked directly in my eyes. "Now listen—you are going to score a ton of goals for us this year." Her tone softened as she moved easily from Marine Corps drill sergeant to mother hen. "It's going to all come together, okay?"

"Okay." I nodded again and she gave me a hug.

"Short memory—and get that looked at." She motioned at the gash on my shin.

"Uh-huh," I replied, still feeling like someone had shot my dog.

"I'll see you on Monday."

Now Cat shuffled over. Catalina Esmerelda Graciela "Cat" Martinez was my best friend on the team, my wingman, and the only one brave enough to approach me under the circumstances. We had known each other since we were twelve and had played Club Soccer together for the DeSoto

Bobcats—now we were Ponies. I went to her quinceañera and famously destroyed her piñata with my first whack. They found candy all the way down the street.

"Come on, choker," she said, putting her arm around me. I laughed. As always it was just the right thing to say.

"You go. I want to sulk." Now she laughed.

"All right. You need a hankie or something?"

"Nah—I got my sleeve."

"We're on for Tuesday night, yeah?" Tuesday was TV night, sacred friend time.

"Of course," I said as she walked toward the locker room.

"Text me later!" she called out over her shoulder.

With everyone gone I sat down and examined my shin. Blood oozed along the entire ridge of welted skin. Another scar—and so little to show for it. In soccer, real scoring chances are rare, and my job as a striker was to make good on them. My failure today cost us a very valuable point. I picked some grass out of the cut, squinted over the edge of Westcott Field into the late August sun, and wondered how things could get any worse.

I wasn't kept waiting long.

"Hey."

I looked up to see my sister, Julia. She was taller and prettier than me, with blonde hair, startling light blue eyes, and creamy, blemish-free skin. Few would guess that we were twins—the clear result of two eggs, not one.

"You see the game?"

She nodded, but stayed several feet away. "Hate to pile

on, but I thought you might want to see this."

Julia handed me her phone, the browser open to *The Dallas Morning News*.

Bluebonnet Club Announces 2016 Debutantes, the headline read. I scrolled through the article. Blah blah blah *proud to announce Ashley Harriet Abernathy, Lauren Eloise Battle, Ashley Diann Kohlberg, Margaret Abigail Lucas, Julia Scott McKnight, Megan Lucille McKnight, Sydney Jane Pennybacker . . .*

Wait, *Megan Lucille McKnight*?! There must be some mistake, because that was ME!

"Did—did Mom call you?" I asked.

"Nope."

"Text?"

Julia shook her head. I wanted to splutter in disbelief. To scream, to rage, to protest violently. But my mother was thirty miles away at the ranch. I read on.

At the bottom were the pictures. Seven toothy, varnished girls soon to take their anointed places in the pantheon of Bluebonnet debutantes, that rare and coveted role in a tradition that dated all the way back to 1882, as Mom had so often reminded us. My picture was a real doozy, taken as an olive branch to her after she complained for years that the only photos she had showed me posing on one knee beside a soccer ball.

For this timeless memento she'd spared no expense. She had hired a stylist, bullied me into a low-cut Stella McCartney, and chosen a photographer who insisted on shooting in the gloaming, down amongst the crepe myrtles along Turtle Creek. Resting my hand oh-so-casually on a branch, smiling at a hundred miles an hour, I looked like a hick who'd lucked into a makeover coupon. Never in my worst nightmares had I imagined it would pop up a year later in the city's most widely read newspaper, beneath an announcement for a virgin auction.

"Maybe it's a mistake?" I said hopefully, handing back her phone. Julia kept silent. She had passed AP calculus as a sophomore in high school and was majoring in structural engineering. Like a lot of really smart girls, she learned early that silence was often a wise tactic.

"All right," I said. "I'll shower and we'll go see what she has to say for herself."

Julia smiled, a tad too brightly.

"I'll make popcorn," she said.

⁘

Julia drove so I could elevate my leg. No stitches required, but the trainers rinsed it liberally with hydrogen peroxide, squirted some Neosporin in, and applied a gauze bandage, telling me to keep it up for a while to stem the bleeding. So on the half-hour drive from Dallas to the ranch, I propped my leg on the dashboard and multitasked by staring out the window and fretting about why my mother would want to ruin my life. Julia, still in the throes of her breakup from her longtime boyfriend Tyler, chose Tame Impala for the gloomy soundtrack. The only thing missing was rain.

It is a truth universally acknowledged that all daughters eventually conclude their mothers are insane, and though I had long heard the rattle of loose nuts and screws in Lucy McKnight's head, even for her this challenged belief. I simply wasn't debutante material. Not even close. And I'm not being modest. I wore faded Wranglers, old T-shirts, and Ropers, except when I mixed it up with baggy nylon shorts and flip-flops. I bought Hanes sports bras and cotton panties in saver packs. I had freckles and a farmer's tan, and my hair, best described as "brown," was forever in a ponytail, except during practice and games when I added an Alex Morgan headband crafted from pink trainer's tape. My lips were permanently chapped, as I lived in a state of semi-dehydration, and my nails were ragged and dirty. My muscular legs were a war zone, and my upper body was lean as a stewing chicken from thousands of hours running in the Texas sun.

"She's finally gone full-on, bat-shit crazy," I said to Julia, who pursed her lips, maintained her silence, and kept her eyes on the road.

Now Julia as a debutante, that made some sense. She was delicate as a Japanese sliding door, and boys fell for her like leaves in the fall—by the thousands. Frankly she was precisely the kind of girl I might have sneered at and despised—a Pi Phi, well-dressed, well-mannered, a successful student, and so good at all those girlie things I could never master, like batting her eyelashes, applying makeup, and flirting. But as she was my only sister and my womb mate, I loved her intensely, and woe to those who threatened her.

She took Exit 47, the only exit on South I-35 we ever took, and turned left onto FM 89. Another mile and we would be at the ranch. When I saw the edge of the buck'n'rail fence that marked the western boundary of the Aberdeen, I set my leg down gently and prepared for battle.

∂e᠎∿

"MOM!" I thundered. "MOMMMM!"

No answer. I stood in the front hallway of the main house. *She's hiding*, I thought, *afraid to show herself. Coward.*

Julia, purse hooked over her arm, came in behind me. She was clearly entertained, like a kid watching floats at an Independence Day parade. I scowled and went around the staircase, down the hallway, and through Dad's closed study door like the Germans through Belgium.

When the door hit the wall he bolted upright.

"Hey," he said, blinking. A college football game played on the TV. Bless his heart, he had been napping on the couch. His dusty boots were under the coffee table.

"Something you'd like to tell me, Dad?" I demanded.

"No," he said, slowly. Julia, content to drift in my wake, wandered in behind me.

"You know, when you offer your daughter up for sale, the polite thing to do is to tell her."

Ahh, now he remembered. He ran his hand through his hair, bought a moment. At forty-six, he had hair that was still tawny and full, with just a swatch of gray at the temples.

A lifetime of squinting in the sun had seared in creases around his hazel eyes, but he was still boyish and handsome. Fit too—the daily grind of cutting cattle on horseback kept him rangy and tough as a fence post. Angus McKnight III looked like exactly what he was—a working cowboy.

"Honey, you are not being offered up for sale, and I was as surprised as you were about the announcement."

"I doubt that," I said, giving no ground. Dad tried his most sympathetic look on Julia, hoping for support.

"Of course we were going to tell you—" Footsteps in the hallway. Dad looked over my shoulder. Could it be the cavalry? Indeed.

My mother, Lucy McKnight, strolled into the study, pulling off her cloth gardening gloves. An inch taller than me at five foot eight, she was still striking, if a little soft around the edges. She was just at that age when women consider the benefits of plastic surgery, and I knew her thinking ran to sooner rather than later, for two reasons. First, you should take your car to the mechanic the minute you hear the engine knock, and second, if done right you might just pass it off on a change in diet and a new personal trainer.

Mom oozed style, and today she managed in that magical, mysterious way only some women can to make jeans, a blue cotton shirt, and a sun hat seem like an ensemble from the Neiman Marcus spring catalog.

"Is that a new purse, Julia?" Mom asked.

"Megan was just asking about—"

"I know why she's here, Angus," she said, then turned back to me. "I apologize for you finding out this way. Of course we were planning to tell you this weekend; I had no idea it would run in the paper today. Still, no matter—it's done and settled."

"But I told you *just last week* I didn't want to debut. Ever. Remember?"

"I took your view into account," she said mildly, "but I don't think you understand that this is truly a once-in-a-lifetime opportunity you simply cannot pass up."

"Not sure if you've noticed, but with school, practice, and games, my plate is full."

"I considered that, but making a debut is draining both physically and emotionally, and you need to be at your best. I suggest you take the fall off from soccer."

Good Lord, this was worse than I thought. I tried to stem the molten anger gurgling inside on its way to full volcanic expression.

"Mom, if you think I would take off soccer to waltz and have high tea, you're more than mistaken—you're demented."

"I understand your feelings—"

"No, you don't," I snapped.

"I am asking for one season out of what, twenty?"

"You're asking for one year out of four of college eligibility. And any chance I have at making the national team."

Her pitying look said it all, but she banged the nail home anyway.

"Sweetie, you're twenty years old. I think that ship has sailed."

"I was invited to the regional camp last year!" I had gone to Kansas City for three weeks the previous summer to audition for the Under-20 Women's National Team, along with about two hundred other girls. Suffice it to say that it was a humbling experience and a quick trip home.

"I know that, current feelings excepted, you will learn so much, grow so much, and make memories you'll cherish for the rest of your life."

"Cherish?" I said. "Learning to match my shoes with my purse? To use *divine* in a sentence?"

"There's far more to it than fashion and manners," she said carefully, "though it will be a great advantage to you to work on both."

"No. It won't. Because I'm not doing it. You want to send me out dressed like a poodle to parties with cash prizes for 'Best Idle Chatter' and 'Most Vacant Smile.' Where I'll be forced to dance with boys I don't like and be nice to a whole slew of people I don't know. And you want me to give up a year of soccer for the privilege?"

I paused, took a deep breath.

"Clearly decades of coloring your hair and chugging SlimFast have taken a toll," I said.

Silence. A step over the line, I realized, as her eyes narrowed and her jaw clenched and her face turned a dark crimson.

"Nobody likes a smart-ass, Megan."

"I do," I said cavalierly. "I *love* smart-asses." I held out fierce hope that one day I would meet a boy who liked them too—or else I was screwed.

Mom, a savvy fighter, ignored my jab and closed the space between us. We were now chin to chin.

"Let's just—" Dad broke in, but Mom stymied him.

"You agreed, Angus." Dad threw his hands up, and she turned back to me.

"Thanks to a good deal of effort on my part, both you and Julia have been invited to debut this year. It's practically unheard of for two sisters, and—"

"I don't care who you bribed."

"Enough!" she shouted.

I gave her the icy, defiant stare, but she held her ground.

"I love you dearly, but you are headstrong to a fault and quite sure you know all you need to about everyone and everything. Trust me when I say you do not. Three generations of women in my family—your great-grandmother, your grandmother, your aunt, and I—all made our Bluebonnet debuts. Your cousin Abby and your sister, Julia, will make their debuts this year, and while you may not realize what this means, I do. One day very soon your soccer career will end and you will find yourself in a much larger and more complicated world than the one you now inhabit, and it is my job to make sure you are prepared for that. So let me be perfectly clear—this is not a request."

"This is so unfair, Mom."

"Is it?" she said. "Is it really?"

The question hung there, and then Mom held the side of her head, obviously in pain. Dad moved in and put his hand on her arm.

"You okay?" he asked. Mom suffered from the occasional migraine, which always seemed to arrive when most useful.

"I'm fine." But she let him walk her slowly to a chair. She sat down heavily and eyed the sun beaming through the curtains like a vampire would the dawn.

I was furious. Tears welled as my anger burned hotter, but I didn't know what to say.

"I-I hate you," I finally mustered. So lame. But committed, I spun and stomped away.

"Honey—" my father started.

"Let her go," Mom said as I slammed the door for good measure. In the hallway I sobbed and heard her offer the old chestnut "She'll come around—just let her get used to the idea."

Not fucking likely.

Two

In Which Megan Ekes Out a Pyrrhic Victory

THERE IS NOTHING MORE COMFORTING THAN THE warm scent of a horse, especially your own horse, one that loves you unconditionally and will let you hang around his neck without complaint. As I pushed my face deeper into Banjo's coat and inhaled deeply, my breath naturally downshifted from a heaving sob to a manageable wheeze. I highly recommend this when your life is in tatters.

I had gone to the barn to hide and think. It was Saturday, so Silvio and the other ranch hands would be off, and I would be alone with my guy Banjo and the dozen other horses there.

Though it burned and I would never admit it, Mom was right about the national team thing. That ship had likely sailed—if you don't make the Under-20 team, your chances of making the Under-23 team are practically nil, and if you're not on that team, well . . . enough said about ever playing with the big dogs. Worst of all, I had choked at the regional tryout and never showed the coaches my best stuff. Sure the other girls were good, but they weren't better than me. I don't even know what happened. It was a maelstrom of bad judgment and rookie mistakes, like the one I made today. I yearned for another shot, and Coach Nash was my lottery ticket—she was a two-time NCAA Coach of the Year and was way connected to the national team. Only if I played like a rock star this season would I maybe, just maybe, get another chance next summer. Days like today didn't help, and now Mom wanted me to quit for a whole season? *Does she know me at all?* I wondered, and not for the first time.

Ironically, the odds of making the actual Women's National Team, the one that plays in the World Cup and the Olympics, were the same as being selected a Bluebonnet deb—essentially nil. Twenty-three women in the whole country are on the top national squad at any given time, and there are only seven or eight Bluebonnet debutantes a year.

You can't *ask* to be invited. You can't buy your way in. You're *selected* by a secret club of very rich and influential men who value tradition above all else. So if your mother debuted, it gives you a leg up. An aunt can help; a grandmother too. Julia and I were serious legacy. When Grandma Rose Alice died a few years back, the headline of her obituary in *The Dallas Morning News* was about her selection as a

Bluebonnet Debutante, 1964. Everything else about her life—parents, college, husband, kids, charities, and social clubs—came after. The subject of our debut started in kindergarten, but until today's juggernaut I'd thought we'd agreed that Julia would do it and I would skip it.

Through my snuffling, I heard the *tick tick* of the diesel engine, the driver's door thumping shut, then the barn latch closing. I hid behind Banjo's neck as the quiet crunch of footsteps on straw grew closer. Long before I heard his voice I knew it was Dad.

"Thought I'd go for a ride. Wanna come?" His voice was perfectly noncommittal.

"I guess," I said quietly, trying not to let on just how hard I had been crying.

While Dad saddled Jasper, and I readied Banjo, there was the rustle of blankets, the creak of leather, an occasional snort, and the clop of hooves, but neither of us spoke—we just went about our business. Before we mounted up, Dad grabbed a shotgun off the rack in his truck, checked the load, and slid it in my saddle holster. This wasn't my gun—mine was a Remington 870 Wingmaster Competition, a real beauty Dad ordered custom for my thirteenth birthday. It was a pump-action twelve-gauge with a front bead sight on a twenty-inch barrel and an eight-load magazine, weighted just a little forward for better tracking. The wood was dark cherry, the barrel and fittings black steel, and the Aberdeen brand was engraved on the stock. But Dad's gun from the truck would do if we startled a rattler, and I was flattered he'd let me handle it.

We set out from the barn, walked out beyond the corral, and loped up the first rise. Dad always stopped here to have a look, and I pulled up beside him.

"Nice up here," he said, after a moment.

"Yeah." And it was.

McKnights have been ranching cattle on the Aberdeen since 1873, the year my great-great-great-grandfather Angus arrived from Scotland to make his way in America. Lanky, gap-toothed, with hair the color of a copper penny, Angus packed only guts and grit when he left Clackmannanshire, and he chose Dallas by chance while standing in the train station in St. Louis. A man he'd never met and never saw again told him he'd find good grass and steady water there. Angus liked the look of him, so he bought a ticket and arrived to little more than a rail junction beside a muddy river, but to the south were rolling hills of fine, tall hay fed by plentiful creeks, and Angus plunked down his life savings for two hundred acres, a steer, and four heifers.

Those two hundred acres were four thousand now, and a thousand head, give or take, wandered through the lush grass, brush cedar, live oaks, and gurgling creeks down below us. As I looked at my dad, hand on his pommel, gaze fixed on an endless prairie dotted with cows all bearing the original *AR* brand, time stopped and it could have been old Angus sitting beside me. That land, the never-changing land, created a deep, primeval connection. For Dad and every McKnight before him, cattle ranching was not a job—it was a calling.

"Hyah!" he belted, and gave Jasper his head. The horse broke into a canter, and Banjo instinctively followed, and soon we were at a gallop, the ground a blur beneath us and no reason or ability to talk above the clattering hooves. We jumped ditches and ducked under tree limbs and rumbled up and over hillocks, only stopping when we reached the far western boundary.

Here the endless prairie ended. Beyond our fence lay El Dorado, a manufactured development bursting with Spanish-style houses butted together like cans of beans on a grocery store shelf. The streets with their picturesque names—Avenida de las Flores, Lomo Alto, and El Camino Real—evoked the land's long history as a working cattle ranch, but the main boulevard and side streets, once cobblestone, were now black asphalt as smooth as a pool table. The development had absolutely everything you needed to forget the past and embrace the future: brightly lit cement sidewalks with code-mandated fire hydrants standing guard over storm drains; power lines and fiber optic cable; playgrounds; a fitness center; a picnic area with gas grills—bring your own propane tank and just plug it right in. There was a water park with a lap pool, a wading pool, and a splash pad. And the spiderweb of dusty trails used by cows for a century was now a network of paved hike and bike trails with strategically placed benches beneath live oaks brought in from a tree farm.

We watered the horses from a creek and caught our breath. A family of four biked by on the other side of the fence, the two young kids on training wheels, the entire family in shiny, sturdy helmets.

"Howdy," Dad said quietly, and tipped his hat.

"Hello," they called back. "Great day, huh?"

"Sure is," Dad replied. The children stared back at Dad like he was a rotary phone.

Dad surveyed the houses across the fence.

"Got another call the other day," he said to me after they'd passed.

"Yeah? Have you called him back?" I teased.

"Nope," he admitted, sheepishly.

"Does Mom know?"

"Not yet." Same old, same old.

"Dad," I said, a tad more serious, "why does she want to sell?"

He paused before answering.

"It's stressful and she knows we can't compete anymore. For a decade or better we've been supporting the cows, and not the other way around." This was a standing joke between my parents. As debt piled up, Dad would occasionally sell off a small piece of land to get square with the bank for a time. But he never reduced the herd, and Mom would periodically wax poetic on the idea that we would finally be left with only the house and a few acres—but a thousand cows.

He looked over the fence.

"'Sides it doesn't take an MBA to see it's better to ranch houses than cattle these days."

"So . . . it's the money?"

"Sort of—it's our future, and yours and Julia's." He looked over at me. "She just figures if we're gonna fold eventually, might as well do it with some chips still on the table."

"Gonna take up golf?" I said, with just a little sass.

"Might take up drinking full-time."

We turned the horses toward home but let them walk.

"You gonna call the guy back?"

"Nope."

I took in a huge breath through my nose. Let it out. Took in another and savored. Switchgrass and bluestem mainly, but layered with swirls of dirt as rich as Swiss chocolate. I picked up hints of lemon mint, bluebells, saddle leather, and sweat. All baked together under the Texas sun, it was the spice cake of my childhood. Nothing would ever smell better.

"Well, I hope we never sell," I said.

"I know."

I knew as well as Dad that the money struggles of the last twenty years were not quite what Mom signed up for when they married, and he didn't begrudge her financial peace of mind. Rather, he honestly feared life without meaningful work. He was a cattle rancher, and it was all he knew. Sure, he might sell the Aberdeen and get a bag of money and buy a house in the right zip code, but what the hell would he do all day? Dad was country, not country club, and always would be.

oe͜ꙩ

We were nearly back to the barn, and Dad still hadn't broached the inevitable subject. I knew he hadn't come out here just to ride, and as we got closer I wondered how he would come at me—would it be "Embrace your opportunities" or the more classic "Do as you're told" approach?

But after we'd hung the saddles and blankets and tack and fed the horses, he came at me with the one surefire, no-fail approach I could never refuse.

"Megan, you know how much I love you, and that I am pretty much unable to function when you're unhappy," he began, standing by the barn door. "And I've got some sympathy for the careless way all this was thrown at you. . . ."

My heart sank and I braced for impact.

"These last few years, since you girls left, your mother and I . . . we've been, well . . . let's just say there will be no peace around here unless your mother wins this one. So I'm asking you—begging you really—as a favor to me, to do this debutante thing."

Oh God, I thought, *is he going to cry? Oh please don't cry!* I suddenly realized there was more going on here, much more.

"Is it really that important to her?"

"You have no idea." He actually kicked at the dirt with his boot.

"Why?"

"Try and understand," he said. "She sees it . . . as your birthright. She worries that you've been cooped up out here in the country your whole life, away from society, such as it is, and you've missed out on . . . well, I'm not sure what. But if you don't do this thing now, there won't ever be another chance like it. And whether it matters to you or not, she's invested, and . . . you can't just throw it back in her face. It's just not the way to handle something like this."

Frantically I searched for an exit, but none appeared.

Dad's a tough guy. I can't remember him ever asking me for anything. And now he was begging me to do something he knew I detested as a personal favor, to take one for the family team. I realized then that he was desperate like he had never been before, and that his "there will be no peace" explanation was only the tip of some enormous iceberg of entangled negotiated settlements that likely spanned my parents' entire married life.

Resigned, I played my sole remaining card.

"I won't give up soccer, Dad. I've only got one more year left." I gave him my super-earnest "You can't ask that of me" look. "I can do both. I'll just have to work harder."

"That seems fair," he said, and I heard myself exhale, unaware until I did that I had been holding my breath.

"I'll offer terms to your mother." He gave me that rueful smile I loved so much.

"Good luck," I croaked.

Dad waved as he walked toward his truck, a mud-stained F-350. He put the shotgun back on the rack and then, with the door half-open, he looked back.

"Hey—thanks." Straightforward. Honest. That was Dad.

I choked back tears as he drove off.

Three

*In Which Megan Reveals a Good Deal More
Than She Intended*

I WAS FLYING DOWN MOCKINGBIRD LANE ON MY BIKE just inches from a red light at Fairfield when I realized the black sedan beside me was an unmarked patrol car. I clamped both brakes and the back tire skidded in gravel and I ended up sideways ten feet into the intersection. I put a single Coach slingback sandal down on the gooey asphalt, backed up, and casually glanced at the cop beside me. He looked over, and chuckled. Really, who could blame him? It's not every day you see a girl on a mountain bike in a Ralph Lauren dress, three-hundred-dollar sandals, and a bike helmet crowned with a giant plastic tiara plastered with rhinestones.

Sweating like Seabiscuit in the final furlong of the Preakness, I blinked at the clots of mascara clouding my vision and worried my heavily made-up face might suddenly fracture and descend in a mudslide of Malibu proportions. Positive I looked demented, but determined to show a brave face, I smiled sweetly at Officer Jenkins in his air-conditioned cruiser and he, being a generous sort, turned away.

I had, of course, planned to blow through the light without a second thought, but a split-second calculation told me the time spent defending a ticket from Highland Park's finest was greater than the duration of the light, so I dutifully paused. That is, if you call jackknifing your bike halfway through an intersection "pausing."

Unable to stop myself, I checked my watch. Again. 4:43 p.m. Yikes.

Just how, I wondered, had I found myself so very late and so very stuck to the seat of my bike? The painful answer was that sadly, all my wounds were self-inflicted. Beginning early that morning I had made a critical error in judgment.

"No, you take the car," I said stupidly at 5:20 a.m. Julia and I shared a blue Subaru Forester. It wasn't flashy, but it was dependable, and Dad chose it based on its impressive safety record.

"You sure?" Julia murmured. Standing in her doorway, I nodded. Turns out sleep deprivation really does affect decision making.

"Practice ends at four, and the orientation isn't until four thirty," I said. "That'll give me time to shower, dress, and make it over to the club—it's only a few blocks."

That Tuesday marked the unofficial start of the Season. Julia and I and the other girls were invited to tea at Turtle Creek Country Club with our governess, Ann Foster. She would look us over, tell us what to expect and how to behave.

"You won't be hot?"

"The weather's cooled off," I said breezily. "And practice is just a walk-through and drills. Besides, if anything does happen, I don't want us both to be late."

"Okay," she replied, falling back onto her pillow. "I'll save you a seat."

Stifling pangs of jealousy—I never get to sleep in—I closed her door softly, went downstairs, and rode to the gym, my sandals hooked over the handlebar and my then unwrinkled, immaculate, and bagged red dress billowing out behind me like Superman's cape.

Alas, things did not go as planned. First, it was hot—blast furnace hot. Summers in Texas are always steamy, but by September the weather usually backs off from freaking unbearable to nearly tolerable. But not that day. By 2 p.m. the temperature hovered at 102 degrees, with rain forest humidity.

Then a series of sloppy passes and general buffoonery sent Coach Nash over the edge, and the whole "drills and a walk-through" was replaced by running the stadium stairs.

"Push it, push it, push it!" Coach Nash screamed as a pack of girls climbed up, up, up. At the top I turned left and sprinted for the next aisle. Then down, down, down the stairs. Up one flight, down another. Rinse and repeat. "It's overtime, you've been running for two hours, you're exhausted, and so are they. Now it's just about will. Who wants it more?"

"Not any harder than climbing Mount McKinley," I managed to wheeze to Cat as we climbed the top section, using three breaths to get out the seven words.

"At least it's cold in Alaska," Cat gasped back.

Word. The metal bleachers were scalding hot to the touch, the stadium was damp as a terrarium, and the sun roared down like a blow torch. When Coach finally released us at 4:15 I was drenched. Worse, my core was hot as a pizza oven.

I entered the shower at 4:19 and blasted myself with ice-cold water for five straight minutes. This wasn't nearly enough to cool off, and as I stood in front of the mirror at 4:28 applying mascara, beads of sweat popped out on my beet-red forehead. I left the locker room, unstuck my dress from my moist ass, and stole a quick peek at my watch. 4:37—I willed myself to stay calm.

"Your highness! Oh your highness," Mariah squealed as I turned the corner by the bike stall. Lindsay and Lachelle immediately started blowing on pink-and-white "princess" kazoos and genuflecting while Cat stood at attention and set off a child's confetti cannon. It went off with as much oomph as a good fart, and the confetti flew up six inches before falling pathetically in the grass.

"Fail," Lachelle said.

"Right? So lame," Cat said, looking at the empty canister. "This thing cost four ninety-nine."

"Funny, guys, thanks," I said. I wasn't that surprised by

the Prank Brigade, as news of my debut had spread quickly through the team. As I unlocked my bike, Cat ran over and handed me my bike helmet.

"Your crown, milady," she said, and then she too bowed before breaking into peals of laughter.

"You shouldn't have," I said. I spent exactly three seconds trying to pry off the tiara she had superglued to the brim, then gave up and stuck it on my head. I didn't even bother to try and remove the glittering streamers flowing off the handlebars.

"Have fun at the ball! Be home by midnight!" Mariah called.

"Let us know if you meet Prince Charming!" Lachelle shouted.

I waved and left to the sound of kazoos. Halfway across campus I noticed they had replaced my nasty old water bottle with a brand-new pink one.

And what I'd remembered as "a few blocks" from SMU to Turtle Creek Country Club turned out to be ten—a solid mile and a half. And there were two lights. Now I was sitting at the second. When I'd arrived at the first, the crosswalk was blocked by a column of toddlers returning from the park to their day care.

Recalling my dress blowing out behind me that morning, I suddenly wished I were Superman, that I could fly or instantly cool the entire world to subzero temperatures. Most of all I wished to spin the earth backward at hypersonic speed, thereby reversing the clocks by, say, an hour. Lacking all of these skills I smoldered, inside and out. One last glance at my watch—4:45 p.m. Best case scenario I would arrive twenty minutes late, flushed and sweaty.

The entrance to Turtle Creek Country Club was, naturally, uphill. Unable to quell the rising tide of panic, I stood on the pedals and cranked my bike up over the crest. Suddenly, as if she were right next to me, I heard my mother offer that "Megan, dear, you *never* get a second chance to make a first impression." Thanks for that, Mom.

Ahead now I saw the shaded portico and the front doors. I imagined the other girls arriving before me—early of course—pulling up in their vacuum-sealed cars, the air-conditioning cranked so high they'd be wearing cashmere cardigans. Exiting oh so carefully—don't muss your hair or chip a nail—they'd take the valet ticket and have a mere eight steps to the cool confines of the club. Not enough time to melt an M&M, much less mar their Kabuki makeup.

Lost in my bitter reverie I hurtled into the entrance, screeched to a stop, and locked eyes with the valet. He was young, dressed in black shorts and a white polo. He was also handsome, ridiculously so, with big brown eyes, wavy hair, and a dimple in his chin big enough to bathe in. I stood waiting, but he didn't move, just hovered with a ticket in his hand.

"Well?" I said. He just stared at me, slack-jawed. *Poor fella, got the looks but not the brains*, I thought. "What, you've never parked a bike before?"

That got him. He stepped forward and held the handle bar.

"Sorry—good afternoon . . . ma'am," he said. Now he smiled. And what a smile—brighter than the lights at Westcott Field. "Welcome to Turtle Creek Country Club."

"Thanks." I unbuckled my helmet and handed it to him. He noticed the tiara, and smiled again. He really was handsome. Must do well with the older ladies. I considered explaining about the tiara, but really, what plausible explanation could I offer?

And then, harried, and distracted by his looks, I caught the hem of my dress on the saddle and tore it as I dismounted. We both looked down at the sound of cloth ripping. My stylish red linen dress now had a tear from thigh to hip, a generous hole through which my sunflower panties and a decent amount of skin showed.

"Perfect," I said. "Just—perfect." He gave me a sympathetic look. I squeezed my dress shut, handed him five bucks.

"Oh, thank you very much, ma'am." I sensed some private joke now, a gentle tease in his voice—probably the tiara.

"You're welcome." I quizzed his face for the answer, and his smile grew. *Definitely the tiara.* I nodded at my bike. "Keep it running?"

"Yes, ma'am," he said, the smile widening. It made my heart thump. He was beyond cute. Typical—on the doorstep of fabulous wealth I swoon for the valet. I walked away holding my dress together.

"And no joyriding," I yelled over my shoulder.

"No, ma'am." As I opened the door I stole one last look. He leaned my bike carefully against the wall, and then a black Mercedes AMG roared in and an older man in a Turtle Creek Country Club polo hopped out. My "valet" went around to the driver's door and gave *my five dollars* to the real valet.

He paused before getting in, looked my way. He smiled even more broadly and waved, clearly enjoying the moment. My shock gave way to amusement. Well, well, color me wrong. Handsome *and* sly. I waved back. *So long, stranger,* I thought as he drove away. Even his car had a great ass.

Inside the club it was dark and cold as an igloo, and I waited as my pupils dilated from midday Sahara to the warm, woodsy tones of high-dollar luxury. Feeling blowing air from an AC vent above, I raised my arms and let the cool draft rush over my wet armpits.

Sweet Jesus, that's heaven.

Having been there a few times before, I knew I was in the main entrance. I looked around to gauge my vision. Gleaming parquet floor? Check. Taupe linen wallpaper and walnut wainscoting? Check. Large potted plants in brass bowls? Crystal chandeliers? Check, check. Woman sitting behind desk staring at me while I air my pits? That was new. Roger and out.

"May I help you?" she inquired, her tone as frosty as the room.

I slowly lowered my arms.

"Yes, hi—Megan McKnight. I'm here for the orientation tea."

"That would be in the Magnolia Room. Down this hall and turn left. All the way to the end and you'll see the double doors."

"Thank you so much."

"Not at all."

"It's very hot outside," I offered.

"Yes, it is," she replied. *Well, I'm certainly glad we settled that.*

I started walking, and clasped my dress.

Then inspiration struck. I turned back to the woman.

"Do you have a stapler I could borrow?"

"I do." She pulled out a beefy stapler from the desk and handed it over. Holding the side seam in place, I squeezed the stapler three times in quick succession—*thunka, thunka, thunka.*

I let my dress fall and, hey, presto, the tear was nearly closed. A flash of yellow still showed, so I hammered in one more staple. Clunky as Frankenstein's stitches, but at least the hole was gone, and with my hand by my side you almost couldn't see it. I handed back the stapler, winked at the stunned receptionist, and ventured off in search of the tea.

The Magnolia Room. Soft, melodic words to be murmured, relished. Just saying it evoked images of all-white-meat curried chicken salad scooped on beds of butter lettuce, linen napkins, gilded china, heavy-gauge silver, and sweating goblets of iced tea garnished with fresh mint. Nothing really bad could ever happen in the Magnolia Room, I reckoned, as the soaring white doors loomed ahead.

They probably haven't even started, I fantasized, squashing the urge to sprint the last twenty yards. I bet they're still standing around, sipping tea, doing the "get-to-know-ya," and nobody would notice I was now *twenty-five minutes late.*

Outside the doors I checked the seam of my dress. The staples were holding. I pulled my hair back tighter in my ponytail, blew air up from my mouth to dry the sweat still lingering on my brow, and reached for the brass handle on the giant door.

Everything is going to be fine, I told myself, and walked in.

Four

*In Which Megan Discovers That Tea Can
Be a Full-Contact Sport*

THE MAGNOLIA ROOM WAS LARGE ENOUGH TO PARK
a Gulfstream in, with room to spare. Instead of a plane, however, the only thing in the hangar was a single round table,
surrounded by seven formal chairs. One was empty. Six
young women filled the others, and a very tall, well-dressed
woman stood beside them. At the sound of the door opening, all seven heads snapped my way. Apparently they had
started.

"Yes?" This from the Amazon in charge. I recognized
Ann Foster immediately. Her gaze was piercing, even from
thirty feet.

"I'm Megan McKnight. Is this the orientation tea?"
Brilliant question, Megan. Your sister is sitting right there.
What else could it be?

"It is." Ann said nothing further. Instead, she measured
me for a casket as I walked to the lone empty chair. I tried

not to cringe openly as I sat. Julia gave me a hopeful look, and I smiled wanly as the woman started speaking again. My cousin Abby winked at me, and I rolled my eyes. The other four girls were stoic, fixated on our host.

"Now, as I was saying, it would be *impossible* to overstate the opportunity before you."

Ann now looked intently at each of us, letting the words land first on the group and then individually. With her eyes on me, I felt my spine straighten as if pulled by a puppeteer's strings. I'll say this for her—she knew the value of brevity followed by silence. She let that sentence dangle for a good fifteen seconds, until long after the silence was downright uncomfortable. *Now there's a trick I need to remember.* I willed myself not to fidget.

"You are on the cusp of an historic journey. This year just seven invitations were extended by the Bluebonnet Club for this, the 2016 Debut Season. In the past century and a quarter, perhaps eight hundred women in Texas have sat where you are now. Some are your relatives—mothers, aunts, grandmothers—the women and families who quite literally built this city through their industry, and their charity. And they have selected you to receive the torch of tradition and excellence and carry it forward."

Ann Foster's face was smooth save for fine wrinkles around her eyes, and I guessed she was sixty, but I could have been off by a decade in either direction. She wasn't a pound overweight, and with her hair pulled back I thought she might have, long ago, been a dancer. She certainly had the posture and the attitude.

In under ten seconds I knew from her honeysuckle drawl she was from Houston, and I quickly filled in the rest: Camp Mystic or at least Waldemar; the University of Texas—either a Kappa or a Pi Phi; decades as a wedding planner and events coordinator for the rich and famous, always around the bubble but never quite inside it. Now she lived in or near the Park Cities, but as she was single (no ring) and still worked, this meant a town house on Northwest Highway or something small west of the Tollway.

"Make no mistake," Ann continued. "Formal traditions demand rigor and sacrifice. Stamina and integrity. They are undertaken not to provide a window in which to display your wares but to prove to yourselves, your family, and others that you will be capable, dependable adults, women of great works—that you will be the very fabric of the next generation of society. If you have come here thinking this will be nothing but a series of silly parties, you are much mistaken. Yes, there will be balls, dinners, luncheons, and teas, and you will attend them all. You will shake hands and curtsy and smile until your cheeks ache—and when it is done you will know everyone in this city worth knowing, and they will know you. But first and foremost your debut will provide you with the means to leave a legacy, a great work of self-lessness. Each of you, if you have not already, will select a charitable organization that you care passionately about, and by the close of the season you are expected to make a *sizable donation* to this organization."

She paused again. I figured it might be lengthy, based on the last one. What with the heat, the bicycling, and the stress, I picked up the glass of iced tea in front of me and tried to take a sip. But when the cold liquid hit my mouth I just kept drinking—*glug, glug, glug.* Halfway through, I realized Ann had not said another word, and she and the other girls watched as I drained the entire thing.

"Sorry," I said, setting the empty glass back on the doily. Ann closed her eyes, took a deep breath, reset, and focused again on the group.

"What do I mean by a sizable donation? Well, last year a young woman raised and donated more than four hundred thousand dollars to Habitat for Humanity, and used in concert with matching grants, those funds built ten new houses for families in need. A girl very much like you, last year managed to put ten families in new houses they now own. *That* is a gift worth giving, a true legacy, and more than most will do in their lifetime. Yet this young woman is just twenty-two and will graduate from college this year. Can you imagine what that's done for her self-esteem? Do you think she will be capable of great works going forward? And wouldn't we all like to have something like that on our résumé?"

She paused again to let this sink in.

"Now I imagine you're wondering just how you will raise this money. The answer is that, in addition to parties given by relatives or prominent organizations such as the Petroleum Club, the Junior League, the Texas Bar Association, and so forth, each girl and her family will also host a party. These should be an expression of who you are, the face you wish to present to the world. They can have themes, they may be at different venues, but you are expected to sell tables to your party, and the money you collect will be the donation you give. The young woman last year sold more than one hundred tables of six to her debut, each at a cost of four thousand dollars."

This caused all of us to look around. One hundred tables? Four thousand dollars each?

"So yes, there will be parties, but these parties serve a greater purpose."

Several girls used this pause for a dainty sip of tea. Prissy bitches.

"Now please open the folders in front of you." I had been so busy acclimatizing that I had failed to notice that on the table were seven linen binders arranged artfully on end— cream with gold accents. Embossed on the cover was *The 2016 Bluebonnet Debutante Season.* In the lower right corner of mine, in fancy gold script, was my name: *Megan Lucille McKnight.*

"This," Ann said, holding hers aloft, "is your bible. Everything you need to know is contained in this folder. In the reference section you'll find stylists, florists, caterers, event coordinators, stationers, dressmakers—all personally vetted by me. Under charitable organizations you will find a thorough, but not complete, list of suitable ideas. There is a section for portraits, and an address book. Familiarize yourselves with this; you will be writing a lot of thank-you notes. Now, please open the 'Calendar' tab, and we'll go over it together."

Books were opened.

"As you can see, I have chosen Abigail Lucas to host the first debutante party, which will be in late October. Lauren Battle will host the second ball . . ."

I breathed a sigh of relief. My aunt and uncle were loaded and had great taste, so the party was sure to be perfect. I glanced at my cousin Abby and she seemed excited. I flipped ahead in the calendar and found our party would be last, just before Christmas. Thank God. Any delay was welcome, as the thought of Mom planning and pulling off a debut party for six hundred of our nearest and dearest friends and family was something I wasn't ready to contemplate yet. Plus, if we made the playoffs, soccer season would be over a week before.

As Ann droned on I tuned her out and had a cautious look around. Six other girls. Julia I knew. And to her left Abby. Abby's dress was navy, with white trim—flattering, understated, geared to appear slimming, as Abby fought her weight. And then the faces went foreign. I tried to remember the names from the paper. A basic blonde—Ashley? An interesting brunette—Sydney somebody—looked vaguely familiar. Had we met somewhere once? I searched my memory to figure out where. She gave me a brief look and I saw something in her eyes—she was . . . uncomfortable. But I couldn't place her. And to her left another brunette—weren't there two Ashleys?

Directly across from me sat another blonde, but this one was *somebody*. Lauren Battle had Queen Bee written all over her. Her hair was curled, her makeup model perfect, and her pale yellow dress played great off a deep, rich tan that strangely brought to mind the Crayola color Burnt Sienna. The Battles had come into the limelight in the 1920s when the oil patch blossomed, and that original fortune had spawned a Texas shade oak of family wealth. They still owned about a third of Fort Worth, and while I had never met Lauren in person I had seen her and her mother and various grandparents, uncles, and cousins in the paper or on the cover of vapid, glossy magazines like *D*.

One trait we all shared was that we were white. I went to public school in DeSoto with a Heinz 57 of kids, and soccer was a meritocracy. If you could put the ball in the back of the net, eggplant was an acceptable skin color. But the girls sitting at that table made it clear that even in 2016 a Bluebonnet debut in Dallas still meant white girls of privilege and wealth—or in the case of the McKnight girls, serious legacy cloaked in the appearance of wealth.

"The final ball, on New Year's Eve," Ann continued, "will be hosted by the Bluebonnet Club. They are, as you know, the founding sponsor of the season, and this ball has been held every year since 1882, an uninterrupted tradition that now spans one hundred and thirty-four years—nineteen years longer than the University of Texas has played the University of Oklahoma in the merry sport of football."

She paused a moment to look around and let this sink in. And it did. Traditions don't get bigger than the Red River Shootout, an annual border war fought on the gridiron. It's held in Dallas, the neutral midpoint between Austin and Norman, Oklahoma, where every October legions of rabid fans in crimson and burnt orange converge for a weekend of boozing and brawling over serious bragging rights. And this Bluebonnet Debut thing trumped that by twenty years? Just kill me now.

"Dress for this event is white gown and white gloves—no exceptions. As each of you are presented, you will be required to bow formally—the Texas Dip. Every young woman who has ever made her debut in the state of Texas has done this, and it is the one skill you must absolutely master. Please remember you will perform this feat alone, at the edge of a runway on a stage under hot lights in front of the entire city—in heels."

She examined each of us for the requisite fortitude.

"I will demonstrate it now."

Ann drew herself up high and tall. And then she put her left leg back and began to bow. Her head reached her waist. Her knees began to fold and her head continued down, down, her face turned to avoid smearing her lipstick.

She's going to fall over! I thought, as she pretzeled herself practically level with the floor. But no, she held steady. And then, with nary a wobble, she began to rise back up.

I watched her face for any expression of effort but it was a blank slate. Having done a little core work in my time, I was impressed.

"Now I want you each to try it. Who will go first?"

Everyone looked around—who would dare?

"I'll go," I said breezily, and stood up. Strength and flexibility were my stock in trade—I did sixty box jumps three days a week and could squat a buck fifty ten times. And by going first I was showing initiative, which might make Ann forget I'd arrived late. A twofer.

"Just relax," Ann said. She held her hands out to me, palms up.

"I'm good." I looked at her hands. Was she there to spot me? "Seriously, I got this."

"You will need assistance."

"I think not," I said. Seriously, how hard could it be?

Ann reluctantly stepped back, but reserved judgment. I closed my eyes, took a breath. Tried to remember just how she had done it. I put my arms out to the side, then began to lower myself.

The first six inches went great, and I let my left leg drop behind my right. The next six inches went pretty well, until my right knee reached parallel. Then a strange thing happened. My left leg ground to a halt behind my right and refused to budge. I tried to force it down with my torso, and then my right leg quivered. I pushed harder, and my right thigh clenched and the muscle spasmed, and under extreme duress the staples in my dress popped. That caused my hip to fly out and I went ass over elbows onto the floor. I had jujitsued myself. Abby died laughing—a full, infectious laugh.

"It's more difficult than it first appears," Ann said drily. She offered me a hand up, but embarrassed, and confused by my failure, I refused. I stood up, held my dress together, and sat down. Julia patted my shoulder, and I grimaced. Lauren gave me the "so sad for you" look.

After my epic fail the other girls went up cautiously, and took Ann's hands for support.

"The key is maintaining your weight over your feet," Ann said, holding Abby's hands as she went three-quarters of the way down before stopping. Sydney went next, and did as well as Abby. Then the Ashleys. Ashley One was clearly a dancer, and with Ann's help reached closest to the floor. Ashley Two appeared to have vertigo and barely budged. Julia came close, as did Queen Bee, but still holding Ann's hands for support.

"Begin to practice right away," Ann said. "Use a dance bar or the back of a chair for support, and try first for enough flexibility to reach close to the floor—then try it only holding on with one hand." Satisfied that we had a newfound appreciation for the task ahead, Ann moved on. "Now please turn to the 'Escorts' section."

Pages turned amid a quiet titter. One of the real perks of the debut was a guarantee of meeting a lot of (hopefully) cute guys over the coming months, and even I was curious to know who they might be. I skimmed a list of sixty or seventy names, read *Bryson Alexander Perriman* and *Benjamin Francis Horton* and my eyes glazed over.

"These young men range in age from early to midtwenties," Ann said. "Some are still at college, but many have entered the world. Many are sons from well-regarded families, but you'll also find attorneys, navy officers, entrepreneurs. Each has something to recommend him. For the formal balls and the debut itself I will match you with an escort, a different young man for each event. The only exception to my choosing your escort is if you are currently engaged, or become engaged during the season, and then of course you will be paired with your fiancé. Now the gentlemen do sometimes make specific requests, and I try to honor those requests when they are sincere, and appropriate. For other parties during the season you are always welcome to arrive with a date of your choice, and it may be that young men from this list will contact you. If so, you may rest assured that I have personally vetted them all. Is this understood?"

Nods all around.

"Good. Now finally, I want you all to understand that individually and collectively you represent a tradition, an ideal, and you will hold yourselves to the very highest standards of behavior. Failure in this regard will have swift and severe consequences. Do I make myself clear?"

Quick nods all around.

"Excellent. I know it will be a successful season. Now

please enjoy the food, get to know each other, and I'll see you in a few weeks' time."

Apparently cued by telepathy, the doors opened and several waiters entered with trays of sandwiches, which they arranged on the table. The scent of dill coming off the cream cheese and smoked salmon finger sandwiches caught me by surprise, and I realized I was famished. Instinct and raw hunger prompted me to make a grab and start throwing down the little suckers, and I was on my second when a voice called from behind me.

"A moment, Miss McKnight?" Damn, snackus interruptus.

I looked back, and sure enough, Ann Foster was speaking to me. She indicated that I should follow her, so I swallowed and stood. In step behind her, I looked back at Julia. Her look, all earnest concern, bucked me up till I noticed Queen Bee smiling to herself. *Petty bitch is probably sad she's gonna miss the barbecue*, I thought. Ann stopped by the massive bay windows across the room. The panorama was all mounded and manicured fairways, pecan trees, water hazards, and flagsticks.

We stood far enough away not to be heard by the others, but clearly in view—whatever was coming, every girl there would see.

"We haven't been properly introduced," she began. "I'm Ann Foster." She held out her hand and I shook it, firmly. She was taller than I'd realized.

"Megan McKnight."

"So nice to meet you, Miss McKnight." She could mean it.

"Nice to meet you too, Ms. Foster." I masked my fear with my most wholesome smile.

"I know your mother and aunt, of course. And I am well-informed about your family's history," she said. "Your sister Julia seems delightful."

She paused and we both understood the distinction she was drawing. I stayed silent, didn't take the bait.

"Miss McKnight, I want to be frank. I am retained by the Bluebonnet Club to plan and execute the debutante season. I have held this position of trust for more than twenty years, and they look to me to make absolutely sure everything comes off without a hitch. I host this tea so that I may, in an informal atmosphere, meet each young woman selected, and not only explain the significance of making a debut but also ascertain to my complete satisfaction that she understands, accepts, and is prepared for the ordeal ahead. Of the utmost importance is promptness—"

"Sorry about that," I interjected. "Soccer practice went late."

"Soccer practice does not concern me, Miss McKnight. What does concern me is your tardy and"—here she gestured to my gaping, sweat-stained dress—"tawdry appearance, which clearly demonstrate your lack of regard for myself and the other young women selected."

"I've already apologized," I said, feeling my cheeks flush. "I promise it won't happen again, and I'm sure given the opportunity I can learn to curtsy just as well as the other girls."

Ann's nostrils flared and she tensed. She now looked

less like a ballerina and more like a Siberian tiger eager for lunch. Her change so shocked me I nearly took a step back.

"*Curtsy*, Miss McKnight," she said icily, "derives from the word *courtesy*, a word and concept clearly foreign to you." *Dang.* "A proper curtsy is neither frivolous nor submissive—it is a posture of respect. Respect—there's another word gathering dust on the shelf of your vocabulary."

"Ms. Foster, I—"

"I see in you, Miss McKnight," Ann went on, "nothing more than the selfish, self-absorbed child so common today. You have no thoughts beyond your own comfort, and what intellect you do possess you employ solely in cheap sport. This is not a game, Miss McKnight, not to myself nor to the people who attend, and I have no intention of working to change your obvious disdain for the institutions I represent and have little hope you will manage it yourself. Therefore, I think it best if you voluntarily withdraw."

I was so derailed by this tart and targeted barrage that a good twenty seconds must have passed before I managed to speak. She waited patiently while I wobbled like a punch-drunk fighter, in danger of going down for the count.

"I think you've misjudged me," I managed.

"I highly doubt it."

My heart thumped against my chest, and my cheeks were red as cherries. Withdraw? We hadn't even started. . . .

"I don't want to withdraw," I began, cautiously. "This is important to my parents, and I am not, and never have been, a quitter. I'll do whatever I have to do to prove myself."

"Moxie," she stated flatly, "while admirable, will not suffice, Miss McKnight."

The *Miss McKnight* thing was starting to grate.

"It is abundantly clear that you cannot walk properly," she continued, "so it would naturally follow that you are unable to dance—and I do not mean Zumba."

"My mom has already signed us up for dance lessons."

"I wish it were that simple. You will need to learn to stand up straight, dress appropriately, and behave with some clear sense of modesty and decorum. You're miles from a satisfactory Texas Dip, and frankly, given the time allowed and the list of requirements, I doubt you're up to it."

Suddenly I was not just insulted, but mad.

"You'd be surprised, Ms. Foster," I stated with reckless confidence, "what I can accomplish in a short amount of time."

She looked me over again, still dubious. Why was I even fighting this? This was my chance to be gone. I could tell Mom that Ann felt I wasn't up to it, that she knew, like I did, that I just wasn't debutante material. But I thought of Dad begging me to do it, and while I wasn't sure why, it was clear he *needed* me to stay.

"Please, ma'am," I said, softening my tone and smiling at her with all the Texas charm I could muster, "I realize today did not start well, but I would very much appreciate you allowing me the opportunity to prove that I belong."

She weighed my "ma'am" and the sentence that followed for a moment, unsure if they were mocking or sincere.

"Miss McKnight, you have a month," she said. "Surprise me."

And with that she turned and left the Magnolia Room.

I staggered over to the table. Julia and Abby stood.

"You look pale," Julia said.

"That bitch is hard-core."

"She is," chimed in Ashley One. "Two years ago she gave my cousin a panic attack—she withdrew and ended up in the hospital."

"Well, what did she say?" Abby asked.

"She asked me to withdraw." An audible, collective gasp. "But I talked her out of it—for the moment. I'm on some sort of debutante probation."

That made them laugh. Me too. I dropped into my chair. Desperate for solid food to calm the toxic cocktail of adrenaline and fear in my stomach, I tossed down a whole finger sandwich. Feeling better, I reached for another.

"It's not too late to change your mind," Lauren chimed in, her voice all singsongy. She smiled at me with emerald eyes and Chiclet teeth, but the effect was more north wind than welcome mat.

"Excuse me? Have we even met?" I asked.

"Megan, this is Lauren Battle," Abby said. "Lauren, Megan McKnight."

"So nice to meet you," Lauren said, and stood halfway to stretch a hand across the table. I half rose too and shook it, resisting the impulse to crush it.

"I'm not trying to be mean," Lauren said, gesturing at the table of girls, "but this is, like, extremely important to all of us. And, well . . . a chain is only as strong as its weakest link."

"Seriously?" I said, looking to Julia. Then back to Lauren. "Well, then I will certainly do my best not to be the weak link."

"Great," she replied. "Honestly, I just want what's best for the group."

"Yeah, I can see that." I resisted rolling my eyes.

She smiled at me and I smiled back. She smiled harder, and I did too, and pretty soon all that warm and fuzzy melted the ice in the tea glasses.

oenO

Outside I stood next to my bike, waiting with Julia and Abby as valets retrieved cars. Ashley One and Sydney were gone, and Ashley Two and Lauren stood "apart" talking quietly, but loudly enough for us to hear.

"She rode her *bike*?" Ashley Two looked askance. "Like, what is she trying to prove?"

"Who cares?" asked Lauren, glancing at me. "She's already on probation. Bet you she's gone by Halloween." Now she smiled. "Love the helmet!" she said too loudly. *The damn tiara!*

"Just ignore them," Julia said.

Ashley Two's car pulled up—a Land Rover, natch. She gave the valet a single dollar, and Lauren stepped into the passenger seat.

"Bye, Julia. Bye, Abby. Bye, Megan. See you soon!" Lauren said, waving.

We all waved back with a good deal more enthusiasm than I felt.

"Okay, bye, Lauren! Bye, Ashley!" we replied. The valets shut the doors—thump.

"Drive fast and take chances!" I shouted, knowing they couldn't hear me now with the windows closed.

"*That* is why I love you so much," Abby said.

"Megan!" Julia admonished. "You can't say things like that."

"I can't?"

"No. Because we understand you're joking. But other people don't know you that well."

"Who's joking?"

"Never change, Megan," Abby said.

Our car arrived. Julia hesitated.

"This is good, right?" She meant eluding my near-death experience.

"Of course," I said. "Now go."

"Dinner at Cafe Express?"

"I already know what I'm having."

Julia drove off.

"I'm glad you're staying," Abby said. "It's going to be a lot more fun."

"That's what I'm here for—to set the bar so low that you and Julia will just step over it."

Her car arrived, and she gave me a hug, then drove off.

The last to leave, I rode my bike lazily out of Turtle Creek Country Club, then stayed on the sidewalk, just taking my time, thinking about my run-in with the "valet" and then about my run-in with Ann. On the one hand, I was glad not to be telling Dad I got booted on the first day. On the other, I was legitimately frightened at the prospect of what lay ahead.

After all, this was just the orientation tea. The real season hadn't even started.

Five

In Which Megan Puts Away Serious Groceries

"JUST BE OPEN-MINDED," JULIA SAID. "WHO KNOWS what might happen, or who you might meet? You might even have fun."

"Please—it's a dog show," I answered, wolfing down a turkey burger.

"God, you're so judgmental."

"But is it really judgmental . . . if I'm right?" I dipped a bouquet of fries in ketchup, then stuffed them in. She rolled her eyes at my question, but I was semiserious. What was the difference between sound judgment and outright prejudice anyway? Wasn't it a function of accuracy?

Cafe Express was crowded for a Tuesday night. This was a regular dinner haunt for us, as it was close to our apartment and not too spendy, and the food was good and came in large portions. Busy now demolishing said turkey burger, I had already polished off an entree of grilled salmon, green beans, and mashed potatoes, and I was eyeing the remainder of Julia's Cobb salad.

Yes, I eat a lot, and with good reason. An average girl can eat fifteen hundred to eighteen hundred calories a day and thrive, but I'm not an average girl. At five foot seven and 135 pounds, every week between workouts, practices, and games I incinerate an astonishing twenty-eight thousand calories. (I know this because the trainers tested me.) My metabolism hums 24/7 like a beehive, and four thousand calories a day just keeps me from losing weight—I need more to add muscle. Believe you me, it ain't easy to find that much food, much less chew and swallow it all. Note to self: stop for chocolate milk on the way home.

"Look," I continued, tossing down the last of the burger, "I get why you're excited. But you're good at this stuff. I'm socially . . . dyslexic."

I reached for her salad, then stopped when I caught the look of shock on her face.

"Sorry, I thought you were finished," I said, confused—I routinely finished off her plate.

"It's not that," she whispered back, with some urgency.

I followed her look and there, at the counter, was Tyler Stanton.

"Crap."

"Right?" She used me as a shield, hoping he wouldn't see her.

"How is he anyway?" I whispered.

"No idea. We haven't spoken in a month."

"Good," I replied. "He's a time bomb and you don't want to be around the next time he explodes." Julia stood as I finished speaking, and I sensed rather than saw his bulk behind me.

"Hi, Tyler," she said evenly.

"How's it going?" he asked. I stood and faced him, inserting myself neatly between them. Tyler, the middle linebacker on the SMU football team, was six foot two with bulging arms and a head the size of a microwave. Standing there in jeans and a T-shirt he looked like a cartoon superhero. But I held my ground even as he looked right over me to Julia.

"Great to see you, but we were just going." I took Julia by the arm, and started to lead her away.

"I heard about your debut thing," he offered. "Congratulations."

Julia stopped, looked back. I pulled on her arm. She resisted.

"Thanks," Julia replied. I could see she wanted to talk to him, though I couldn't fathom why. "How are you?" she asked. I huffed audibly.

"Fine. Good. You know . . ." he replied, his voice dripping with self-pity.

Unhappy that she had stopped, but content that they were now ten feet apart, I gave her some space.

"I'm gonna get a to-go container," I said, and started

toward the counter, eyes locked on Tyler, warning him not to get any closer to her. They kept talking.

Julia and Tyler started dating the first week of senior year in high school. Tyler, a heady brew of clean-cut good looks and imposing brawn, was a consensus all-American on the field as well as a straight-A student, and that fall he graced the cover of *Texas High School Football Magazine*—a sure step on the path to sainthood. The students voted Julia homecoming queen, and as proof that she was more than a pretty face, she gave a commencement speech as the salutatorian in a class of six hundred. Awash in scholarship offers, inseparable, and in love, they were the envy of the school and pretty much every parent who knew them. They chose SMU together, and it was widely assumed they would reign there as before until they graduated, married, and went off to end world hunger.

The first year went according to plan, but last fall Tyler tore his ACL, and during the long rehab he grew moody, often downright angry, and month by month began to shut her out. By May their relationship was on the shoals. Desperate, sure something bigger was going on, she confronted him, begged him to let her in, to trust her, confide in her. For an answer he grabbed her by the shoulder, shouted "Leave me the fuck alone!" and slung her away. Her journey across the room stopped when her head connected with his bedroom door.

Both in tears, they showed up at our apartment and woke

me. After one look I screamed at him to get away, then drove her to the ER. The doctor sewed the three stitches, and I pleaded with her to press charges. She refused, but did break it off with him. That was four months ago, and as far as I knew they hadn't seen each other since, though they texted occasionally and he had called a couple of times.

I returned with my to-go container, dumped everything with calories in, and closed the lid.

". . . so, I don't know, maybe we could get a coffee sometime," Tyler said. Then he went all misty. "I miss you . . . I'd really like to see you, just—catch up."

"Thinking it's gonna be hard to squeeze you two into a booth big enough for the restraining order," I said, again moving between them.

"Megan—" Julia said, but Tyler interrupted.

"Same old Megan," he sneered. "How's your love life?"

"Anxious about prison?" I responded, not giving an inch.

"Megan, let's go," Julia said. I didn't need to be asked twice.

"Look." Tyler softened, casting back to Julia. "I just really care about you, and I don't want to lose touch. Okay?" His eyes pleaded his case.

"We'll see," Julia offered.

"Okay, then, fun catching up," I said breezily, and pulled Julia firmly toward the door.

"See ya," Tyler called after us.

"Hope not," I whispered, to myself but loud enough for Julia to hear.

Outside, I marched Julia to the car.

"Are you insane?" I asked. "That maniac sent you to the hospital, remember?"

"He feels terrible about—"

"He should. And he got off easy."

"I just hope he finds a way to turn this into a positive. He's really a good person."

I looked at her. She meant it.

"You're the good egg, Julia." I held her by the shoulders. "And I know that you want to think the best of him, but trust me when I tell you that Tyler did a very bad thing and deserves whatever grief comes his way. Promise me you won't see him alone?"

"Promise." I hugged her, and she hugged me back.

"I love you and I don't want to see you hurt. Ever."

"I know. I love you too."

We got in and I started the engine. Glancing over I noticed the slump in her shoulders, her downcast eyes. The last few months had been tough on her, and seeing Tyler clearly brought back the misery.

"Hey, this deb thing is gonna be great for you," I said, brightly. "Four months of shopping, dates, and parties . . . just what you need to forget all about him."

༒

Tyler had done us one solid. He was responsible for our awesome two-bedroom apartment less than a quarter mile from campus. When two football players, Quinn and Brady, had pulled a midnight move, Tyler gave us the heads-up, and we ran over, checkbook in hand. We found it a wee bit less than awesome when we opened the door.

"Oh God!" Julia screamed. She stepped back as the stench hit her.

Picture this: an enclosed space where two large offensive linemen and their copious clones ate frozen pizzas and Chinese takeout, drank Lone Star, and never cleaned the bathroom or really any surface for two years. Add in various native bugs and fetid laundry cooked by seven months of summer, multiply by a thousand, and you have a filthy crockpot of stale and crusty testosterone—aka our new home.

"I can't," Julia said.

"But we can stay three years," I pleaded.

We called the landlord and set off for Home Depot, where we bought rubber gloves, industrial cleaner, sponges, a bucket, a mop, bug bombs, and a box of paper masks. We bombed every room, then scraped food from the baseboards, washed the walls, the floors, the windows, and even the ceiling fan. Quinn's bedroom was empty and in need of nothing more than the same routine we'd given the living room. Brady's was a post-apocalyptic toxic waste site doubling as a location for *Mad Max: Fury Road*.

"This is your room," Julia said, sniffing the air.

Two contractor bags to the Dumpster later, and we were nearly done. The last item was a futon, which rested on the floor. We hiked up the rubber gloves and each grabbed one side and lifted. Gasping, we heaved it toward the door, and that's when we saw it: the March 2015 issue of *Pistol* magazine hiding underneath.

"Is that . . ." Julia asked, staring at the cover. A very muscular and very naked man stared up at us. In one hand he held a pipe wrench, and in the other . . . well.

"Oh my," I said, dropping my end and bending down to pick the magazine up.

"Don't touch it!" Julia screamed, but I ignored her. I was wearing rubber gloves, after all. I leafed through a few pages.

"Brady, Brady, Brady," I said, thinking of the football player who had lived here. "What a naughty boy you are." I offered it to Julia but she declined.

We manhandled the futon down to the Dumpster and shoved it in, along with the magazine.

Julia shuddered. "We will never speak of this again."

"Agreed."

After an IKEA run with Dad, we bought linens and a woven rug at Target, hung some pictures, and put Fiestaware in the cabinets, and the place felt like ours. That first night we were watching TV and I noticed Julia looking all sad.

"What's wrong?" I asked.

"I feel bad for him."

"Who?"

"Brady." The gay football player. "He must be so . . . lonely."

Like I said, Julia's the good egg.

The night we saw Tyler at Cafe Express, Julia came and stood by my bed.

"Still thinking about Tyler?" I asked.

She nodded so I moved over and she crawled in and we lay there, back-to-back, each lost in our own thoughts. I had been thinking about him too. Not about what a dick he was, but about his snide comment regarding my pathetic love life. I would never admit it, but it burned.

I liked boys. I just had no idea how to attract them. Flirting was an absolute mystery to me. I was categorically incapable of the unspoken communication that drew boys in, piqued their curiosity, or flat out turned them on. I had several theories for this. The first was that Mennen Speed Stick deodorant, which I slathered on because it actually worked, neutralized female pheromones.

The second was that boob tissue actually imparted the ability to "speak boy," and if you didn't have enough, it left you somewhere between a nasty speech impediment and positively mute. Mine were decidedly on the lean side—perky, but they lacked real heft, a pair of plums vying for attention in a market bursting with oranges, grapefruits, and ripe melons. I sometimes worried that a decade of lashing them in sports bras had stunted their growth.

"Don't worry. I'll be right there with you," Julia said, reading my mind.

"I'm not worried," I replied way too quickly, unsurprised by her clairvoyance.

"Uh-huh." Julia was unconvinced. More than any other person, she knew that fathoms beneath my surface bluster lurked a gushing vent of anxiety about dating, boys in general, and the now-looming debutante season, which would be the ultimate public test of my femininity.

Spectacular failure is by far the most likely outcome.

Six

In Which Megan Proves Sir Isaac Newton's
Second Law of Motion

WHEN MOM ADDED "SHOW DOG" TO MY OTHER identities as "college junior" and "Division I athlete," my already busy days became a nonstop sprint of workouts, classes, shopping, practice, dance classes, shopping, homework, games, and—oh yeah, shopping.

Mondays, Wednesdays, and Fridays began at five o'clock in the a.m. with breakfast—a cup of oatmeal loaded with blueberries, peanut butter, and honey. Then I rode my bike to the gym, where I lifted weights and did box jumps until drained and often dizzy. After showering, I downed two chocolate Muscle Milks for second breakfast on my way to my eight o'clock class. With no workouts on Tuesdays and Thursdays I slept in till the luxurious time of 7 a.m.

Because of my soccer schedule, I only took morning

classes, and though that semester I took the required twelve hours for my scholarship, I went light on substance—my only real course was History of Ancient Rome, and I padded with electives in Mayan Art, theater set building, and personal finance. After class I crammed in a few thousand calories at the athlete's cafeteria, and then had practice five days a week from 2:30 to 4:00 p.m.

After an early dinner (never forget food!) the second half of my day started. Monday and Wednesday nights were reserved for homework, and Tuesday and Thursday nights for a month, Julia and I waltzed around the Studio 22 dance floor. There were eight of us in the Intro to Ballroom class— two middle-aged couples looking to rekindle the pilot light, and a wedding couple nervous about that first dance.

Ernesto and Gloria, our instructors, had four weeks to get us on our feet. The women wore dresses and heels, the men slacks and leather-soled shoes, and the first time I stepped onto the waxed floor in my pumps I immediately concluded that walking in those shoes on the dance floor was not for the faint of heart, and dancing in them was downright perilous. For two weeks I clung to Ernesto, terrified he would let go and I'd spin off like a rogue planet into the outer galaxy— or worse, out the door, over the railing, and into the parking lot below.

Julia, a veteran of ballet and jazz from childhood, and a stalwart in heels, used that month as a tune-up, and several nights after class she led me around our living room slowly counting the steps. With her help and a lot of encouragement, sometime in week three it clicked. I wasn't going to win *Dancing with the Stars*, but I was capable of moving in a gentle circle around a room without careening into the furniture. It would have to do.

On the weekends we shopped—relentlessly. Julia and I met Mom and her Chase Platinum card promptly that first Saturday at quarter to ten, before Northpark Mall opened.

"I've hired a stylist," Mom announced as we stood outside Neiman's. "She comes highly recommended." I cringed. *Recommended by whom?* I wondered, and then recalled my Debutante Bible. No doubt our stylist featured prominently in there.

Mom seemed harried and distracted, like a young mother at the grocery store trying to push the cart, read her list, find the Cheerios, and keep an eye on a couple of toddlers. She eyed her watch again. "She said she'd be here at ten."

"Still five till," I offered, but in Mom's world five minutes early was still late.

"She charges a fortune . . ." Mom said, and sighed.

I was now on the lookout for a severe, heavily made-up woman past fifty, a bloodless vulture in a black knit dress and pumps wearing little glasses on a chain. Her eyebrows, long since tweezed away, would be drawn on with eye black, and her pursed lips would be as wrinkled as scrunched-up aluminum foil. Once squired away in the sanctum sanctorum—the ladies' dressing rooms at Neiman's—she'd examine us with a cold and calculating eye like we were sweaters on a sale rack, and behind her back Julia and I would speculate that she enjoyed spanking naughty men and made extra cash as a dominatrix on the weekends. Her name would be Doris.

A dusty brown Vanagon, circa 2005, squealed into the parking lot sporting Minnesota plates and a faded *Widespread Panic* bumper sticker. It stopped with a jerk, and a very tan white chick emerged. She was in that gray area between thirty and forty. Her hair was a nest of dreadlocks, and she wore heavy, horned-rimmed glasses, an Irish flag wife-beater, shapeless jeans, and the clunkiest green shoes I had ever seen. She flung a nylon, caution-yellow Marmot backpack over her shoulder and slammed the door, but it didn't close, so she slammed it harder until it shut, then locked it with the key, which she shoved in her front pocket. *Probably stopping by to stock up on patchouli*, I thought. But when she saw us she walked straight over. Mom stiffened as she approached.

"Mrs. McKnight?" she asked. Her voice was very low, raspy, and she spoke in a heavy French accent. *She probably smokes cigarettes!* I thought. *And weed out on the lawn during the summer tour. Cool!*

"Yes?" Mom answered unhappily.

"I'm Margot Jaffe." She stuck out a hand and we all saw she had full underarm hair. Mom was torn between pointing and falling to her knees in shock.

"Oh," Mom managed, trying desperately not to stare at her unshaved pits, and Julia and I shared a look. If Mom was looking to score backstage passes to Coachella, she'd hit the jackpot. For cocktail dresses and gowns to wow a Dallas debut crowd, maybe not so much.

"You must be Julia." Her pronunciation of *Julia* was so exotic I half expected a plume of blue smoke to come out of her mouth.

"Yes—so nice to meet you," Julia said, holding back an impish smile. As they shook hands we both enjoyed Mom's obvious discomfort. She was absolutely mesmerized, and probably a little queasy, that Margot didn't shave her underarms and had the brass to wear a tank top in broad daylight to go shopping at Northpark with clients.

"I'm Megan—great to meet you!" I said, delighted to keep Mom squirming.

"Megan—*enchantée*." She said my name with a long *E*— Meegan—then looked at Mom without a speck of discomfort. "*Bon—allons*." When nobody moved, she said, "Shall we go?"

"Yes, of course," Mom answered distantly, and Margot held the door for us. We entered in the cosmetics department, and the poor saps who lived there were just opening the shop. They looked wan and thirsty in the harsh daylight. At the second counter a tall black woman with square shoulders smiled when she saw Margot.

"Margot! *Ça va?*" she asked, waving like she was on a float at a parade.

"*Ça va, cherie. Et toi?*"

"*Comme ci, comme ça*," the woman said, shrugging her enormous shoulders. "*À bientôt.*"

"*À bientôt,*" Margot answered.

In a strange way this worked to establish Margot's bona fides, and Mom mulled her next move as we worked our way past handbags toward the couture stuff.

"So you helped Claire Munson's granddaughter Mackensie with her debut last year?"

"*Oui,*" Margot said. "She's a real doll, no?"

"Yes, she is—her pictures were absolutely fantastic," Mom answered. And that would have to do for Mom's interview, though clearly she harbored reservations.

"Now, we won't need white gowns for the final ball. My sister and I are taking the girls to New York for those with their cousin . . ."

Julia and I exchanged a look. Shopping trip to New York? Perk!

"But both girls will need cocktail dresses and gowns for the other balls, and many have themes, so we'll need to be aware of that. And what the other girls are wearing, of course. And then they'll need shoes and handbags and—"

"Mrs. McKnight," Margot interrupted, and stopped in the aisle. Mom faced her.

"Lucy, please." Margot tilted her head down and looked up, so she could see Mom above her heavy glasses.

"Lucy. Let us just start with measuring them. We must let our eyes and minds be open to their natural beauty, and then hope that will tell us their style. Later, we will discuss exactly which parties and which dresses. Okeydokey?"

Margot waited while Mom absorbed all this.

"Okeydokey," Mom answered, and smiled for the first time.

In the dressing room Julia and I stood in our underwear. Of course Julia was wearing a matching bottle-green silk set, while I had gone with my habitual Hanes cotton bikini and a gray sports bra. We were similar but never exact copies, and the years had pushed us further apart. Julia was slender, feminine, all gentle curves. I was more—uneven.

Margot removed an orange tape measure shaped like a snail and a box of pins from her backpack and went to work. First she measured Julia—precisely, to a sixteenth of an inch.

"A perfect size four!" Margot exclaimed to no one in particular, and then took a pink Sharpie and began making notes in a brown Moleskine notebook. "Five foot seven inches, breasts thirty-four B, waist twenty-seven, hips thirty-five." Now she walked back and looked at Julia from ten feet. Mom went and stood next to her, and Margot had a stream-of-consciousness dialogue with herself. "*Alors*, blonde hair, wonderful complexion, warm eyes, green with yellow, neck long, legs slender—well, we can do practically anything with her, but I think we should first stick with the classics. She will look fantastic, of course, but the clothes will speak about her, tell everyone who she is, and not just what she is wearing." She turned to Mom.

"*Oui*," Mom said, and Margot smiled. Now she measured me.

"Five foot six and three-quarters," she said.

"Five foot seven!" She ignored my protest, wrote *5' 6 ¾"* in the book.

"Thirty-four A," she said, after measuring my chest.

"B!" I cried. *Bitch is gonna cheat me out of a cup size?*

But she wrote down *34A* in her book.

"Waist twenty-eight, hips thirty-six, hair brown." It all went in the book. I was starting to sweat, realizing that I was not a perfect size four, and we hadn't even gotten to the really bad stuff, like my farmer's tan and my scarred, muscular legs. Margot went to the back of the room and did her gazing thing, and Mom fretted beside her like a guy who had bet big on a bad horse and was now forced to watch the damn thing run.

"We can get her a push-up bra. And cutlets for the gowns," Mom said.

"I'm not wearing those!" I said.

"And a spray tan—"

"Nope," I said.

"A haircut and color and—"

"What's wrong with my hair?" I asked, but Mom was ignoring me.

"We can get her eyebrows waxed and colored and maybe her lips dyed and—"

"Not gonna do it!" I cried out.

"This is how she is," Mom said to Margot. "She'll fight you the whole way and have something to say about everything."

"Only seems fair," I said. "I'm the one that has to wear this stuff so I think it's pretty damn reasonable that I should have some say."

"You see," Mom said to Margot, who had been watching us intently.

"Lucy—I think there is a Starbucks in the mall," she said. "Would you mind terribly going and getting me a small coffee?"

"Um, all right," Mom said. "Just a coffee?"

"A venti macchiato with cream, light on the foam."

Mom left to go get Margot's coffee, and when she was gone Margot walked over and led me to a bench in the dressing area away from Julia, who made herself scarce by looking at dresses. She sat me down and held my hand.

"Megan, please listen to me now. Your mother has hired me, and is paying me, to style you impeccably, and I will do it. But the most beautiful dress in the world will look horrible if you are not comfortable in it. And yet there are a lot of parties and you must wear something, yes?"

"Yes," I said.

"So please, you must trust me. I promise there is a middle of the road, a place where your mother is happy, but you are too."

"Promise?" I asked. If I had to put myself in someone's

hands, better this French lunatic than my mother.

"I swear it," Margot said, and looked as if she meant it. "You are full of fire, and we will find a way to bring that out."

"Okeydokey," I said, and Margot laughed.

"Now, what do you absolutely hate, the things you cannot wear?"

"Nothing pink," I said. "And no bows."

She held out her hand and we shook on it.

It turned out that Margot had a great eye and brought me loads of stuff over the next month that I would never have picked, in colors I would have shunned, but when I tried them on they looked way better than I expected. I relaxed a little, and she and Mom chatted the weekends away as the four of us stormed Neiman's, Saks, Barneys, and Nordstrom in a blitzkrieg of eyeing and buying that soon approached the GNP of a modest European country. It was ultimately embarrassing, and exhausting.

"Did you like the lavender for the museum luncheon?" Mom asked a few weeks in, as I slumped in a chair. Margot and Julia and the salesgirl had gone off for the fortieth time that day.

"Mom, seriously, I'll wear anything you want. Please just make it stop." The room was littered with shoe boxes, and dresses filled several large metal racks.

"You must have some opinion."

"My opinion is that you and Dad are spending way too much money on all this."

"You girls don't need to worry about that. Your grandmother left me a small trust specifically for your debut."

"I don't think a small trust is gonna suffice," I replied, but I knew my grandmother would have been tickled that her girls were blowing her cash on hats, gowns, purses, and heels.

Just then Margot appeared with a crushing armload of cocktail dresses. The salesgirl followed with a stack of shoe boxes so high and so precarious I thought the Cat in the Hat had arrived.

"Lucy, wait till you see the Versace!" Margot crowed. She somehow found room for the dresses on a rack and started rifling through them.

Mom jumped up.

I slumped deeper in the chair.

ᢒᡝᡅᠵ

"Please, Megan, can't you skip this one game?" Mom begged me that evening. It was the night before Abby's party.

"Mom, the party doesn't even start till seven. That gives me three hours, which is forever for a low-maintenance girl like me."

"But it's the kickoff to the entire season," Mom badgered. "You never—"

"Get a second chance to make a first impression. I know. Trust me, it's going to be fine."

The next afternoon I opened my locker and found my jersey, shorts, and socks neatly folded with my shin guards on the top shelf. But no cleats, no sports bra, and no underwear on the bottom. Instead, someone had left a Victoria's Secret box.

I looked over my locker door and, sure enough, Cat and Lindsay and Mariah and Lachelle and half the others were watching, waiting for me to discover their latest "gift." Since the tiara incident, I had been the victim of endless pranks. And they all knew today I was playing in an unusual doubleheader: starting striker against the Colorado State Rams in the afternoon, entitled fashionista at Abby's party that evening. I tore off the ribbon with a flourish, opened the box, and held up a pink satin push-up bra.

"Cute," I said, modeling it over my T-shirt to cheers and clapping.

"We knew you didn't have one," Cat said coyly.

"Actually, I do. In several colors."

"No you don't!" Cat gasped.

"I do. I've even got the chicken cutlet things you put inside. And tonight, I'm using them. That's right, ladies, tonight, for the first time in my life, I'm gonna have"—I squeezed my boobs together and bent over—"cleavage!"

This brought on huge laughter, with some whistles thrown in.

"I'll let you borrow them if you want," I offered to Cat.

"Ewww, hand-me-down boobs—no thank you," Cat said.

"Just rinse them off!"

"Okay, let's stop talking about this now," she said.

I smiled and realized that right now the other debs would already be deep into some serious primping—blowouts, massages, manicures. Mom and Julia were enjoying a spa day. I felt pretty certain I was the only deb strapping on shin guards right then.

Two hours later I bent over and adjusted those shin guards. We were now in the eighty-eighth minute, tied 3–3, and I had just earned a corner when, after a long run down the right side, a defender blocked my cross beyond the endline.

Strangely, though I'd run nonstop for an hour and a half, I wasn't particularly tired. My legs felt strong and my mind clear. Jogging toward the edge of the goal area, I glanced back, saw Mariah would take the corner kick, and was suddenly overcome by a slurring of time and a powerful out-of-body sensation. This had happened before and I knew then, with absolute certainty, that I was just seconds from scoring.

Giving myself over to the flow, I stopped above the penalty area with my back to Mariah. I felt the tug on my jersey as the CSU girl marked me—she was now between me and the ball. I closed my eyes, took a deep breath, and started to follow a low, imperceptible-except-to-me homing signal that I knew, just *knew*, would end with the ball in the net.

First, I threw the defender's hand off my jersey and took two quick steps toward midfield. I felt rather than saw her confusion as she wondered why I was moving away from the goal. Then I whirled and started a hard run on the outside, toward the far post. She went with me, satisfied that she was still between me and the ball.

Stride for long stride we ran, then I planted hard and pivoted directly back toward Mariah. My defender tried to reverse course with me, but I picked her off with another girl and now I was free, running parallel to the goal mouth.

Mariah always hits the ball with a lot of pace, and I heard the *thunk* as she launched it, saw it rise into the air, curling over a defender's head. I kept running as it continued to curve gently toward the goal.

The goaltender, to my left, sensed danger and angled forward. The ball was just too high for another inside defender, who jumped but missed, and I took one more step and now the goalie bolted forward, alarm bells ringing. Too late, I knew, but she was determined to try and clear it.

I leapt as high as I could and cranked my shoulder and hips, storing kinetic energy like a twisted rubber band. The ball soared toward me, and I hovered, waiting for it to arrive. When it did I gave it a clean, crisp flick with my head, turning my face directly toward the goal. I caught the blur of gold from the goalie's jersey, saw the ball blast past her outstretched fist and into the white mesh, captured like an amberjack in a trawler's net. Then, with more than a little shock, I saw the goalie's fist. Having missed the ball entirely, her brick-sized clenched hand was now aimed at my very fragile and exposed face.

In that split second I remembered the day my high school

physics teacher took us outside to demonstrate Newton's second law: force equals mass times acceleration. We all put trash bags over our clothes and adjusted our goggles while he put a cantaloupe on a metal table beside two hammers. He first tapped the melon with a ball-peen hammer—nothing happened. Then he hit it harder and faster—more acceleration but still low mass—with the same hammer. It barely dented the surface. Then he took the sledgehammer—more mass—and he tapped the melon. It bulged but remained intact. Then we stood back, and with a mighty swing he crushed the cantaloupe with the sledgehammer, sending pulp and rind and juice across the assembled class.

I hadn't thought of it since, but staring at that fist it came rushing back and I realized that if force did indeed equal mass times acceleration, this was going to hurt.

Seven

*In Which Megan Finds the Best Defense
Is a Good Offense*

I SAT AT THE KITCHEN TABLE, A BAG OF FROZEN PEAS pressed against my face.

"Let me see," Mom said.

I removed the bag.

"Oh dear God."

Her hand went to her mouth and she squeezed out another tear. Not exactly sure why she was crying, as I was the one who'd taken the heavy overhand right, but whatever—it was something to see. My right eye, purple and swollen half-shut, provided the centerpiece, but the entire right side of my face was puffy and mottled blue. The right side of my upper lip was so large it looked like I'd had a haphazard and badly aimed collagen injection, and it was bisected by a nasty split that still oozed blood, despite two very painful butterfly stitches tacked on by the trainers.

I pressed the frozen peas back on my face, more as

a kindness to Mom than for the healing effect. After two hours, whatever swelling could be prevented had been. Still, probably best not to remind her of that just now.

"Look on the bright side, Mom. I didn't lose any teeth," I said through the bag.

"No jokes right now, please." Mom emptied her glass of chardonnay, and refilled it.

Who was joking? If she'd hit me an inch lower I would have been in dental surgery right now.

"I don't know how I'm going to tell Camille," she said, more to herself than me.

"Tell her what?"

"That you're not going," Mom replied.

"Who said I'm not going?" I asked. Honestly, it hadn't actually occurred to me that a black eye and a probable concussion gave me a "Get Out of Debutante Jail" card for the evening, or I might not have been so quick to answer.

"Megan, you can't go to this party like . . ." She trailed off.

"Yes?" I offered, baiting the trap.

"Well. Like that."

"Why not?"

"What will people say?"

Typical. While I was sweating the little things like keeping all of my teeth and if it was safe to go to sleep, Mom was focused on the more important issues of my appearance and how it would affect her socially.

"Oh, I'm going," I said, suddenly feeling a rush of energy. I chucked the peas in the garbage can. They landed with a satisfying thump. I stood and poured myself a glass of wine.

"Are you *sure* you feel well enough?"

"Never better," I said, heading upstairs. "Besides, no sense in wasting the dress." I took no small pleasure in the fact that I was now defying my mother by attending Abby's party.

Once upstairs in my room, however, I had to reckon with reality. My eye throbbed, my jaw ached, my lip was on fire, and a clutch of drummers had taken up residence in my right temple. Stef, the head trainer, had given me eight hundred milligrams of Tylenol, and then, as I left, a single Vicodin—just in case. I reckoned if hours of dancing and revelry didn't count as "just in case," I didn't know what would, so I washed the pill down with chardonnay. Alcohol and pain medication: that should liven things up a bit.

In the large upstairs bathroom Julia sat in a director's chair facing the mirror. The theme of Abby's party was "Hollywood's Golden Age," and Margot had channeled young Grace Kelly with simple, dramatic makeup that brought out Julia's classic features.

She let loose a single giant curler from Julia's hair, and it fell to one side in a beautiful curve. She brushed it vigorously until it glowed like warm honey, then cupped it with her hand and shellacked it.

"You look fantastic," I told Julia.

"So do you," she replied, eyeing me in the mirror.

"Right?" I said. We all laughed.

"*C'est le pied*," Margot said to Julia, and then turned to me. To her credit she didn't flinch as she held out the chair. I sat. We looked at each other in the mirror.

I took a healthy swallow of wine and set the glass on the counter.

"Do what you can."

The four of us sat in the living room, dressed and ready, in stony silence. Mom's anger at my condition, and my decision to go anyway, hung palpably in the air.

The doorbell rang.

"I'll get it," I said, anxious to escape. I strolled in the general direction of the front door. For some reason, I couldn't feel my feet.

On the other side of the door would be my date, Hunter Carmichael. We had spoken a couple of times in the past week, but I had not met him in person. He was an attorney, apparently, in a downtown firm. I approached the door with a whiff of anticipation—after all, I wasn't against the idea of meeting someone, and on the phone he sounded gracious, if a bit nervous. Who wouldn't be?

I turned the doorknob and got my first look at Hunter Carmichael, dressed in a vintage black tuxedo, his hair slicked down with motor oil, boxed corsage in hand and smiling like a beaver. I instantly concluded that, while well-scrubbed and earnest, he wasn't my type—not by a country mile.

"Megan?" he asked, and of course he also had his first look at me. I had turned my face to the good side, just a bit, to delay the shock.

"You must be Hunter."

"So nice to . . . finally meet you."

"Thanks."

"You look . . ."

"I know," I said, content to leave it at that.

He tried not to stare, but that proved impossible. Sad too, because from the one side I looked good. Margot had achieved more than I thought possible, and in my lavender dress, with my hair back in an elegant chignon, I was tolerably pretty—except for the train-wreck part.

Mom and Dad stood to greet Hunter, who glanced back at me one last time. I smiled sweetly.

"This is my mother, Lucy, my dad, Angus, and my sister, Julia. Mom, Dad, Julia—Hunter Carmichael."

"Hunter," Dad said.

"Sir." They shook hands.

"So pleased to meet you," Mom said, offering her hand.

"It's an honor to meet you, Mrs. McKnight," Hunter purred. "And what a lovely dress." He was laying it on thick as peat moss. Julia and I exchanged looks behind his back, as if to say, "Oh well."

"Why thank you, Hunter," Mom said, blushing slightly.

"Very nice to meet you too, Julia," he said, turning.

He offered me the box he still held.

"I brought this for you."

"How thoughtful," I said.

"May I?" he asked.

"Of course." He opened the box and his fingers shook slightly as he tied a gorgeous violet orchid on my wrist.

"It's lovely, Hunter. And the color goes perfectly with my face," I said, without a trace of irony. Hunter tried to laugh, but it came out more like a late-stage tubercular cough.

"Hunter, would you care for a glass of wine, or . . . a drink?" Mom asked.

"No thank you." He looked at me. "We should probably be going."

"We should."

Julia's date, Simon Lucas, arrived as we were leaving. Simon was Abby's older brother, and we had spent family vacations with him and Abby since we were all kids. Simon was the perfect escort—he was fun and funny, and as they were cousins, there was exactly zero romantic pressure.

"We'll be right behind you," Dad said, waving from the front door.

Hunter gallantly held the door for me and in a supreme waste of resources two couples boarded two huge limos right next to each other, both headed for the exact same place. Securely seated inside, Hunter finally asked.

"Megan . . . what happened to you?"

"I was carjacked," I replied drily. Hmm, was that the sauce or the pills talking?

"It must have been gang-related," he said, excited. "There was an article about this just the other day. The police have noticed a big uptick in carjackings in the metroplex. They said lots of these incidents are younger members out to 'make their bones.'"

Make their bones? I sighed. It was going to be a long evening.

✺

The thirty-minute trip in to Dallas cemented my initial impression of Hunter Carmichael. Passably smart, too eager with a compliment, and not nearly as worldly as he imagined, he would do well in the sterile if rewarding corporate law world, which was his passion.

In that brief span I learned more than I ever hoped to about his firm, Kemper Dean, the sort that has little to do with practicing law and everything to do with the business of making money. Hunter was already plotting his ascent from slave to master. As he prattled I tried to feign interest, but this was not a strong suit.

Too bad he's not hot, I thought, gazing out the window at the passing buildings, *because if there was ever a night I might be reckless . . .*

We exited the freeway, turned on Harry Hines Boulevard, and immediately stopped, becoming the caboose in a train of limos delivering guests to Brookline Country Club. Bumper to bumper we crept along until we finally entered the gates. Built in the forties on the site of an old nursery, Brookline was the most beautiful club in town—an oasis where ancient Italian stone pines towered over long, low brick buildings draped in ivy. In the daytime it was shaded and calm—at night dramatic and cool. Tonight was beyond dramatic.

"Holy cow," Hunter said. Indeed.

Up ahead swirling klieg lights fired shafts of light deep into the night sky. Under the portico, valets rushed forward to hold the doors as High Society clambered out while photographers, dressed in 1940s-style suits and armed with antique Speed Graphic cameras, swarmed the red carpet. Guests posed, teeth flashed, flashbulbs popped and fizzled. It could have been a movie premiere at Grauman's Chinese Theatre seventy years earlier.

With just a few cars left in front of us, I realized I would soon be out there under the hot lights. And in this corner . . . Rocky Marciano.

"It's so *exciting*." Hunter leaned forward and gaped through the windshield.

Not the word I would have chosen.

"You know," he said, turning to me with a toothy smile, "I worked the partners hard to be an escort to this season's parties."

"Really? Why?"

"I'm in the market for a wife."

"Seriously?" I asked, now unable to hide my disdain. "Aren't you a tad young?"

"I'm twenty-six—lots of people get married at my age. And debutante parties are a terrific way to meet educated, well-bred girls from the best families."

"My dad talks about cows in much the same way," I said.

"You know," he went on, oblivious to my sarcasm, "some of the guys go through the deb announcement like it's a racing form. Rate the girls on their looks, try to pick the winners, stuff like that. But not me." He caught my reaction and realized what he'd implied about my own looks, then hastily added, "I'm all about finding someone for the long haul. Getting married is a very big step on the way to making partner at a firm like Kemper Dean—it shows you're solid, committed."

I had never met anyone with so many unromantic phrases in hand—*racing form? Long haul? Solid?* Marriage to Hunter sounded a lot like a life in trucking.

"I see. I don't suppose love figures into your . . . equation?"

"Love is very important—I'm not insensitive." *The jury's out on that one, Counselor.* "But love isn't just about fireworks. It can also result from shared values and goals, a common outlook on what's important in life—don't you think?"

The limo stopped and a valet opened the door.

"Well, I hate to disappoint you," I said, "but I'm just here for the sex."

Eight

*In Which Megan Rues Her Decision to
Mix Pills and Booze*

AS WE APPROACHED THE RED CARPET, HUNTER GAMELY held my hand. Once there we smiled like idiots, and it wasn't until the cameras came down that I saw the photographers' puzzled faces.

We walked on and waited while Julia and Simon arrived for their moment. Their pictures would be everything mine were not—gorgeous, timeless, something you'd keep.

Dad and Mom arrived behind them, in his truck. As a sweetener to Mom he had washed it, but it was the only non-limousine in sight, and Mom tried hard not to look mortified stepping out of the cab. From her expression I guessed they had been arguing—no doubt about why Dad had failed to rent a limo for the event. Dad took the valet ticket and led her onto the red carpet, and they stood for pictures. He looked dashing in a black tux, and when she felt the cameras on her she relaxed and I saw for a brief moment the elegant, intelligent woman he had married.

We gathered in front of the doors under a violet deco neon sign flashing *Mocambo*. The women adjusted their wraps, the men straightened their jackets, and we all gave each other a quick look of reassurance. Mom wilted a bit when she looked at me, but Dad didn't. He smiled at me, and I smiled back.

"Shall we?" Mom asked of no one in particular. We walked in.

If the outside was fun and glamorous, the inside was beyond belief. Passing through the doors we entered a throwback world to the supper clubs of the 1940s. Cockatoos squawked from banana trees, a gleaming maître d' waited, and big band music wafted like smoke through the curtains behind him. We checked our coats with a girl dressed in a short silk halter dress with a matching hat perched on her head. In her heels and fishnets, she might have sprung from the pages of *Life* magazine.

"Welcome, welcome," the maître d' crooned, and held back the curtained entrance.

Through those curtains a fantasy world waited, a time warp of such epic proportion it took my breath away. The main ballroom of Brookline, a dull and utilitarian space, had been transformed into "The Mocambo Club." We all gawked in silent wonder at the period booths, tables, dance floor, bar, bandstand, and a forest of glistening jungle trees. A phalanx of debonair men and sophisticated women jammed the immense room and scores of uniformed waiters delivered Cuba libres, brimming martinis, and champagne. Cigarette girls wended their way through the crowd offering cigars, handmade candy, and fresh yellow roses, while out on the parquet dance floor, couples swayed to a Latin-flavored "Mack the Knife," pumped out by a thirty-piece band in matching blue tuxedoes.

Gobsmacked by the spectacle, I felt a shard of fear stab me. I knew Aunt Camille and Uncle Dan were loaded—he was a senior partner in a very large law firm—but this was beyond imagination, and one day in the not too distant future we would have to host our own party. I wasn't sure exactly how much our grandmother had stuffed under the mattress, but if it was less than a quarter million, Dad would need to hock some cows to cover the difference. As he looked around I wondered if he was thinking the same thing.

We joined the receiving line. At the front, Abby, Aunt Camille, and Uncle Dan greeted guests. Abby wore black, elbow-length gloves and a black velvet gown overflowing at the bosom. The dress hugged her in all the right places, and with her long, curly red hair piled on top of her head, she looked extra fabulous. All three displayed that easy gracious manner that simply cannot be faked or bought. It is either encoded in your DNA, or it is not. Sadly, I had missed that sequence.

Until now I had escaped any brouhaha over my appearance by staying inside our scrum, but we were moving inexorably forward toward the hosts, approaching full exposure.

Mom licked her lips, and her mouth twitched in a half-smile/half-grimace that subtly betrayed her anxiety. Hunter squeezed my hand, and once again I turned my face slightly in an effort, if only for a few seconds more, to delay the reckoning.

And then Ann Foster appeared behind Abby.

Screw me, I thought, and the urge to turn and run gripped me. But boxed in by guests I stumbled forward. Aunt Camille caught sight of Mom, and Abby saw Julia.

"Julia!" she cried, happy to see a truly familiar face. Julia stepped forward and they hugged. Abby embraced Mom.

"Abby, this is amazing. You look gorgeous," Julia said. Abby beamed.

"Thanks. It was all Mom's idea." That made sense. Aunt Camille had unerring judgment, and she had clearly thought hard about the best venue for Abby's substantial "assets."

Julia and Mom moved on to Aunt Camille, and Abby searched for me. Behind her, Ann's eyes narrowed as she sensed something not quite right about my face.

Oh, what the hell, I thought, and stepped forward.

"Abby, congratulations!" Abby's face dimmed as she stared at my eye.

"Oh my God, Megan. What happened to you?" she asked, truly concerned. I considered the truth, tried a few one-liners out in my head, saw Ann cock her head, hoping for some adequate explanation.

"I, I—well, I'm so sorry, I got—"

"She was carjacked. By a gang."

I think if I, or really anyone but Hunter, had said it, everyone would have burst out laughing. But he was so ploddingly sincere, so clearly incapable of humor on such a grand scale, that it simply had to be true.

"Did you go to the police?" Abby asked, aghast.

A voice inside my head screamed, *Don't do this!* I knew I should reverse course, pronto, and clear up this vulgar, offensive lie. Delay could only lead deeper into the swamp. Still, I couldn't help myself.

"I . . . not yet," I stammered.

The wine and Vicodin clouded my judgment. In fact, mixing wine and Vicodin was bad judgment. I probably did have a concussion. Whatever the explanation, in the moment I just smiled and went with it.

Ann Foster didn't believe it for an instant. She practically had steam blasting from her nostrils, but she wasn't going to question me publicly.

"Oh you poor girl," Aunt Camille said as she hugged me.

"If they find them," Uncle Dan advised, "you can sue for damages. It's civil as well as criminal." I nodded, disgusting person that I was.

Fortunately, other guests pressed up behind us, and I shuffled on with some last hugs and final looks of concern. Hunter, my brave defender, had stood by me gallantly, and I sensed him mentally tick off the box for "loyal" on his partnership application.

"I need a drink," I said. Three or four hundred people filled the room, and it took some doing to squeeze through. We passed the bandstand, now piping out "The Boogie-Woogie Bugle Boy of Company B," and bellied up to the bar. The bartender winced when he saw my eye.

"Yes, ma'am?" he asked.

"Tequila. And leave the bottle." He raised his eyebrows—*seriously?*

"Kidding," I said. "Just a white wine please."

"And for you, sir?"

"Chivas and soda."

Hunter smiled at me. I smiled back, and looked around. Behind the bar hung a large antique mirror. In the mirror, to my right, stood a tall, broad-shouldered guy with wavy brown hair, chocolate eyes, full lips, and a square, dimpled chin. It couldn't be . . . but it was! My valet, the gorgeous man who'd parked my bike! *Now there's someone I could get reckless with.* I followed him in the mirror as he turned and walked away holding two champagnes.

"Thank you so much," I said to the bartender when he brought my wine, and immediately bolted some down. It was cold and bracing, just what I needed. Still feeling a little reckless I turned, anxious to see where the hottie had landed. Alas, I didn't have to look far. Directly in front of us Lauren Battle held court, and I sighed as he handed her a champagne.

Lucky her, I thought. *I get Hunter, and she gets this tall drink of water as her escort. Ann Foster really has it out for me.*

In a floor-length black dress, Lauren was a stunner. Beside her stood another guy—fair-haired, jovial, and they shared a nose, so I figured he had to be her brother. Ashley Two hovered to her right, completely ignoring her date, a douche-bro plucked from a beer commercial. I took another sip of wine and another secret sip of Lauren's date.

Lauren hadn't seen us yet, and with the room so packed there were lots of places to hide, but Julia and I were debutantes, two of only seven, and we were expected to mingle. Julia looked over at me and, knowing we couldn't stand there indefinitely, stepped forward.

"Hello, Lauren," Julia said.

Lauren coolly surveyed her competition for the spotlight. Their outfits that night told the whole story—Lauren had gone all-out on sex, while Julia parried with pure style. Her gown, pale silk the color of straw, hung straight from her shoulders on wispy straps, then cascaded down her long, slim frame like a waterfall to the floor. It was somehow both incredibly sexy and tastefully demure.

"Julia," Lauren replied, "what a fantastic gown!"

"Thanks," Julia said. "Yours is gorgeous too."

"Oh, thank you!" Lauren said. "This is my brother Zach—Zach, Julia McKnight." The fair-haired one stepped forward and took Julia's offered hand.

"Hey," he said.

"Great to meet you," she replied, paused, then looked down. "Um, can I have my hand back?"

"In a sec," he said, still holding on. What a flirt!

I immediately liked this guy, so clearly Lauren's antithesis. His eyes were bright and mischievous, and his hair had already come unglued in a boyish tumble. Judging from Julia's reaction, she liked him too.

Zach finally let go of Julia's hand.

"Sorry, man," he said to Simon, "but your date is . . . gorgeous. Zach Battle." They shook hands.

"No worries," he replied. "Simon Lucas." He indicated Julia. "We're cousins."

"First cousins?" Zach asked hopefully, eyes still on Julia. Simon nodded, Zach smiled broadly, and Julia glowed.

Lauren now turned to Handsome Man.

"And this is Andrew Gage—of the New York Gages." Beside me, Hunter tensed. His name meant nothing to me, but it clearly meant something to him.

"Andrew," Julia said, offering her hand.

"So nice to meet you, Julia," he replied. Andrew Gage stood very still and yet he hummed like a generator—you could feel the energy burning off of him.

Lauren didn't introduce him as her boyfriend, I thought. *Good sign—maybe he could be my escort to one of these things.* My heartbeat went from four to six at the thought.

Julia introduced Simon, and they shook hands.

"Lauren, you remember my sister, Megan," Julia said now. It was time for my close-up.

"Hello, Lauren," I said, stepping into the group.

Lauren took one look and burst out laughing.

"Oh, Megan." She tried, not very hard, to cover her delight. "I didn't think you could possibly outdo your appearance at the tea, but I was wrong—so wrong."

"Careful, Lauren," I said, loud enough for everyone to hear. "You should see the other girl."

"Zing!" Zach said as I leaned in to Lauren for an air kiss. Her eyes crinkled, not sure if I was kidding. I let her ponder and turned to the two men.

"Megan McKnight. Nice to meet you," I said to Zach.

"You too," Zach said, and he shook my hand with real feeling. "Does it hurt?"

"I've had eight hundred milligrams of Tylenol, a Vicodin, and half a bottle of wine. Honestly, I don't feel a thing."

Zach roared, but Lauren and Ashley Two sneered.

"Classy," Lauren said.

"Really," added Ashley Two.

"So it's Megan," said Andrew.

"So nice to meet you—again," I said.

"You've met?" Lauren asked, her hackles up.

"Not formally," replied Andrew.

"But he has seen my favorite sunflower panties," I said.

His shoulders went stiff.

Lauren pulled him closer.

"It was a misunderstanding," he said, still looking at me. "I met her outside after I dropped you at the orientation tea. She ripped her dress."

"Oh," Lauren said, working hard to find any hidden meaning in all this.

He dropped her off at the tea?

"So you're twins?" Zach asked Julia.

"Yes," Julia said.

"Fraternal," I explained. "She got the pretty egg." Zach laughed.

All this time Andrew stared at me, and my cheeks burned. I realized my face looked awful, but his scrutiny bordered on rude.

"You're staring," I finally said to him.

"Sorry," he said, looking down quickly. He was incredibly awkward, nothing like he'd been the day we met. Hunter, straining like a dog on a leash, stepped forward.

"Mr. Gage. May I call you Andrew?" Hunter gushed, offering his hand. "Hunter Carmichael. It's great to meet you."

"Thank you," Andrew said distantly.

"I know all about your family. I read your mother's memoir. The section about your father's death was absolutely heartbreaking."

Now the name popped, and the face, and I realized why Hunter was so effusive. Andrew Gage appeared occasionally in weekly magazines under headlines like "America's Hottest Bachelors" or "Thirty Billionaires under Thirty." Not that I bought that kind of trash—like most self-respecting people, I thumbed through them in line at the supermarket, then put them back.

Hunter reached in his pocket and handed Andrew a business card, said a few words. Andrew's withering look said it all, and I felt a pang of sympathy for Hunter. Sure, he was a tool, but Andrew didn't have to let him know it so publicly. Uncomfortable, I saw Dad at the bar.

"Excuse me." I smiled and walked away. Hunter stayed behind, unwilling to separate from Andrew Gage so soon.

I asked for a refill, and Dad and I stood side by side, backs to the bar, enjoying the circus.

"I am so damn proud of you," he said after a moment.

"Really? Why?" I asked, genuinely curious.

"I don't know one other girl—young woman," he corrected himself, "with the guts to come to a party like this looking like that."

He raised his beer bottle.

"Here's to you, Megan McKnight, the brassiest woman I know."

I accepted his toast. *Clink.* My evening brightened, until I caught Mom scowling at us from across the room, resentful that we might be having a good time in this moment of family tragedy.

"I'm not sure Mom feels quite the same way," I said.

"Look, you didn't make her day, but she's not really mad at you. She's mad at me."

"Why?"

"She found out I haven't called that fellow back yet."

"Why not?"

"'Cause I know what he's gonna say."

Hunter now looked over, and I saw the tumblers in his head fall into place: *Rule 4. Must not leave date alone.*

No, please, feel free, I thought, *leave date alone.*

He excused himself and walked our way.

"Dad, do something," I whispered. "Anything."

Hunter arrived.

"Would you like to dance, Megan?"

"Really, Hunter, you don't have to dance with me. I know how I look."

"But I want to."

I did not. Taking classes had not blunted my opinion that ballroom dancing was silly and outdated, and I would gladly have skipped it altogether. Especially tonight.

"Of course, then, thank you," I said, and gave my dad a "thanks a lot" glance, only to see him smile and raise his beer in mock salute.

Out on the dance floor Hunter gripped me like a ladder and waltzed me off at a good clip. *Slow down, sailor, I've got a head injury*, I thought as we lurched around, but Hunter plowed forward, oblivious to my misery.

"Zach and Andrew are business partners," he said, breathless with excitement. "Rumor has it they're engaged."

"Zach and Andrew are engaged?" I asked, my brain all muddly. We flew past Julia and Zach dancing, and then Lauren and Andrew. I focused on the horizon, praying it would cure my nausea. I was now actively regretting my quixotic decision to mix booze with downers.

"No—Andrew Gage and Lauren Battle," Hunter replied.

Engaged? I thought. *He may be handsome and occasionally*

witty, but he must be deeply broken if he wants to spend the rest of his life with her.

"His great-grandfather was a steel tycoon, you know," Hunter continued, "and his father was an advisor to President Clinton—he died a few years ago and left behind a fortune. His mother is practically the queen of New York. Even her dog, Mitzy, is famous. They go for walks in Central Park, with a bodyguard."

"Imagine!" I said, but Hunter again ignored my sarcasm altogether, still caught up in the thrill of the Gages and their first-class lifestyle.

"I gave him my business card," he continued. "You think that's all right?"

"I'm sure it is." Lying to Hunter was becoming a regular habit.

"I think it went over well," he said, his face a wall of concern over just how this chance encounter had gone.

The music stopped and Hunter slowed to a halt. I held on to him for an extra few seconds, waiting for my head to stop spinning. I took a deep breath, let go of his hands, and did not crumple to the floor.

"Thank you, Hunter, for such an . . . exuberant waltz."

"My pleasure." He smiled. Bless his overly earnest heart, all stink was lost on him.

"Would you excuse me for a moment?" Debutante code for "I gotta go pee now."

"Of course. I'll find our table."

"Great," I said, and took my first step. Teetering, I put my hand on Hunter's shoulder, steadied myself, and set off. Just a little farther, and I would be alone. I hoped they had a chair in the bathroom. I needed to sit down.

Someone fell in beside me. Ann Foster. I served her my best smile and she returned a stern, unhappy look. God, what now? She held the door for me, and followed me into the empty hallway beyond.

Ambushed.

Nine

In Which Megan Takes a Long Look in the Mirror

"THIS," ANN SPAT, INDICATING MY FACE, "IS NOT WHAT I meant by *surprise me.*"

"*This* was an accident—I got punched in the face in a soccer game this afternoon."

"How interesting. Because eight hundred party guests believe you were carjacked by a gang." Ann was seething, a lioness on the attack.

"I said that as *a joke!*"

"I am not amused."

"Well, I had no idea my clueless date would take it seriously and tell everyone."

A long look of reproach.

"We are rarely in control of other people's actions, Megan. We are, however, in absolute control of our own. And so, with your ridiculous appearance and this fantastic story, you have made yourself the talk of the party. I do hope you are proud of yourself."

"I scored the winning goal," I ventured.

A sharp intake of breath.

"I should have followed my instincts," she said, shaking her head. "You are simply not cut out for this. I expect your written withdrawal in the morning."

"You said I had a month. I have a week left!" I blurted. "I'm sorry, but I'm—well-rounded . . ." I wasn't entirely sure where this was going, but it felt good to try and defend myself. "I'm smart. And athletic. And I think it's a good thing that I can play soccer and go to school full-time and do this too. These other girls would wilt in a week with my schedule. I don't deserve this, so if you want me gone now, kick me out. Otherwise I still have a week to *surprise you!*"

Ann considered this outburst, but for a long moment made no reply. She was harder to read than symbols on a crumbling Assyrian temple.

"I agree that your varied interests are an asset," she said finally. "To a point. And I do admire your spirit. But your judgment is deeply flawed. Why didn't you just call me? If you had told me about the black eye and how it happened, I would have told you to do a good job on your makeup, and for God's sake make sure your cousin knows you're all right *ahead of time.* Do your best not to take attention away from her on her big night, but be there in support. I could have spun you to the guests as one of our most accomplished, dedicated debutantes, and this whole mishap would have turned in your favor. Instead you lied and made it an offensive joke, and in the process damaged an evening your cousin worked tirelessly to perfect."

"I'm sorry—again. That was not my intention."

"Whether intended or not, you have fallen further than even I expected, Miss McKnight. You may have your week, but I suggest you fill it with fervent and regular prayer."

"Yes, ma'am."

She left me there with my aching head and my big fat black eye, feeling like I'd been punched in the face for the second time that day.

Getting dressed for the evening had been an adventure. It started with my underwear, or what Margot offered me for underwear.

"What is that—a washcloth?" I asked.

"Spanx," she replied. "They will make you look smooth and perfect, and give you a nice silhouette."

They were the tiniest pair of shorts I had ever seen. I protested that they would never fit, but Margot coaxed and Julia nodded, so I pulled, hopped, crammed, and finally got them halfway up. Then I lay on the bed and kicked and squirmed and heaved until they somehow cleared my hips. With Margot's help, we yanked and smoothed some more, and at last they were on—an iron vise from mid-thigh to just under my boobs.

I walked slowly around the room, then felt an unexpectedly cool rush of air down below.

"Oh great, mine are ripped," I said to Margot, showing

her the split in the crotch. Julia and Margot giggled at my ignorance.

"That's for going to the bathroom," Julia offered, already comfortably ensconced in hers.

"You've got to be joking," I said. "I would need an Air Force bombsight to accomplish that, and there would definitely be collateral damage. Besides, I'm not hanging out like this for the whole party."

"Nobody will know," Julia said.

"I'll know."

"You can wear panties underneath if you like," Margot offered.

With a great deal of effort I somehow got the Spanx off, slid on the tiniest thong I had ever seen, then struggled back into the damn things. My central organs under siege, we moved on to my cleavage. Margot hooked me into an extremely tight strapless bra, then fit in two silicone cutlets to give me boost. Finally I stepped into my dress, and Margot zipped me in. Feeling like I was wearing a wet suit, I thought we were done. But no—next came the taping. Margot used double-sided toupee tape and sealed the edges of my dress to my skin to eliminate any gaping or crinkling. Twenty-five minutes of effort to get into a pair of man-trickers and fake boobs, and tape me to my dress. Sexy.

Now, an hour into the party, I had to pee. I raced up the stairs to the ladies' room, and there realized that what I had done in a large room with assistance, I now had to undo in a closet alone, with a water hazard. I lifted and bunched material until I could hold my dress up in one hand, and with the other hand I wrenched and pulled at the Spanx. They wouldn't budge. Gasping, sweating and desperate to go, I was finally able to roll them down below my ass. I collapsed onto the toilet seat in joyous relief.

Choosing maneuverability over modesty, I went outside the little tinkle cabana to get them back up again, only to discover that I'd popped my tape. I spent a good three minutes hoisting my bra back into place and smoothing and re-taping myself. I should have tried to pee through the hole.

I went to the sink to mop my sweat and wash my hands.

Shutting off the tap, I had a good long look in the mirror. I turned my head from side to side. Not quite Dr. Jekyll and Ms. Hyde, but close. One half was a rather attractive and stylish young brunette who looked ready for a night on the town. The other half was a fearsome beast with swollen purple features who looked hungry for a live squirrel. I bared my teeth in the mirror—*grrrrr.*

I mentally replayed my run-in with Ann. The worst part was that she was right. I couldn't avoid the beating I took that afternoon, but I could have handled it better. *And why hadn't I?* I didn't consider myself selfish and self-absorbed, but maybe I just wasn't looking hard enough. I felt horrible about taking attention away from Abby, or spoiling her party in any way.

There was no getting around it—I had to apologize: to Abby and Aunt Camille and Uncle Dan and Hunter

Carmichael—my, that was quite a list. I'd better get started. Figuring out just how to surprise Ann with only a week remaining would have to wait until my head cleared.

The ladies' room was on the second floor, and as I neared the top of the staircase I heard voices below and the name "Julia." Stopping, I peeked over the balustrade and saw Zach Battle and Andrew Gage below. The heavy carpet had muted my footsteps, and they had not sensed me above them. Like any girl would, I paused to listen, hoping to hear a few kind words about my sister.

"She's freaking gorgeous, right?" Zach asked.

"Granted. But—"

"I really like her," Zach went on.

"You just met her."

"So? She came with her cousin—that's a good sign." Zach was on the hook! I couldn't wait to tell Julia. "I'm gonna work it out to be her escort to the next thing."

"I think you should."

"And what about her sister?" Zach asked. "With that eye and that attitude? Total boss deb." *I'm a boss deb? Thanks, Zach.*

"Lauren thinks she's into chicks," Andrew said.

What? Is that the way I came across?

"No way," Zach countered. I glanced over the railing.

"She does play soccer," Andrew continued. "And drives a Subaru. Just saying . . ."

Now I was pissed. I had been dealing with this stereotype

my entire life—yes, there are lesbians in women's sports, but *playing sports does not make you a lesbian.* And anyway, what if I was? I knew lots of lesbians—my coach, for starters, and Mariah, one of my best friends on the team. *First he acts like we've never met and he can't wait to get out of talking to a plebe like me, and now this?* Andrew Gage was a snob who needed to be brought down a rung or two.

I started down the stairs—CLOMP, CLOMP, CLOMP. Their heads snapped up, and they knew they were busted. As I came down, taking my sweet time, the burning question lingered: just how much had I heard?

Let 'em squirm, I thought.

Andrew seemed particularly uncomfortable. Good. *I'll roast him on a spit with an apple stuffed in his mouth.*

"Hey, Megan," Zach managed. "I was just telling Andrew how much I like your sister."

I paused on the last step, smiled wickedly at Zach.

"Really? What a coincidence." I stepped down. "I really like your sister too." I sauntered past him, then winked at Andrew with my good eye. "She's smokin' hot."

I kept walking, determined not to look back. Behind me Zach laughed, and I'm pretty sure he punched Andrew in the arm.

Suck on that, I thought, and with the flame he'd lit a month before now firmly extinguished, I silently wished Andrew Gage good riddance.

꿈

When I returned to the table, Julia and Simon were eating. Hunter had waited for me. What a peach—he probably would make partner someday.

"So sorry. Ann Foster cornered me and wouldn't let me go."

"Is everything all right?" Julia asked.

"Fine. But I need to go talk to Abby. And Hunter," I said, turning to him. "You do realize I was not really carjacked?"

"You weren't?"

"No. I got punched in a soccer game."

"Oh," he said, pondering this new information. "But why would you say you were?"

"Because I'm psychotic. I knew we weren't a good match."

Hunter and I stopped by Abby's table, where I performed an act of penance worthy of our savior Jesus Christ. I told them the truth and apologized profusely and sincerely, both for the way I looked and for causing a scene. Abby laughed it off, and everyone was relieved to know I wasn't involved in a real felony, just a legal mugging. I told them again how wonderful the party was, and we went off to the buffet line.

Calling that spread a buffet was damning with faint praise. Casinos and cafeterias have buffets. This was a feast. Famished, I opted for everything. Smoked tenderloin? Yes, please! Grilled lobster tail? You betcha! Alaskan salmon? Don't forget the sauce béarnaise! Chophouse salad? Extra bacon! The guys serving enjoyed watching this chick with a shiner load up her plate, but it left Hunter shell-shocked, not that I cared. I stopped for rolls and butter, noted the home-made ice cream sandwiches.

As I returned to our table, I saw Andrew Gage staring at me and my gigantic plate of food. He didn't approach, made no gesture, said nothing, but just looked at me for a good ten seconds as I walked past. *Weirdo.*

For the next twenty minutes I ate steadily while Hunter, Julia, and Simon kept up the small talk. Afterward I felt much better. My thoughts drifted and I realized the evening had turned out much as I had feared. I didn't want to be here, didn't fit in, and had little hope that things would improve in the near future. Maybe I should take Ann's offer to withdraw while a shred of dignity remained.

"Would you excuse me, Hunter? I want to go browse the desserts."

"Of course," he said. His brow furrowed at the idea of me and more food, but he stood nonetheless and smiled gallantly as I marched back toward the buffet.

In fact, my dessert search was a ruse. I was beyond full, and I went straight past the buffet to the veranda doors and outside for some fresh air.

Texas nights in October run cool but rarely cold, and that night held to form. I wandered across the empty terrace toward a stone wall that held back Turtle Creek. Happy to be alone I kicked off my heels, hiked up my dress, sat down on the wall, and dangled my feet over the water. I took several deep breaths, exhaled, and for the first time since the game, my head really cleared. I stared into the black water below, where the round white moon floated like a china plate, and realized it really had been an action-packed eight hours.

As a little girl I never missed a chance to skip rocks, so I dug for a flat stone and skimmed it hard across the water. One, two, three hops and a "splash." The moon shimmied in the ripples, and my mood brightened slightly. My fingers searched for another rock. It too danced out into the darkness. Another satisfying splash. I considered making a wish.

"Good arm."

Startled, as I had neither heard nor felt anyone approach, I swiveled and found a guy standing behind me. He wore khaki slacks below a dark green military jacket replete with army buttons, epaulets, and a few decorations on his chest. He held his hat flat under his arm and stood straight without seeming rigid. He was cute enough if you go for crew cuts and spit shines, but jarheads aren't usually my type.

"Thanks," I replied, and turned away, wondering just what I had done to attract his attention.

"Mind if I join you?"

"Free country," I mumbled, "thanks to you, Captain."

He sat down beside me.

"Lieutenant." He pointed to his tunic. "One bar. Henry Waterhouse, ma'am," he said formally as he offered his hand. "My friends call me Hank."

"Nice to meet you . . . Hank. Megan McKnight." We shook hands and I noticed his strong grip.

"Is that a real uniform or do you just like to play soldier?" I asked, indicating the cropped battledress jacket and matching serge trousers.

"Both. This is a genuine World War Two dress M44, with the Eisenhower jacket," he stated.

"Natty," I said. "So you're in . . . the army?"

"I was in the Corps at A&M." He pointed to the Corps Stack medallions on his lapel. "I miss it sometimes, so thought this would be a good opportunity to bust it out."

"Aggie, huh?" I asked, without enthusiasm.

"'Fraid so," he answered. "You?"

"Pony," I said, using the slang for SMU. "Majoring in history, but mostly playing soccer." We rested there, both content to bask in the moon's glow and the cool draft off the water.

"You know," he said, after a bit, "that eye is the talk of the party."

"Really?" I answered. "I hadn't noticed." This was an outrageous lie, of course, as pretty much everyone at the party had either stared or pointed at me.

"It's caused a good bit of speculation. Some have it that you were carjacked by a gang, and others are saying it was an alley fight over a boy. One lady told me she heard that you faked the whole thing and it's nothing but makeup."

"People do talk."

He laughed and I was surprisingly happy that I made him laugh—almost everything till now had been a downer, and though he really wasn't my type, he was pretty cute when he smiled.

"So which is it?" His tone managed to walk a line between playful and curious.

"D. None of the above. Some girl I've never met punched me in the face."

"Well, that's plain rude. What did you do to her?"

"I scored a goal. And she didn't like it."

"Ah. Tough, sweaty girls running around smashing into each other," he mused. "I gotta admit, that's a bigger turn-on than any of the other explanations I heard."

"Plus, afterwards? We all shower together." He raised his eyebrows. *Whoa, Megan, you just met the guy.* But I couldn't help myself—the words had just rushed out. It occurred to me that Hank Waterhouse brought out the flirt in me.

He grinned back and we sat beside each other in a comfortable silence.

"So, are you a deb or family?" he asked.

"Both. Abby is my cousin, and my sister Julia and I are both debs too."

"Well, clearly you're a fighter. I think you'll make it," he said.

"I appreciate the vote of confidence," I replied. I thought about telling him how tenuous my hold on debdom was at the moment, but figured it would spoil the moment. "What about you?"

"Oh, you know, home on leave," he deadpanned. "My

company's about to ship out for Germany, save the world from the Nazis and all. Just hoping I might meet some nice girl who'll take pity on me, maybe give me her picture. I don't wanna die a virgin."

I busted up. He had such an open, honest look about him, so apple pie, that I hadn't expected anything so sly and downright funny. I looked closer and noted his gray eyes were full of humor and intelligence.

"Well I'm a patriot and all," I managed a moment later, "but that's a pretty forward request, Lieutenant, seeing as we just met."

"You're right. How about we start with a dance?" he asked.

"You really gonna dance with a bruiser like me? Could lower your reputation."

"I'll risk it."

"Then I accept."

He stood, then helped me up. I put on my shoes and we walked back across the veranda. He held the door for me and as I stepped through I ran smack into Andrew Gage, on his way out.

"Oh, excuse me," he said.

"That's all right," I replied, and we locked eyes.

"I really wanted to talk to you, Megan."

"Okay." What could Young Master Gage have to say to me?

"I just wanted to tell you how—" He stopped as he saw

Hank come in. Hank stopped too. Clearly they knew each other, and not in a good way. Their clenched jaws dueled right there in the doorway. *What the hell?*

"Um, Andrew, this is Hank—"

But Andrew turned and walked away before I could finish, without a further word to me or any explanation.

"Uhh, sorry," I said to Hank. "I have no idea what that was about."

"It's all right," he said.

"Honestly, I just met the guy tonight and, well, he's a bit of an asshole."

"I know," Hank said. "We were friends for a while—but not anymore."

"Lucky you."

"You still want to dance?" Hank asked.

"I do."

He took my arm and once on the dance floor held one hand and placed his other at the small of my back. Standing in front of me, gazing down with his dove-colored eyes, he seemed taller, and suddenly quite handsome. I felt a small surge pass between our hands as the band began to play "What a Wonderful World," and we set off easily to the slow, romantic song. As we moved around in a lazy arc I was impressed by Hank's graceful, measured steps, and in contrast to Hunter's banter he seemed content not to talk.

I zigzagged between enjoying dancing close to Hank and a nagging curiosity about the scene between him and

Andrew. Andrew had been looking for me: why? And the look on his face when he realized I was with Hank—it was almost . . . protective. He looked like he wanted to hit him before he left. I considered asking Hank about it but knew it would break the mood.

"I love this song," Hank said, interrupting my quandary. So he was good-looking, funny, a fantastic dancer—and a romantic too? *Lucky me.*

"Me too," I said softly, and smiled up at him.

I closed my eyes and listened to the music. I held on to Hank and let my feet go wherever he led. Thoughts of Andrew Gage skittered away like brittle autumn leaves in a brisk wind.

Julia and I slept in our old rooms at the ranch that night. Just as I turned out the light she crawled into bed with me. I knew she wanted to talk about Zach, but she was never one to be open about her feelings, even with me. Fortunately, I had just the tool to pry it out of her.

"I overheard Zach talking about you." She bolted upright.

"Really?"

I nodded, and she waited expectantly.

"He was telling Andrew Gage just how gorgeous you were, how much he liked you—"

"He was not!"

"Was too," I said. "So—do you like him?"

"I do," she said. "He's funny and cute, and that cowlick—woof."

"Well he's going to be your escort for the next dance." Looking at her I could tell that hope bloomed, but Julia always kept her emotional cards close.

"We'll see," she said finally.

A moment passed.

"How about you?" she asked, not so subtly changing the subject. "Any prospects?"

"Hmm," I said. "The evening started out rocky with the brown-nosing, wife-hunting bore, then deteriorated with nasty insults from the scion of America's first family."

Julia frowned at my unhappy tale. I smiled at her.

"But it ended with a handsome and intriguing young officer in uniform."

"That doesn't sound all bad," Julia said.

Not bad at all. For the first time since discovering my name and picture plastered across *The Dallas Morning News*, I thought, *This whole debutante thing might not be a complete waste of time after all.*

Ten

In Which Megan Nearly Tosses Her Cookies

WA-OO-GAH! THE SOUND OF AN OLD CAR HORN WOKE me with a start.

"Megan."

"What?" I said sleepily.

"It's your phone!"

I was hunkered down in my bed under a thick down comforter. Julia lay beside me, her head resting on her hand.

"Leave me alone," I said.

Wa-OO-gah!

"Aren't you going to see who it is?" she asked, clearly not pleased that the sound had woken her. My phone was across the room on a chair, much too far away.

"No."

"Are you really my sister?" She sank back down and rolled over. This drove Julia insane and was a long-running point of contention between us, as texts and calls from her often went unanswered for hours, even days. Like most girls she was umbilically attached to her phone, and not reading and responding to a text immediately was inconsistent with life as she knew it.

But I was thirsty. I sat up very slowly, treating my head like a rare Fabergé egg. It ached, and my lip felt as big as a croissant, but I was alive. I stood and shuffled to the bathroom and poured a drink of water.

On my way back, I leaned over carefully, and retrieved my phone.

"It's from Hank," I said, sitting on the bed.

"Who?"

"The Aggie jarhead."

"Really?" Julia sat up, intrigued. "What does it say?"

"*I have a problem,*" I read off the phone. "Car trouble, I bet."

Julia sighed, audibly, as if I were a dodo bird working a math problem in the sand.

"Megan, he's not texting you at nine in the morning with car trouble."

"He's not? Then what's wrong?"

"Ask him."

"I don't know how," I whimpered.

"Seriously?" she asked. I nodded.

"You know I suck at this." I offered her the phone, and she took it.

I looked over her shoulder as she quickly typed, **Oh no, what's wrong?**, then hit send. *Whoosh*—off it went. We waited, and in a moment we could see that Hank was typing. *Wa-OO-gah!*

I can't stop thinking about you.

"Oh my," Julia said, showing me the phone. I took the phone, read and reread the message. Julia smiled at me. I smiled back. *Wa-OO-gah!* indeed.

How's your head? he wrote next.

"Okay, so just answer," Julia coached.

I typed **Good** and showed it to Julia.

"Oh my God, Megan, you are hopeless."

"Then what should I answer?" I whined. Julia sighed for the second time.

"Be playful."

"How do you make *this* playful?" I asked, indicating my face.

She thought for a moment.

"Okay—tell him *Better than expected. But my lip is very tender.*"

My look said it all—"I am not writing that."

"You want to flirt, right?" she asked.

"Yeah, but don't you think that's too . . . forward?" Cause for another sigh.

"If I'm not mistaken, *forward* is the direction you're trying to take things, Megan."

"Okay, okay." I typed. I checked with Julia one last time, then pushed send.

"What now?"

"See if he comes back."

In the bathroom I brushed my teeth, anxious to scrub off

the film left by the night before. I wasn't much of a drinker, and never did drugs, and I vowed that morning to be more cautious going forward. His next text arrived as I was rinsing, and I surprised myself by rushing back to see what he had written.

"*Tender lips—I like the sound of that*," I read. "Julia, you are a genius! Now what? More about the lips?"

"Yeah, but not romantic," Julia said. "Change the subject."

"How?"

She considered. I waited. She looked at my lip.

"How about *Trust me, it's the wrong kind of tender.*"

"You're so good at this!" I exclaimed, tap-tapping away. I sent the message and looked at her.

"Now, before he texts back, ask him a question. Something basic, like *What r u up to?*"

I typed away happily, and pushed send.

I'm at the office working. :(

"Ask him what he's wearing," Julia said.

"Are you sure?"

"Megan, he's at the office. He's fully dressed, and knowing what he's wearing will give you some insight into what kind of guy he is. Plus, you get points for spicing your text with a harmless but semi-sexy question."

"Wow."

What r u wearing? I typed.

A suit.

Color?

Gray.

Tie?

"Why do I care about this?" I asked Julia, after I sent it. "Just trust me, okay?" she said. *Wa-OO-gah!*

Crimson.

So professional. I'm sure you look very handsome.

Come see! I'm in the crappy junior exec office.

"He wants me to come see him!"
"You can't go," Julia said emphatically. I stopped typing.
"I can't?" She shook her head.
"It's too soon, and your lip looks terrible. And saying no will be teasing, and therefore perfect flirting."
"I have no idea what you are talking about," I said, but dutifully typed . . .

Can't. Too much homework. :(

But I want to see you!

You'll just have to wait!

:(do u have a date for picnic next Sat?

"Bingo," Julia said.

"That was magic." I was genuinely impressed. "You are the puppet master."

"It's not rocket science, Megan."

"Maybe for you, but I just don't get this."

"There's nothing to get. You just have to act interested, give him some clues now and then. You know, let him know he's on the right path."

"Can't I just tell him he's on the right path?"

"No."

"Give him a thumbs-up?"

"No! Megan!"

"Why not?"

"Because that's not the way the game is played. You have to, oh God, I don't know. Just smile at him, play with your hair, bite your lip, whatever. And text him when he texts you, and occasionally when he doesn't, but don't answer too quickly, and don't agree to anything too easily, especially in the beginning. Tease him, put him off—like today, you can't see him, even though you could, but agree to see him next weekend so he has something to look forward to, and so he'll think about you all week."

"So . . . even though I'm interested, and he's interested, don't tell him directly I'm interested but act sort of interested and hope that he knows I'm interested by texting him back today but not agreeing to see him until next week?"

"Exactly!"

"I can't do this."

"You just did!"

"No, you did. What if you're not there?"

"I will be. But you've got to make some effort because if you don't, you know what will happen—he'll stop trying, and go away."

I didn't like the sound of that. Julia stood up.

"Where are you going?"

"To get some coffee."

"But I haven't answered him yet."

"Oh, right. What was the last thing?"

"Do I have a date for next Saturday's picnic?!"

Not yet

You do now. I'll pick you up at 2.

:)

Address?

That big stadium on Mockingbird. U can't miss it.

See u then!

:)

After Julia left I sat on my bed. With her help I suddenly had a date next week with a really cute guy I liked who seemed to like me. And last night he had seen me at my absolute worst, with a face left over from a cage fight, and then texted me the next morning.

As I chewed on all that had happened in the past twenty-four hours, the encounter by the stairs with Andrew Gage still burned. I now wished I'd mustered up something more self-righteous and crusading, something like, "How dare you act as if that's something to be ashamed of—I know lots of lesbians, and they're great people, not like you, you small-minded and prejudiced man! And let me tell you something else—Subarus are very dependable cars!"

I smiled to myself, happy to have it out with him once again, even if only in my mind. And then, in a flash, I realized just how I knew Sydney, the uncomfortable debutante from the orientation tea. She had dated Mariah last year—she came to all the games, they hung out, I'd even seen them making out once. They broke up sometime last year, and I hadn't seen her since, but it was definitely her.

No wonder she had looked nervous when she saw me. A lesbian debutante—I was pretty sure the dinosaurs at the Bluebonnet Club would not be down with that.

✑

"Just coffee," I said. Mom poured while I sat at the table. Next to me Julia worked on a bowl of cereal while Dad read the sports news on his iPad.

"I have eggs, bacon, fruit, bagels . . ." Mom offered.

"Not hungry, thanks." She let this unusual reply pass without comment, but Julia glanced over.

"What?" I whispered.

"Nothing," she said, and buried her smile in her spoon.

It made me think—why wasn't I hungry? Probably because my head ached, I had at least a mild concussion, and I drank far more last night than almost ever on top of pain medication. And this morning I flirted for half an hour with a cute guy who seemed to like me. It was a lot to digest, without adding in real food.

"Megan, we need to talk," Mom said, sitting beside me.

"Sure—what's up?"

"Last night was . . . a disaster."

"What?!"

"You humiliated me, Megan. Publicly, to a group of people I've known my whole life, who haven't seen you since you were a little girl, who saw you there looking like—like you had been in some kind of *bar fight*."

Speechless, my mouth hung open. In my version of events I was the hero. I scored the winning goal, overcame a head injury, and still managed to chat and dance my way through my cousin's debut party.

I wished Margot were here to provide a welcome buffer between me and Mom.

"Now when this all began," Mom continued, "I asked you to give up soccer for the fall—and under pressure"—here she glanced over at Dad, who did not look up—"I agreed for you to do both. If yesterday proved anything, it proved that was a mistake."

"Mom, I'm not giving up soccer. I'll give up the debut," I said. "Gladly."

"Megan, be realistic. It's too much, and we are spending

a fortune for you to put your best foot forward, and—"

"I didn't ask you to do this!" I nearly screamed. Julia, who hated conflict, picked up her cereal and left for the den. Before Mom could get back in, the phone rang. She picked it up without answering, looked at the number, then held out the phone for Dad.

"Who is it?"

"It's Sam Lanham—about the offer."

"Tell him to call back," Dad said, and went back to the news.

"No, Angus—you tell him." Mom's tone had some real edge now. Dad looked at her.

"It's Sunday morning, Lucy, I'm not—"

"Since you won't call him back, he probably thinks it's the only time he'll reach you."

The phone rang for a third time—one more and it would go to voice mail.

"I'm not taking it," Dad said firmly. Staring right at him, Mom answered the call.

"Hello? Yes, it is. Fine, Sam, thank you—how are you?" A pause here. Dad was staring daggers at Mom, but she didn't care a whit. "Why yes he is—hang on just for a moment, will you?" She handed the phone to Dad, who grimaced.

"Hello." He stood and walked toward the hallway. "Real good, Sam, thanks. Mm-hmm."

Mom turned back to me. My parents' tiff had given me time to plan my next move.

"Ann Foster didn't ask me to quit soccer."

"You spoke to her?"

"Of course. She agreed that this was . . . unfortunate. But she thinks soccer makes me well-rounded."

"Really?"

"Mm-hmm."

I heard a series of mumbles, the occasional "Yep" or "I understand" and now a final "I sure will" before Dad hung up.

As Mom had chosen this morning to fight a war on two fronts, she now turned to Dad, who handed back the phone.

"Well, what did he say?"

"Just what I thought." Mom waited impatiently for the details.

Dad walked to the kitchen window, which provided a magnificent view across the Aberdeen to the west. He looked out.

"That's right, Lucy, for a truckload of cash, XT Energy will happily put up their wells and pipelines, pump it full of sand and water, and blow it to all to kingdom come." He turned back to her. "Is that what you want?"

"No, of course not. Nobody wants to see our family's land destroyed," she said hurriedly. "But we are stuck. You already sell off little pieces of land every few—"

"Little pieces! Not the whole thing! And not to vultures!"

"I'm tired of this, Angus. This cycle is wearing me down. Feed bills come in, we sell thirty acres; tuition's due, we sell some more; can't meet payroll—"

"I get it!" He cut her off. By now Mom was crying, and Dad's jaw tightened.

"I can't keep living this way," she sobbed.

"I'm not taking the deal. *We're* not taking it. And knowing it's out there just makes it worse."

"Well, I'm sorry you feel that way," Mom said.

"Well, I'm sorry you answered the phone." Dad left without another word.

Nauseated at what I'd just seen, I took my coffee and went upstairs. My parents *never* fought like this—they bickered, sure, but this was something new.

I remembered my dad asking me to "do this debut thing" in the barn, telling me how much it meant to Mom, and when I'd asked why, his cryptic reply was, "You have no idea." Since Julia and I had gone off to college, Mom had definitely seemed out of sorts, but I hadn't known just how unhappy she was. They were fighting like never before, and I worried their marriage was in real trouble.

Last night Ann had made it clear that short of a miracle, I was out in a week. But Dad was depending on me—when he'd asked me to do it for him, he meant for *them*.

I took a sip of coffee, and my stomach clenched.

I *had* to make this work.

Eleven

In Which Megan Throws a Hail Mary

THE PROBLEM WITH JULIA'S BRILLIANT PLAN TO MAKE Hank wait a week to see me was that I had to wait a week to see him too. And I am not good at waiting—I'm more of an instant-gratification girl. Fortunately, it was beyond a busy week: I had two tests, morning workouts and practices, and a game Wednesday afternoon, and while dance class was finished, the Season had officially started and events were lined up on the horizon like planes on approach to DFW airport. Monday, the Junior League hosted a lunch at Brookline, and I barely made it back to practice. Tuesday, the Petroleum Club held a dinner in Renaissance Tower, which meant I had now missed six Tuesday nights watching TV with Cat. And Thursday, Highland Park Presbyterian Church put on an afternoon "social," and I do mean social. The church boasted three thousand members. My right hand felt blistered from greeting so many new people, and my cheeks ached from smiling nonstop for three hours.

Worse, my week to "surprise" Ann Foster was a day from over, and I had yet to think of one decent idea. I wondered if she would accept a cow as a bribe—I figured, given the stakes, Dad would let me have one, and delivery of a live cow to her door had to qualify as a surprise, though perhaps not the kind that would impress her. Desperate and exhausted, I scoured my deb bible at midnight on Thursday with Julia, but couldn't find anything helpful. I was doomed.

And then, on page 16, buried deep in the details, Julia found the answer: Young Ladies' Etiquette & Decorum with Ann Foster.

"Deportment class?" I asked. "She said *surprise me.*"

"It's the best you're gonna do—you're showing willingness. And initiative," Julia said. "And how can she kick you out if you're *her* student?"

I was impressed. This was socialite judo at its finest.

"It starts tomorrow afternoon," I said, after looking it up online.

"Perfect, just in time," Julia said.

So at 2:30 Friday afternoon I stood in a silk bra and panties in our apartment contemplating just what to wear to Young Ladies' Etiquette & Decorum. Julia and I had so many outfits, along with instructions from Mom and my debutante field manual to never, *ever* wear the same thing twice, that we had transformed our living room into a vast closet. We had pushed the couch back against the wall, removed the coffee table, and installed two dress racks, one "to be worn" and one "already worn," each labeled half "J" and half "M." The shoes were stacked in boxes, each with a picture of the shoe inside pasted to the outside, because Julia was obsessive about this kind of thing. Handbags, scarves, and various accoutrements hung from a hat rack made from native cedar and longhorns we had cadged from the ranch.

I considered the gently used "already worn" rack. I tallied the cost for that first week alone and decided it would feed a Kansas family of four for a year—and they could shop at Whole Foods. In the developing world it would feed an entire village and their cattle too.

Disgusted, I focused on what to wear for Ann Foster and chose the full armor: an ivory merino wool Calvin Klein top, a mocha silk skirt that ended decidedly below the knee, and matte black pumps with conservative two-inch heels. I accented the demure ensemble with Julia's diamond earrings and a string of freshwater pearls I'd inherited on my sixteenth birthday. *Everything except a bulletproof vest*, I thought.

Next I worked on my face. The swelling around my eye was nearly gone, and to mask the latent bruising, now delicate shades of green and yellow, I put on a coat of base and smudged in some rouge. I swept my hair back and up, brushed a thin film of Vaseline and an overcoat of reddish-brown lipstick on my cracked lip, dabbed my eyes with mascara, and squirted myself with Jo Malone Vanilla & Anise. Wide Prada sunglasses provided the final touch. I looked in the mirror and thought, *Perfect*.

I arrived at the Crescent Hotel at precisely 3:45 p.m., cool, crisp, and fifteen minutes early. I smiled at the doorman, and passed through the lobby to the concierge desk.

"May I help you?" she asked.

"Yes, hi, I'm here for the—young ladies' etiquette class."

The woman paused, seemed about to say something, then changed her mind.

"Is something wrong?" I asked. "Has it been canceled?"

"No, no," she said. "That will be in the Bordeaux Room. Left past the front desk and then down the hallway to the end."

"Thank you."

"You're very welcome."

The Bordeaux Room? What was it with all the fancy-sounding rooms at these places? The Crescent complex was built on a Parisian theme, great soaring blocks of graying concrete with slate mansard roofs, so I guess they took the French thing seriously. As I walked down the hallway I laughed to myself—*If I had asked for the bathroom, she would have directed me to the Salle de Poo Poo.*

⌒e⌒

Outside the Bordeaux Room I smoothed my skirt, checked my sweater for lint, and glanced at my watch. I was early and dressed impeccably, and I opened that door with confidence, not a bead of sweat on me.

"Hi," a girl said, standing and smiling and smoothing her dress just as I had done outside the door. She had a pile of blonde curls and wore a red silk dress embossed with roses, white leggings, and shiny black Mary Janes. *She can't be a day over ten*, I thought, and all my plans for surprising Ann and saving my bacon crashed down around me. Clearly I had misunderstood the definition of "Young Ladies."

"Hello," I replied.

"I'm Carli!" She held out her hand gamely. I smiled to mask my panic and we shook hands.

"I'm Megan, Megan McKnight."

"It's very nice to meet you," Carli said politely.

"It's very nice to meet you too."

Another girl, of a similar age, smiled eagerly. She was dressed in a shiny white frock with a lace petticoat and glittering white sandals festooned with Diamelles.

"I'm Hannah. It's very nice to meet you."

"Megan McKnight. It's very nice to meet you too, Hannah," I replied, and we shook hands demurely. There were three more—Isabelle, Jayla, and Paige.

"Are you the teacher?" Carli asked.

"No, I'm not the teacher." I looked back at the door, thinking there was still time to split before Ann arrived. She was going to think me the dumbest person she'd ever met if I didn't get out now.

"So you're here for the class?" Carli continued pressing.

"Um, well . . ."

"Are you doing Junior Cotillion?" Carli couldn't stop the questions.

"No, I'm making my debut."

"Really?" Hannah asked. "At the symphony?"

"No, I'm in Bluebonnet."

All the girls gawked at me.

"Really?" Paige asked, in awe.

Somewhat surprised that they knew the difference, I nodded. This was the great divide in Dallas debuts. The Dallas Symphony Orchestra debut was a much shorter season—far cheaper and more of an application than an invitation—while the Bluebonnet debut was known as "the One."

"How did you get chosen?" Carli asked, agog. She said the word *chosen* pretty much the way someone would refer to Jesus.

"Ah, well, my mom debuted, and so did my grand-mothers, and an aunt, and my great-grandmother. My family's been part of it for a long, long time."

"Cool," Hannah said.

"So you're doing Junior Cotillion?" I asked.

All the girls nodded.

"My sister Julia did Junior Cotillion." In fact, probably Lauren and the two Ashleys and all of the other debutantes except me had done Junior Cotillion. I had to admit, the pictures were the cutest ever—all the girls in white dresses dancing with boys in tuxedoes, so deliciously awkward. Half the girls were taller than the boys.

"Did she make her debut too?" Carli asked.

"We're doing it together this year—we're twins."

"*Both* of you were chosen?" Paige asked.

I nodded.

"Your family must be a really big deal," Jayla said.

"Well, we have been in Texas for a long time."

"What happened to your eye?" Carli asked now. She had been looking at my face.

"I play soccer for SMU, and a girl hit me in the face in a game last week."

"You play college soccer too?!" Isabelle asked. Apparently, I was now the coolest person on earth, and it gave me a jolt of pride and confidence. At least I had impressed someone, if only a pack of tweens.

"I play soccer!" Isabelle said.

"Me too," Carli added. "Do you *love* Alex Morgan?" She looked at the ceiling as she said her name—Alex Morgan was a religion with little girls.

"I do. She's great," I said.

"I want to be her," Isabelle said with nary a trace of hesitation.

"Work hard," I advised.

I checked my watch. It was one minute to four. I started for the door, but before I could move, it opened and in walked Ann Foster. She saw the little girls first and then her gaze fell on me. She stopped cold.

"Miss McKnight. What are you doing here?"

I had been planning to cut and run. This class was clearly not meant for me and I had no intention of looking more like a fool to Ann, but the look on her face right now, *that* was the look I needed—a delicious swirl of shock and astonishment. I pushed my chips in right then.

"Surprise!" I said, vamping a little. She quickly composed herself.

"How nice of you to join us," she said very formally, and turned now to the girls. "Good afternoon, ladies. Let's begin with introductions, shall we? Miss McKnight I already know."

I watched her introduce herself to each of the girls—first Hannah, then Carli, Isabelle, Jayla, and Paige. She was hiding it well, but I had definitely surprised her, and I loved it.

"Now, who can tell me what deportment means?" Ann asked.

"Um, it means, like, how you act," Jayla offered.

"It does. And more so how we carry ourselves, the image we project to the world through our bearing and behavior. Proper deportment can be summed up in one word: poise."

Here she looked at us.

"*Poise* is from the French 'to weigh.' It signifies a state of balance, or equilibrium, like two things of equal weight. Think of a scale." Now she held out her hands like scales. "Poise is characterized by composure, steadiness, and stability, but do not confuse this with a lack of effort. We are not slack or lazy when we are poised. Rather, we are in balance, in perfect control of our emotions and our actions, our thoughts, and especially our bodies. Imagine a ballerina." Ann stood on one leg, and let the other rise effortlessly behind her— now I was sure she had been a dancer. "When she stands on her toes on one leg, and maintains that posture, we say she is *poised*. But attempt it and you will find it takes maximum effort to remain so, and to keep your face calm and not waver is most difficult." She returned to both feet. "This talent does not come easily—it is the result of hard work and long hours of practice. So poise is a muscle that must be exercised. And that is the purpose of deportment class—to exercise poise in all of its variations until you have built the confidence to carry that composure out in the world."

My worlds had now officially collided. Ann's sermon on poise might well have been given by Coach Nash, if you added a Euro tracksuit and occasional spitting. Coach lectured us about composure pretty much every day. In a game we had only a millisecond to make decisive plays, so success demanded the utmost poise and absolute control, no matter the circumstances. Regardless of fatigue or injury, when the moment presented itself you had to be prepared for it. Coach had made it clear that my missed goal at the end of the University of Oklahoma game had shown a tragic lack of poise, not unlike my late arrival and ripped dress at the first tea.

"Today, however, we will focus on the basics. Please stand in front of your chairs." We did.

"Most people believe that good posture involves pulling your shoulders back and raising your head, which is true. But that begins with your feet and flows through your hips. Now I want you all to stand with your feet solidly underneath you, right below your hips."

We all stood and checked our feet. Ann made minor adjustments.

"Good. Now turn your left foot out slightly. And here is a most important thought: our shoulders are not *back* because we hold them there with our muscles, our shoulders are naturally back and our head sits on top of our shoulders when our spine is properly placed in our hips. So now, I want you to let your spine sink into your hip sockets, and that will allow that gentle curve in the small of your back. Can everyone feel that?"

Nods all around. As a sloucher this was uncomfortable, but when I did it, right away I felt my shoulders retreat comfortably and my butt naturally pooch out behind me. *Who knew? I bet that looks good from back there!*

"Now, with your feet solidly below you and your spine in alignment, I want you to imagine your head is a balloon, filled with helium. It rises effortlessly, as if on a string, and hovers."

I took a deep breath in and imagined my head was filled with helium. To my surprise my head did just what it was supposed to do—rose slightly and floated.

"Good. Now, breathe from your stomach and just stand."

Okay. I stood, and breathed, as did all the girls. Ten seconds. Fifteen. Ann didn't move.

Thirty seconds. Forty-five.

"Hannah, your chin is dropping." Hannah raised her chin. "That is one minute. We are going to stand for five minutes."

I ran for hours, lifted weights, rode my bike everywhere, and now this broad was threatening me with *standing* for five minutes? *Bring it on!*

But a strange thing happened. Before two minutes were

up, my legs began to ache and I itched in places I didn't know I had places. By three minutes I was screaming inside my head, and the little girls were sweating. *This is ridiculous*, I thought. *It can't be that hard to stand for five freaking minutes.* By four minutes I was panicked, counting the seconds in my head as my ears buzzed and my ass went numb and my ankles quivered.

"Jayla." The single word stabbed the little girl upright, as she had begun to wobble.

"Thirty more seconds." Ann stood as still as we did, just watching us. My face flushed, my feet tingled, and my pupils dilated. *All of this just from standing?* It was agony and I was begging for it to end. The only thing that kept me from collapsing in a heap and scratching myself all over was pride. I refused to do worse than a room full of ten-year-olds.

"You may sit," Ann said finally. I exhaled sharply, and happily sat down. "Don't flop—stay in control!" We all sat up straight. "Now, sit firmly on your bottom, with your spine still locked into your hips. Knees together, feet together. Head up, Miss McKnight." I perked up. "Put your hands in your lap. Good. Now we will sit for five minutes."

Sitting was worse. I didn't understand how, but it was worse. After two minutes my head felt like a bowling ball and my shoulders ached. After three I felt nauseated and clammy. Just sitting without moving was brutal. After four minutes my shoulders began to quiver and I was breathing through my mouth. I now had massive respect for princesses and celebrities who stood stoically for hours at a time on balconies or the red carpet.

That first day all we did was stand for five minutes and then sit for five minutes. Stand for five minutes. Sit for five minutes. Stand. Sit. Don't fidget. Don't scratch. Don't sigh. Don't scream! Don't jump up and beat Ann Foster senseless with my chair! It was one of the hardest days I had ever endured. My calves were on fire, my feet ached, my shoulders throbbed, and I felt dizzy and queasy all at the same time. Ann did everything we did, and she didn't seem to mind at all—she looked as if she could sit and stand for a week. Occasionally, she would reprimand one of us for swaying, or leaning, and on the fourth round of standing, Isabelle locked her knees and nearly passed out. Ann gave us a talking-to about the dangers of locking your knees, and we went back to standing and sitting.

The entire hour Ann spoke of nothing but poise. Poise did not happen by chance, was not granted or gifted to you—it resulted from a strong mind and body bent to a purpose, and the hardest part was to achieve it *effortlessly*. As we neared the hour mark, on our fifth round of standing, I nearly cracked. Again, only cheap pride kept me in check.

As class ended Ann said simply, "I hope we all now have a little bit better understanding of poise, and I will see you next week."

I stumbled toward the door with the other girls.

"Miss McKnight? A moment?" Her questions were not

really questions but statements. Carli gave me a last sympathetic look and the door shut and we were alone. I waited.

"I appreciate you coming here today, really, but—"

"No buts! Admit it, you were surprised." My voice was slightly hysterical, but I stood firm.

"I was surprised—a little."

Ann gathered herself, chose her words carefully.

"Miss McKnight, I can see that you are a very competitive person, but outside of *surprising* me, why are you here? *Why* do you wish to make your debut?"

"Because my dad begged me to and he never asks me for anything and I think it might help save their marriage," I blurted out before I could stop myself. "And I promised him I would try, so I'm trying."

Ann considered my outburst.

"Megan," she said, and I noted that this was the first time she had ever called me anything but *Miss McKnight*. "That's the first honest thing I've heard you say."

Afraid to ask if this meant what I thought it did, I stayed silent.

"I'll see you tomorrow at the museum lunch," she said, and began to pack her bag.

"Okay, see you then."

Tempted to run for the door and get out before she reconsidered, I held it together and walked with my head full of helium.

"And Miss McKnight?"

I turned, did my best not to huff. "Ma'am?"

"Now that you have righted the ship, try not to hit any icebergs."

"Yes, ma'am."

Once in the hallway with the door shut I crumbled and leaned against the wall and heaved and sniffled. At home I soaked in the bath, and Julia came and sat on the closed toilet and I bawled while I told her all about it. I bet I wasn't the only little girl who cried that night.

Twelve

In Which Megan Takes a Dose of Culture

PRACTICE ON SATURDAY WAS THE LAST THING ON MY list before the Dallas Museum of Art picnic, and I was cruising a little, just going through the motions in our scrimmage, when I looked over and saw Hank sitting in the stands. He gave me a little wave, and I idiotically waved back. What the hell was he doing here? I mean, he was supposed to be here, but *after* practice, in thirty minutes!

Suddenly my legs felt weak and I had to think about how to run, which made me run funny. Then I hit a cross thirty yards too long and it sailed into the stands.

"Megan!" Coach Nash yelled, and I waved, letting her know it was my bad. It took all of thirty seconds for Cat to realize he was here for me.

"You got a brother?" she asked him as she ran by. He smiled and shook his head.

"Sorry!" he yelled back.

"You got a sister?" Mariah yelled, getting in on the fun.

"Only child!"

"Game's over here!" Coach Nash shouted, and that put an end to the overt stuff, but boys never came to practice. Ever. It was a thing, for sure.

When practice ended I walked over nervously, and he stood to greet me. He looked very handsome in a light gray checked suit. Cat, Lindsay, and Lachelle sidled over to listen.

"Hi," I said.

"Hey."

"You're early," I said.

"Just thought I might watch a little."

"Why?"

"Because I like you?"

Lachelle whimpered.

"Two-one-four-seven-six-two . . ." Lindsay started calling out her phone number.

"Lindsay!" I shouted, and she stopped. "Um, thanks," I said to Hank. *Thanks? C'mon, Megan, put some oomph into it.*

"I looked you up. You're the star of the team."

"Hardly," I said, but I was warming to his unflappable enthusiasm.

"You scored nine goals last year," he said. "I bought tickets to the Houston game."

"You did?" He held up his phone—confirmation for two tickets to see us play the University of Houston next Tuesday. Cat and Lindsay sighed, swooned, and then fainted dead away in the grass.

"Are they always like this?" Hank asked, clearly amused at the general buffoonery.

"Ignore them. They're unused to royalty." I smiled at him. "I should go change."

"I'll wait for you."

"You better," I called over my shoulder, and then I bit my lip—sadly, and stupidly, as my back was turned to him so he didn't even see my lame attempt at sexual innuendo.

"Totally doable," Lachelle said on the way into the locker room.

"Thanks," I replied.

"I'll wait for you!" Cat teased, and I punched her in the arm. "So he's the reason we can't watch TV on Tuesday nights."

"Cat, you know how busy I am—I'm sorry, and it's just until January."

"I know," she said, but I could tell her feelings were hurt.

Twenty minutes later I exited the locker room with my hair blown out, wearing a strapless violet-and-cream Tory Burch dress and the cutest pair of sandals ever. Margot found them—they were Alexander McQueen and, best of all, they were flats. She was really looking out for me.

"Wow," Hank said as I walked up. He was standing beside a very expensive-looking car.

"What—this old thing?" I said, holding out the hem of my dress.

He held the door and I got in. It was all leather and walnut, very grown-up and cool inside with the AC already running. After a moment I felt air coming through my dress—were the seats air-conditioned? He backed the car out.

"Are you really coming to the game?" I asked as he shifted to drive. He nodded.

"You gonna score a goal for me?" he asked with a wicked tone. I figured since he was doing the heavy lifting in the flirting department, the least I could do was try.

"Just one?" I asked, trying out the flirtiest thing I could imagine. "Why not a brace?"

"A brace?" he asked.

"Two goals," I replied, holding up two fingers.

"Why not a hat trick then?"

"Why not!" I said impulsively.

"Deal." He drove out of the parking lot and onto campus. We reached the light at Mockingbird and waited for it to turn.

"Did I just agree to score three goals for you on Tuesday?"

He nodded slowly. "Is that a problem?" He smiled at me—again. I don't want to say his eyes twinkled, because that would be corny, but they did shine. And I was beaming.

"Well, only that I've *never actually scored a hat trick* in a college game."

"Then I'll be there for your first one!"

There was no getting around it: Hank Waterhouse was persistently interested in me. It was, well, pretty sweet. Supersweet, actually.

"*Andrew!* Over here! Andrew! Mr. Gage! Andrew! *Andrew!*"

A dozen paparazzi crammed against a steel barrier shouted as Andrew Gage emerged from his Mercedes—the same car the valet had brought to him that first day. Even I knew these guys weren't hired for effect, as at Abby's party. No, they were the real deal, middle-aged scavengers firing away with their digital cannons. Andrew looked surprised, then annoyed, when he heard them. He ducked his head and hustled around the car to grab Lauren's hand. The photographers shouted and clicked, begged him to turn toward them. Lauren did, smiling, clearly relishing her moment, but Andrew never wavered, and moments later they were safely inside the Nasher Sculpture Garden.

Hank and I arrived for the Dallas Museum of Art luncheon right behind them, and enjoyed front-row seats to the spectacle—routine in Beverly Hills or NYC, but unusual in Dallas.

"Is he that big of a deal?" I asked Hank as we rolled to a stop. Valets opened our doors.

"He thinks so," Hank said, stepping out.

The photographers showed zero interest in us as we walked up the steps, but I stole one more look before we went through the entrance. Some examined their shots and others were already on the phone. Hank stopped too, and his lip curled ever so slightly at them.

"What?" I asked, noticing Hank's expression.

"Nothing."

I pulled on his hand.

"You know something—tell me."

"He calls them—or his publicist does."

"Really?"

Hank nodded.

"He makes out like he's surprised and doesn't want them there, but it's all a game—they're told ahead of time where he'll be, what time, what car he's driving."

What kind of person does that? I wondered. It was so . . . fake, so calculated.

"Gross," I said, with some feeling.

"Come on." Hank took my hand, and we went inside.

The Dallas Museum of Art gives an outdoor luncheon at the Nasher Sculpture Garden each year for the Bluebonnet debs, knowing many of them will become major donors. The Nasher has a small gallery building for exhibitions and some of the small stuff, and as we entered it was already full of heavy hitters, their wives, debutantes, and their dates. It was all very money.

"Diet Coke," Hank said when we reached the bar.

"Not drinking?" I asked.

He shook his head, smiled at me. "Driving precious cargo."

I smiled at him and realized that might be the most romantic compliment I had ever received. *Me—precious cargo?* "White wine, please," I said to the bartender.

"Have you been to the Nasher before?" Hank asked as we waited.

"Um." I squinted in embarrassment. "If I say no does that make me lame?"

"No, it means you're in for a treat!"

"Really?"

"Prepare . . . to be amazed!" he stated with the bravura of a circus barker. "May I?" He offered his arm and I took it. The sea parted, and he led me out the back doors and down the steps to see the big stuff—the permanent collection.

A chamber orchestra played on the veranda, and the music floated out over the grounds like a gentle mist. The garden itself was gorgeous, immaculate, all manicured lawn and shaded stone pathways. A phalanx of tables and chairs occupied the central green, but nobody was sitting or eating yet—everyone was strolling along admiring the very large sculptures. Many must have been placed by a crane.

"Now I realize that Dallas has its fair share of *culture*—a ballet, a symphony, many small theaters, even a fine aquarium," Hank said, still holding my arm and leading me out along a path. He had taken on a humorous air of showmanship that was both charming and engaging. "There is also, of course, the Dallas Museum of Art, which is a solid if uninspiring home for assorted pre-Columbian pots and spoons, the odd Chagall, and an early Basquiat or two."

"Pre-Columbian pots and spoons?" I asked, laughing.

"Okay, so I'm not wild about history," he said. "I mean, it's all in the past." He knew history was my *major*, right? "Anyway," he continued, "add it all together and you have a rather pedestrian assortment—a crown perhaps, but lacking the crown jewels." Now he stopped and held his arms out expansively. "But fortunately there is the Nasher, which makes up the balance and then some. Yes, in these few paltry acres lies a king's ransom of world-class art—which I will be pleased to show you."

"Lead on, sir," I said, and relaxed a little. We walked down the pathway toward the first piece, three gigantic clubs of rusted metal perched on a forge.

"This," Hank said thoughtfully, "this is Ulrich Ruckriem's *Three Cheetos Dancing*." He paused dramatically to consider it, one hand on his chin. I played along, studying it too while fighting back the urge to laugh. "Notice how tempting, how tasty it looks—an excellent example from his afternoon snack period."

We walked farther and reached another sculpture, a spiderweb of black metal that looked like a jungle gym that had partially collapsed.

"Ah," Hank said. "This is"—and here he bent down to see the artist's name—"this is David Smith's *Something I Found in the Alley*."

"Really?" I asked, barely holding back laughter.

"Yes, yes, this is one of his most famous pieces, inspired, or one might say cadged, by his regular morning walk through downtown Sacramento."

Without prelude, he took my hand.

We passed Zach and Julia near a fountain, and then Ashley One and her date studiously reading a brochure. Typical, she was taking it all seriously. We kept on and went into a far corner of the garden, where Hank showed me Schist's *Half Finished*, Picasso's *The Chisel Slipped*, and Giuseppe Penone's masterpiece—a ripped-open box called *After UPS Delivers.*

On our way back we examined one of the larger pieces, two huge curved rectangles of metal the color of roasted cumin. I gazed at it mock-admiringly and waited for Hank to tell me about it.

"Oh, oh, oh," he said. "This—words fail me." I giggled. He took a step toward it, reached out as if to touch it, then withdrew his hand. He wiped at his eyes, as if wiping away a tear. My giggling increased. "This is Richard Serra's magnum opus, his final word—he calls it *My Curves Are Not Mad.*"

He said the title with a silly Spanish accent, and I burst out laughing. "Stop it!"

"I'm serious," he said, and I looked at him.

"*My Curves Are Not Mad?*" I mimicked the accent. "No you're not."

"Have a look," he said, and I stooped to see the plaque. Sure enough, it was Richard Serra's *My Curves Are Not Mad.*

"But you made up the other titles!" I said.

"Did I?" he answered, smiling mischievously. It was a conjurer's trick, and I felt like somehow it made it even funnier that he had somehow mixed and matched it all, and then ended with one that was just silly enough to catch me out. Hank Waterhouse was sharp—sharper than me.

Later we stood in line for food and took our plates and

sat with Mom and Dad, and I introduced them. Mom liked him because, well, he was cute and was with me. End of story. And Dad and Hank both went to A&M, which practically made them first cousins. Fifteen minutes into lunch, Mom was patting Hank on the arm, and he and Dad were deep into the haze of Aggie glory days.

"Ahh, I should have joined the Corps," Dad said. "It's . . . well, I had the ranch, I knew I wasn't going into the military, but now, looking back—should have done it."

"Best thing I ever did," Hank said. "It gave me something to be a part of, for sure, but more than that—a value system, something to believe in, you know?" Dad nodded. For a moment I thought he might salute.

"How do you like the sculptures?" Mom asked.

"Oh, they were great," I answered. "I particularly liked *Three Cheetos Dancing*." I glanced at Hank.

"I've got a blowtorch and some scrap iron lying around. Thinking I could whip something up in an hour or two that would really get these yahoos going," Dad said.

Mom gave Dad *the look*.

"Angus, as you may have gathered, would rather be home watching the football game right now," she said tartly. I could see the rift from last week had only widened.

"Fourteen–seven Aggies," Hank whispered to Dad after checking his phone. "Early second quarter."

"All right. But don't tell me any more—I DVR'd it."

Talk of the football game was the last straw for Mom.

"I'm going to go peruse the auction items," she said.

"Try not to accidentally buy something," Dad said. It was a cheap shot, for sure, and Mom took it that way.

"I'm sure we can still afford for me to window-shop." Mom gathered herself and headed toward the gallery building, and her body language—annoyed—was pretty easy to read.

"Still mad, huh?" I asked.

Dad sighed and folded his arms. He nodded.

"She's still hot about this damned land thing. I came here today, missing the game and all, as a peace offering. You can see how that's working out for me."

"I don't get it, Dad. She said she didn't want the ranch to be fracked, either. Why is she still mad?"

"Because it's a lot of money, Megan. You convince yourself it would make things easier, and in some ways it would. And you know, when they hold it out to you, even if you're not gonna take it, you think about it—you hope."

Hank, to his credit, had remained silent while our tacky family drama played out in front of him. Now I turned to him and smiled the way I'd seen Julia smile at Zach, and I carefully pushed my hair back behind my ear.

"I'm sorry, Hank—this isn't the right time for this conversation."

"That's okay," he said, and then to Dad. "Oil and gas?"

"Yeah," Dad said.

"What is it with those guys? I mean, what part of 'No' don't they understand?" Hank asked. "You gotta realize there really are times when folks just don't want to sell."

"Yeah, you know, it's more complicated than that. I would sell, frankly, if the right deal came along. I'm not gonna ranch forever. Megan, Julia—they aren't gonna run cattle for a living. But I won't sell it for . . . *that*. To have it destroyed."

We all sat with this for a moment.

"Well, couldn't you develop it for houses or something?" Hank asked mildly.

"Sure. I wouldn't mind something like that."

"It'd be less money and all, but . . ." Hank said.

"Enough is all I'm looking for. But those guys aren't calling me. That land's too valuable to build houses on."

"Not necessarily. You'd be surprised how deals come together. I see it all the time at my job. Just because it doesn't work one way doesn't mean you can't figure it out another."

"Well, like I said, nobody's ever talked to me about that."

"Honestly," Hank continued, "you're in a great position. When a developer brings you a deal, they've got preconceived notions of what they want, how they'd do it. And if you don't like that, then you've got to talk them around to the way you see it. But if you plan the development the way you want it, then you're just looking for a buyer."

"Well that's interesting. I never thought of it that way." Dad took a swig off his beer. "Got yourself a smart one, huh?" he asked me, and I beamed. You want to win a girl over, win over her dad. I smiled again at Hank, and this time it wasn't put on.

"You want another beer, Dad?"

"Sure, thanks."

"I'll go," Hank said, but I stopped him.

"You stay. Would you like something?" I asked.

"Another Diet Coke?"

"You got it."

I practically floated to the bar. I had just ordered a mimosa, a beer for Dad, and a Diet Coke when Sydney came up next to me.

"Hi, Sydney," I said.

"Hey." Another bartender appeared. "Two white wines please," she said, and then we were alone at the bar.

"Sydney, I, I remember where we met." She looked over. "I just want you to know that, you know, if you were worried—nobody's gonna hear it from me."

The bartender set her two wines down. She picked them up.

"Yeah, thanks," she said curtly, and walked off. Not the gracious reply I expected. I leaned against the bar and looked out—Andrew Gage walked toward me, and our eyes met. He promptly spun around and walked away. *What's wrong with him?*

"Here you go," the bartender said, setting my drinks down.

"Thanks." I scooped up the three drinks, turned, and found Andrew now blocking my way.

"Megan," he said formally.

"Hi, Andrew."

"I've been meaning to speak with you." *What could Andrew Gage possibly have to say to me?* I wondered.

"I tried to apologize at your cousin's party," he began, "but I couldn't find you alone, so I thought it best left for another time. Anyway, I want to apologize for the *comments* you overheard. I was just repeating what Lauren had said, but that is no excuse. It's really not who I am, and I'm so sorry I said that. And that you heard it."

"Um, okay—thank you." It was a decent apology, but it sounded oddly . . . rehearsed.

"You're welcome."

I stood there with the drinks in my hand, and he looked this way and that, but didn't seem to have anything more to say. God, he was Captain Awkward standing there, shifting from one foot to the other.

Lauren Battle had seen us and came over.

"I've been looking for you," she purred to him. She ignored me completely.

"Hi, Lauren," I said, standing deep in the shade she threw.

"Oh, hi, Megan—how's *charm school* going?" *How could she know about that?*

"I'm crushing it, thanks for asking."

"She's learning to walk," Lauren said, as if it were just the cutest thing ever. I ignored her and looked at Andrew.

"Was there something else?"

"No—that was it."

"Okay—see you around."

On my way back, I stopped and watched Hank and Dad deep in conversation. They could have been talking about land, or Aggie football, or the Corps. It was damn sexy and I thought about what might come later. Hank would drive me home, and based on all the little cues that day, I felt certain he would walk me to the door. I tingled at the thought. Should I invite him in? Would that be too forward? Would he kiss me?

I certainly hoped so.

Thirteen

In Which Megan Shops for a Raincoat

WHEN WE ARRIVED AT THE APARTMENT, HANK CAME around to open my door, but I was halfway out before I realized he was there. We met somewhere in the middle, with me standing there, and him opening the door the rest of the way.

"Oh, sorry. I should have waited," I said.

"That's okay. Sometimes it's inefficient." I thought again, *He's so normal.*

He took my hand as we walked slowly toward the door. Mildly anxious in the car, I was buzzing now.

"My dad really likes you," I said.

"I like him too," he said.

"What I meant to say was—I like you." My heart trilled at the words, so rarely said. But he took it in stride, still comfortable and smiling.

"I like you too."

"Mind if I ask why?" I could have kicked myself, but the question was out.

"Are you kidding? You're made of awesome. Pretty, smart, athletic—I'm not kidding when I say it turns me on to think you probably squat more than I do."

I laughed an easy, comfortable laugh.

"Really? That simple?"

"That simple." He paused. "What do you squat anyway?"

"Max?"

"Five reps."

"A buck seventy-five."

"No way! You do squat more than me!"

"But you said it turned you—" His hand covered my mouth.

"It does." And then he removed his hand, and his head bent forward. He stopped inches from my lips, and I nodded. His mouth came down on mine and I closed my eyes. He wrapped his arms around me, nearly lifting me off the ground, but the kiss was soft.

We broke apart, still just inches away. I felt he had stolen my breath.

"You want to come in?" I gasped.

He kissed me again for an answer.

Inside I dropped my purse, and Hank and I kissed again, deeper. He walked me toward the couch and we fell together, side by side. We kissed some more, and then he rolled on top of me. His hands swept my hips and came up to my hands, and he pinned them back, looked down at me. He was very strong, and his body weight pressed into me.

"Hi," he said.

"Hi." He pressed his lips against mine, pushed his tongue through my lips. I responded, dizzy with lust. His hands went to my breasts just as Julia's keys jingled in the door.

She nearly fell over when she saw us on the couch. Hank, understandably, was not in a rush to stand. I just lay there with him on top of me, looked over at Julia, and laughed.

"So sorry!" she said, and started to back out of the door.

"No, stay," I said, still laughing.

"Yeah, stay." Hank laughed too.

"Are you sure? 'Cause this looks . . ." I could tell from Julia's smile that she was actually happy for me, and was perfectly willing to go if I wanted.

"I'm sure," I said, and squirmed out from under Hank. I straightened my clothes, wiped my hand under my lips to clean up my lipstick. Hank sat up and . . . adjusted.

"I should go," he said.

"Don't go," I said. "Not yet."

Julia put her purse in the kitchen, rummaged in the fridge for a soda, giving us time to get it together.

"You want something to drink?" she called out.

"Uh, sure, a Coke. Or whatever," Hank said.

"Fuzzy water!" I yelled.

"Fuzzy water?" Hank asked.

"Oh, yeah. As a little girl I mixed up fizzy and fuzzy, so . . . *fuzzy* water."

"How cute are you?" he said. What could I answer to *that*?

Julia brought in a soda for Hank and a sparkling water for me. I opened it and took a quick sip, then another. Whew, it was hot in here.

"Where were you?" I asked, aiming for nonchalant.

"With Zach. We went for a drink after."

"Nice."

"We talked about Lauren's party—weekend—at their ranch in Pilot Point," she said.

"I can't wait," I said, not brimming with enthusiasm.

"Then I guess you don't want to share the private cabin he offered me?"

"He offered you a cabin at their ranch?" I asked. She nodded, smiled.

"Sounds . . . nice," I said, glancing at Hank.

"I was gonna talk to Ann about being your escort," Hank said to me. "If that's okay?"

"Um, yeah!" I paused. "I wasn't sure if you were going."

"Why wouldn't I go?" he asked.

"Just, you know, it's Lauren's big weekend. . . . Andrew will be there."

"So? I don't avoid him. If I want to go somewhere, he can deal with it."

Tough-guy talk. I took a gulp of cold sparkling water.

"I really should go," Hank said.

I walked him to the door, where he kissed me again, and I blushed a little.

"I had a great time," he said.

"Me too. Call me."

"Promise." And he was gone.

I closed the door and leaned against it, shut my eyes, and dreamed my little dreamy dreams of lust and romance.

"So, where was that going?" Julia asked, breathless to know.

"I don't know . . ." I giggled like a sixth grader, grinned, and fell back on the couch. I took a deep breath, and I could still smell him there. My body tingled and my ears were ringing.

"Were you going to . . . ?"

The question hung there.

"Um, maybe—probably." My answer surprised me—were we about to?

"Do you have a condom?" Her tone, slightly mother hen, brought me down to earth.

"No," I answered honestly. "But I'm sure he did."

"Okay, he probably did, but you cannot rely on the guy."

"You're right. Can I borrow some?"

"Ewww, Megan, you don't *borrow* condoms."

"You know what I mean. Not borrow, but like, give me some?"

"You are twenty years old. Go to the store and buy a box of condoms—there is no shame."

❧

The next afternoon I walked into the Tom Thumb full of confidence, secure in my purpose, ready to plunk down my money for a box of condoms. Contrary to Julia's opinion, however, there was shame in buying condoms. Massive shame. Because there is massive choice—really overchoice.

I worked my way down the pharmacy aisles to "Contraception," which shared an aisle with "Shampoo." And there I found the Great Wall of Condoms. Racks and racks of boxes stacked, hanging, a blur of words and images so diverse I thought I had mistakenly stumbled into the cereal aisle, except the boxes were far too small. I frowned, bent forward, and examined the first one that caught my eye, realizing as I did that my errand might take a tad longer than I'd imagined.

The overchoice started with the brands. Sure, they had Trojan, and Durex, and Crown, but they also had Lifestyles, Kimono, and Rough Rider—this last one did not sound appealing. And next to these were generic condoms with a sign that read, "Compare to Trojan and other leading brands," and a sticker price half of the others. Now I'm not a label snob, and I appreciate a bargain, but I don't think condoms are the place to save a buck. And it would take a girl made of tougher stuff than me to present a condom to a guy, any guy, whether it was the first time or the fiftieth, and say, "I went with generic."

Worse, they came in different *sizes*. Should I text him and ask, "Hey, what size is your doppelgänger?" Or *assume* he was a big guy and then be faced with the unforgettable and ruinous possibility I had bought a size-twelve sock for a size-eight foot? If only I had paid more attention to his shoes! But the other choice was "Regular." This too led down a slippery slope—I imagined the conversation in the semidark. "You bought me the small?" "Not a small! There is no small! It's a *regular*!" And while I felt pretty certain the elastic qualities of latex would win out, who on earth wants to have this conversation?

And there were near-endless permutations. "Ultrathin"— as opposed to what, an oven mitt? Red, blue, pink, purple, or clear? "Pleasure for her?" "Pleasure for him?" Wasn't the idea to get both—must I choose that now? I had now been on this aisle for five minutes, and I was more confused than when I arrived.

"Hi, Megan."

Ashley Two stood beside me, for how long I didn't know.

"Ashley—hi." We shared a look. I was, after all, standing in front of a few hundred boxes of condoms, and held a box of Kimono MicroThins in my hand. I glanced around for help and made a break to the nearest item not in the promiscuous section. "Aussie shampoo! Don't you—I just love Aussie shampoo!"

"Never tried it," Ashley Two said coolly, clearly enjoying watching me sweat.

"Well, you should—because you'll love it. And the conditioner too!"

"Thanks for the tip."

"You're welcome!" Was I shouting? I really couldn't tell.

"Well, gotta go." Now she looked pointedly at the condoms in my hand. "See you at Lauren's?"

"Yes you will. With my shampoo, that I'm here to buy!"

I prayed that Ashley Two would just show mercy and move on, though I knew word of my purchase would be passed to Lauren the second I turned my back.

"Okay, see you there."

"Bye now!"

I waited for her to turn the corner, counted to ten, and went back to the wall of condoms. I had to decide, quickly.

$$\sim\!\!e\!\!\curvearrowright$$

When I arrived home, Julia was practicing the Texas Dip. She wore a weight belt to simulate the train and still used a chair for support. She began to bow and flowed down, down, down to the floor, just one finger on the chair. And then rose back up with only a tiny wobble.

"Very nice," I said, and went into the kitchen, threw the bag down on the table, and started rifling through the fridge.

Julia poured the bag out onto the table—six boxes of condoms, a Mountain Dew, and the Aussie shampoo, which for some strange reason I'd felt obligated to buy.

She examined the receipt—$96.43.

"Jeez, Megan, what are you planning? To sleep with the marching band?"

"I couldn't decide—it was . . . crazy. So I just grabbed a bunch." I picked up a box. "Like this one is purple, and ribbed, but I'm worried—does that make me playful, or a slut?"

"It's fine," she said.

"What about—the ribbing? Good idea?"

"It's, God, I can't believe you're asking me this. Truthfully, it doesn't make much difference."

"There were so many flavors." She rolled her eyes. "But I wasn't sure—there was tropical punch and bubble gum, but I just thought they sounded fruity, so I went with grape because, well, I just thought he would like that better."

She gave me her very best withering look.

"Megan, the flavor—it's for *you*." She walked out and went back to practicing the Texas Dip.

I knew that. I did. Really.

"Damn. I should have bought the bubble gum."

Fourteen

In Which Megan Waxes Patriotic

LIKE MOST ATHLETES I'D HEARD "THE STAR-SPANGLED Banner" about a million times, and there were times, standing with my hand on my heart, mouthing the words, when my mind wandered. Sometimes it wandered to tactics for the upcoming game, other times to the butterflies the song brought on. But so much had happened in the past three days that today, my mind whipped and snapped this way and that like the big American flag in the north corner of the stadium.

Sunday afternoon Dad had called me to ask if I would invite Hank out to the ranch.

"What for?" I asked.

"Well, we got to talking at the museum and he gave me a different way of looking at this whole thing, so I'd like to drive him around, give him a look, and see what he thinks about it."

"Wow. You're serious about this."

"I'm serious about thinking about it. Your mom won't let it go and we're kind of stuck here, and if there was a third way, well—I just don't want to leave stones unturned."

"Sure, I'll ask him."

"Thanks, honey. We'll throw in dinner too."

Dad wanted my help with ranch and family business. I swelled with pride. Even sweeter, I now had a reason to call Hank, which I wanted to do every few hours anyway, but had so far resisted. Our game on Tuesday ended at five, and Hank had already bought a ticket, so I figured we could go after.

"Going to my girlfriend's soccer game and then having dinner with her parents," Hank said when I asked him. "Not bad for a Tuesday."

Girlfriend! Had I hoped? Of course. Had we talked about it? No. And then he just threw the word out so casually— GIRLFRIEND! I was afraid to speak, sure it would just come out a squeak.

"So I'll see you after," I managed.

"I'll be there. And remember, you promised me a hat trick!" Grrr. I was hoping he forgot!

Now I glanced at the stands where the crowd stood. Normally friends or family at games didn't bug me, but today was different. Up there somewhere were several of the girls from my deportment class, and for the very first time my honest-to-God real "boyfriend." *Why* had I said I'd score three goals? He must have known I was kidding, right? *That's what I get for trying to flirt.*

The crowd clapped, and the team huddled for a last pep talk.

"Keep your spacing—trust your teammates," Coach Nash said. We all nodded. "You're prepared, you're ready. Relax and be the best version of yourself today." Nods again. "Okay—*team* on three."

Seconds later I stood at the center line, one foot on the ball. *Relax.* The whistle blew and I kicked the ball back to Mariah.

⤴

"She was amazing," Hank gushed to Dad.

Hank rode shotgun and I sat in the back as we bounced and bumped along a dirt road on the Aberdeen in Dad's truck. A cow raised its head as we passed, then went back to grazing.

"I got lucky," I said.

"Three goals is not luck."

"A hat trick?" Dad asked, glancing back. I nodded, and then blushed from the jolt of Hank bragging on me to my dad.

"The first one was from, like, thirty yards away," Hank said.

"It was just outside the eighteen," I corrected him.

"Well, it was from *way far away*, and she blasted it with her left foot right into the corner of the net."

"She's always kicked harder with her left," Dad said. "Even when she was just tiny, when we'd go out and kick the ball around, she preferred that left foot."

"Well, it was a crazy-good shot," Hank said.

It was freaking unconscious. I had received the ball on a run toward the top of the box, and thought I'd slide it right to Mariah but my defender shaded that way. So I flicked it back onto my left foot and caught a glimpse of daylight between the crush of bodies and let it fly. The ball knuckled slightly and then peeled back into the top left corner as if controlled by a homing signal. The keeper never moved.

"Then just before halftime she scored again."

"That was all Cat." It really was. Cat had beaten a defender to the end line and then curled a perfect pass back over the keeper and into the goal mouth. It was a simple volley home.

"But you scored it." Hank looked back at me and smiled.

"Even blind squirrels find nuts," I said.

"And the third one, that was the best goal I've ever seen!" Hank said emphatically.

"Okay—how many soccer games have you been to?" I asked.

"One," Hank admitted, and we all laughed.

"They were behind, and pressing, and were just open to that kind of counter off a long ball," I said mildly, but I knew it was the best goal I had ever scored.

I broke forward as soon as Lindsay stole it, one-touched and settled her looping pass, then chipped it over the keeper all in a split second. Goals like that were instinctive. They resulted from thousands of hours of practice, and afterward you could never quite explain just how you did what you did.

I hadn't actually been trying to score three goals. Once the whistle blew I forgot my rash boast and really didn't think about Hank in the stands the whole game. But it happened just as I'd promised. Coach Nash was seriously impressed—she told me it was a watershed game, that my confidence and composure really showed in all three situations.

"People were chanting her name!" Hank said. "Afterward two girls asked for her autograph."

"They're from my deportment class!"

"Anybody ask you for your autograph this week?" Hank asked Dad.

"Nope. Sounds like a helluva game, honey. Sorry I missed it," Dad said. I could tell he was happy I scored the goals, and also that I had a guy who wanted to brag about it.

"I got so excited I bought a foam finger," Hank said.

"You're sweet." I smiled at him, and put my hand on the big blue SMU foam finger on the backseat. It was pretty romantic.

Dad stopped the truck and as we got out I grabbed the scatter gun off the rack. Hank took my hand and then noticed the shotgun in my other hand.

"Should I be afraid?" he asked.

"Only of snakes," I explained, holding it up.

Hank looked down suddenly and noticed Dad and I were both wearing boots.

"Wrong shoes," he said, nodding at his sneakers.

"I'll protect you." I smiled at him and squeezed his hand.

Planted deep in the earth by time and gravity, the barn in front of us was as much a part of the Aberdeen landscape as any tree or hillock. It was a western raised center, wide on the bottom with a narrow second floor. It had shed roofs to either side, big double doors at either end, smaller doors in the haylofts, and a paddock on one side. The red cedar, stripped and refinished dozens of times in the past 140 years, was now pumpkin orange with dark knots.

"My great-great-grandfather built it around 1873," Dad said. "He built it first, before any house, 'cause back then job one was taking care of the cows—if they died, there was a good chance you died. He lived in here with the cows for a decade or so." Hank checked to see if he was serious. He was. "Different times," Dad added wistfully.

Hank took my hand and we walked closer. He reached out to touch the wood—it was as smooth as marble.

"We don't use it much, just some tack in here and some old hay, but I thought we'd start here because from up there"—Dad pointed to the hayloft—"you get the best view. He built here 'cause it's the highest point."

"It's . . . amazing," Hank said.

Dad opened the doors, turned on the lights, and we went in. Empty stalls. An old saddle perched on a rail. He walked over to the ladder, which led up to the hayloft. There, nailed to one of the original timbers, was a rattlesnake skin six feet long. Hank stared at it.

"You weren't kidding," he said.

"That was a special one," Dad said. "When Megan was eight or so, we came out here for something or other and she startled that fella."

Hank looked at me—*really?* I nodded.

"What'd you do?" he asked breathlessly.

"Exactly what she was supposed to: nothing," Dad said proudly. "He was chattering away, coiled up, and she's staring right at him—most girls, hell, grown women and some men even, would have screamed and jumped around and probably got bit. But not her. Just stayed rock still and whispered, 'Daddy, there's a rattler over here.' I grabbed a shotgun, came up beside her, and blew its head off."

Hank looked stunned. Dad patted me on the shoulder.

"I skinned him and pinned him, so she'd always remember."

"He's only told this story a hundred times," I said sarcastically. "I'm surprised it hasn't turned into a whole nest of rattlers by now." But I was secretly proud he'd told it, and it had clearly impressed Hank.

Upstairs, Dad threw open the doors on either side, and light flooded in. It really was an amazing view. To the north the horizon lay unbroken by man, and it felt like you were looking straight to Oklahoma. On the other side was a good stretch of the Aberdeen, the main creek, and a number of cows, and it felt like staring into the past.

"Wow," Hank said. He had his phone out and was taking pictures. "This is special." Hank looked directly at Dad.

"This has everything you want in a first-class development: great land, lots of water, history, perfect location, far enough out from the city but not too far." Hank held Dad's gaze. "People would eat this up."

Dad pointed to El Dorado in the distance. It marred the effect.

"That there's the kind of thing I hate," he said. "The houses are all built on top of each other—it's like China."

"That's just density," Hank said, still snapping away in all directions. "I wouldn't do anything like that here—no way. I'd go with big lots, forty or fifty acres, and where that creek runs I'd forbid any development on either side, let it be a greenbelt."

"You can do all that?"

"Sure—you can do whatever you want, impose any kind of restrictions because you're in the catbird seat." He swiped through a couple of pictures. "Besides, it fits. The people that want this want to have space. Let 'em have horses, keep this barn, keep the name the Aberdeen. They'll feel like they're buying a piece of history."

"How do you deal with the mineral rights?" Dad asked.

"You just exclude them. It's done all the time. If you don't mind, Mr. McKnight—"

"Angus," Dad said firmly.

"Angus—if you don't mind I'd love to just sketch some ideas, give you an idea of what it could look like."

"I don't want you doing any work for free," Dad said.

"I don't mind. I'm just starting out, and I need turns at bat. It's always great to have the first crack at something. And that way, you'd have something to look at."

"All right, then, I'd appreciate it."

⤳⤳

Mom served dinner on the terrace—steak, of course, thick marbled rib eyes that Dad grilled over coals. There were baked potatoes, a wedge salad, and hand-twisted rolls.

"That was the best steak I've ever had," Hank said when we were done, and I believed him. Most people who ate steak at our house said the same thing.

"Well, if I can't put a good steak on your plate, then I'd better get out of this business," Dad said.

"As if that would ever happen," Mom said drily.

"Hank seems to think a development could really work, Mom," I offered, hoping to break the tension.

She rose to clear the plates.

"I hope you're not just running this poor boy around," Mom said to Dad.

Clearly whatever had been going on between my parents was still going on.

"Can I help?" Hank asked, starting to stand.

"No, you stay," she answered, but I stood and began stacking dishes.

When I got to the kichen, Mom stood at the sink with the water running, looking out the window to the patio where Dad and Hank were still talking. Was she crying?

I set the plates on the counter, came up behind her, and gave her a hug. I pressed my head against her shoulder and she tilted her head till we were touching.

"Mom? Are you and Dad okay?" I asked.

She patted my hands and breathed deeply and I heard the low sniffle it caused.

"Your father and I have been married for twenty-three years, and that is not easy. It's hard work. It's compromise. There are different stages—for a long time you girls were my job, and I don't really have a job anymore. Your debut is keeping me busy but that will be over in January. Your father has the ranch and I don't . . . have anything."

"Yeah. But you still love each other, right?"

"Of course." She dabbed at her eyes. "Please don't worry, sweetie. Things will be fine."

She began loading plates in the dishwasher while I tried to digest what I had just heard. It was the most adult conversation we'd ever had, and if that's what lay ahead, I wasn't anxious to grow up. When she shut the dishwasher, she smiled and reset.

"We need to talk about your party," she said, and I happily let her change the subject to something far less serious. "We have less than two months now and we have to decide on a theme. It was very inconsiderate of the Battles to take Denim to Diamonds—we're the cattle ranchers, and it would've been a perfect theme for us."

"I know, Mom," I said mildly, trying not to get her really going. She was aggravated no end that Lauren Battle had chosen Denim to Diamonds as her party theme, and had already let both me and Julia know it on several occasions. Not only was it a perfect theme for us, it also would have saved us a little money. We could have held it out here, at the Aberdeen, rather than having to rent a space.

"Really, they're *oil people*. But I suppose there's nothing to be done now." The phrase *oil people* implied that somehow the Battles had not *earned* their money; rather they had lucked into it. It was a phrase that non-oil-moneyed Texans used to convey mild disdain while also offering themselves cover for not being able to afford things—"They bought a yacht, don't ask me why, but well, they're *oil people*."

I tried to get her on track.

"Do you have any other ideas?"

"We could do Bollywood. I think that would be festive and colorful," Mom said.

I rolled my eyes.

"Mom, no. What are we going to wear—saris and bindis?" I didn't even bring up the wrongness of cultural appropriation, not that Mom would have been all that sensitive anyway. Her debut party twenty-five years ago had been *Gone with the Wind*, with her as Scarlett O'Hara and the men as ruffled Rhett Butlers and even Confederate officers. It was tough enough to talk to my soccer teammates about why making a debut was important, and why I was doing it, without outright offending any of them with the theme of my party.

"A Night in Paris?" Mom asked.

"Ewww. No."

"Why not? It would be so romantic!"

"Trust me, Mom—it would not be romantic."

"Okay—then how about Cleopatra?"

"There are two of us, Mom—who's going to be Cleopatra?" I hoped this answer would halt any further talk about what I felt was a just plain dumb idea. I truly wanted to get through the debut season with my pride intact, and gallivanting around in thick black eye makeup in a gold sheath dress and crown wouldn't help.

"It's all well and good to shoot down ideas, but we have to decide on some theme, and it has to be soon. There is so much to plan, and the designers can't begin to work on swatches and color and decorations, linens, food—anything—until we come up with a theme."

"Look, Julia and I are driving out together to Lauren's on Friday. We'll discuss it then and I promise we'll come back with at least two solid ideas. Then you can pick—okay?"

"Saturday then. And if not—a Night in Paris," she threatened. "Go on now, go show him around."

⚬⚬⚬

Hank and I stepped off the terrace and walked out across the side yard and then down the gravel road toward the barn. The air was fresh and the October sun, a butterscotch candy halfway down in the western sky, turned the tall grass shades of tangerine and marigold.

"It's really a great place," Hank said admiringly.

"Thanks. It was awesome growing up here."

We heard the clatter of hooves behind us, and three dusty men rode up on horses.

"*Hola*, Megan!" Silvio called out, smiling warmly. A former professional bull rider the same age as Dad, Silvio was the ranch foreman, and my favorite uncle. The two others were hands, a little closer to my age.

"Silvio! *Cómo está?*"

"*Bien, chica. Y tu?*"

"*Bien, gracias.*" I looked at Hank. "This is my friend Hank," I said.

Silvio reached down and they shook hands.

"Silvio Vargas."

"Hank Waterhouse."

"*Con mucho gusto*, Hank," Silvio said, tipping his hat.

"*Mucho gusto*," Hank replied, smiling.

"Mom saved you some dinner," I said to Silvio.

"Okay. We're gonna put the horses away, and then I'll come to the house."

"Great to see you!"

"*Adiós!*" he said to us. "*Vamos, gringos,*" he called to the hands, and they rode off.

Hank and I turned back.

"He seems real nice," Hank said.

"He's the best. Silvio's been the ranch foreman here since before I was born."

When we reached the house we walked through the shade trees to the north and came up to the side of the main house. He looked in through a pair of French doors.

"What's in here?"

"That's the study." I opened the doors—we never locked our doors on the ranch, even at night—and we went in. The study was part of the original structure, and all the furniture in it was ancient. A mission-style desk dominated one side of the room. Behind it sat a leather office chair. There were bookshelves full of musty ledgers, and two seriously old leather chairs in front of the desk. A lot of business had been done here, back when buyers actually came out to the ranch and sat and went over prices per head and delivery schedules, and a handshake meant something. Now the ledgers had been replaced with laptops, and they just called from their cell phones.

Hank ran his fingers along the bookshelves, looked up at the old brands on the wall, then wandered over to a wall of pictures.

"The rogues' gallery," I said, and he laughed.

"Cool," he said. It *was* cool. There were at least two hundred photographs, and they told the Aberdeen's story. Practically all my ancestors were up there somewhere, as well as assorted foremen and hands who had worked on the ranch. There were wedding pictures and roundups, family rodeos. Lots of pictures featured bygone celebrities: Tom Landry, Neil Armstrong, Kitty Wells.

"That's the original Angus," I said, pointing to a black-and-white. Angus looked very stern in this picture, standing next to the barn. "And that's his wife, Jemima." I pointed to another.

"And who's this?" Hank asked, pointing to a very little boy sitting on a very big horse. He had on jeans, boots, and a hat, and the stirrups had been cinched right up to the edge of the saddle. It seemed neither safe nor possible that a boy that size should be on a horse that big.

"That's my dad."

"You're joking."

I shook my head. "They put 'em on horses early back then. My granddad rode around with him on his saddle starting when he was two, and he got his own horse at four. And if you fell, you got back up and got back on the horse."

Hank moved slowly through the pictures, stopping at a woman wearing jeans, boots, a sombrero, and crisscrossed shoulder holsters with two pearl-handled pistols. She was smoking a cigar and looking at the photographer like he'd better hurry up with it.

"Who is that?"

"My great-great-aunt. She fought in the Mexican Revolution."

"On which side?" Hank asked.

"I'm not sure. Probably both. I don't think she really cared who won, she just wanted the adventure." I pointed to a picture of two very young girls in white tennis dresses holding racquets, side by side. They were clearly relaxed, entitled. "That's my mom and my aunt Camille—Abby's mom."

"Cute," he said.

We stopped before another photo—this one Mom when she was young, in a massive, off-the-shoulder white dress.

"Your mom?"

I nodded.

"Is that her wedding?"

"No. It's her Bluebonnet debut."

"Who's the dude?" Hank asked. The guy beside her was huge, broad-shouldered, and very handsome in a slick sort of way.

"That's Hardy Rowan—he's the Texas railroad commissioner. They were engaged but Mom broke it off."

"For your dad?"

I nodded. "Dad was the wild card."

Hank moved on, gazing at the pictures, but I stayed with this one. Looking at her younger version standing next to the man she might have married, I saw Mom's alternative life flash past: married into a politically connected family, a membership at Turtle Creek Country Club, afternoon tennis or bridge and Junior League lunches, a weekly trip to get her hair and nails done. It was the life she probably imagined during her four years at Hockaday, and the four more at SMU. *Does she regret it?* I wondered. Was all her anxiety and pressure to make me debut and the trouble between her and Dad less about money and more that she chose a life on the ranch rather than in the Park Cities?

"I remember this one!" Hank crowed. It was my deb announcement picture. *Ugh.*

"We're done here," I said.

Dad and I walked him to his car.

"Thanks for coming out, Hank," Dad said.

"Thank you," Hank answered. "I'll get on those drawings."

"No hurry."

Hank stood right in front of me, took my hands, looked in my eyes.

"See you Friday?"

I nodded, and then he kissed me, and not a peck on the cheek—it was a "kissing your girlfriend" smooch right in front of my dad that shut my eyes and left me woozy.

Dad and I watched as he drove out to the main gate and made the turn. He put his arm around me and we started back toward the house.

"I think you got a good one," he said.

Fifteen

In Which Megan Suffers from Stockholm Syndrome

"NEVER RUSH OR BE RUSHED," ANN SAID. I CHECKED MY watch furtively: 4:40 p.m. "Consider every action. A well-mannered young lady moves with purpose, with direction, but never in haste."

The third week of Young Ladies' Etiquette & Decorum was held at Ann's house, a modest one-story on Edmonson Avenue, at the far edge of the Park Cities across the North Texas Tollway. Technically this gave her the correct zip code, but it made it clear that Ann worked and was not "from money." Nobody with a choice lived west of the Tollway.

The girls and I were seated at her dining room table, which was laid out for tea. Ann took tea very seriously, and on the table were silver forks and spoons, white linen napkins, bone-china plates, and a matching teapot, creamer, and sugar bowl with its own corrugated silver spoon. "Brewing good tea requires three things—high-quality tea, preferably loose leaf; very hot, but not boiling, water; and agitation," Ann continued.

Agitation, I had plenty of. On the verge of leaving for Lauren's weekend, I still needed to shower and pack and I had a term paper that was already a week late. I'd have to pull an all-nighter to write it before I left. I looked at my watch again. A single minute had passed, and I let out an audible sigh.

"Is there somewhere you need to be?" Ann asked, pointedly.

"No." I knew I was being rude, but I had a thousand things to do and a million places to be, and none of them included watching her boil water. I mean, *not quite* boil water.

"Preparation is key, so lay out everything you will need beforehand," Ann continued, pointing at all the stuff on the table. "Know how many guests will be coming, and for loose-leaf tea you will require an infuser. Make sure it fits in the pot. You will also want to have lemon, honey, sugar, and cream. Some people like lemon and honey, some sugar and cream, so you should have both. *Never* mix lemon and cream."

"Why not?" asked Hannah.

"The lemon will curdle the cream," Ann said. "Tea should be added, one teaspoon for each cup," she said as she demonstrated one *agonizingly slow teaspoon* at a time.

Now she went into the kitchen and we followed. A kettle steamed away on the stove over a large burner. I stood at the back tapping my foot. *Come on!*

"Boiling the water reduces the oxygen, so take great care to remove the kettle just prior to bubbling." I sighed while she turned off the burner, found a pot holder, and lifted the kettle. The girls moved aside and we all followed her back into the dining room, where we sat and watched as she carefully poured the water into the teapot.

"Steep for precisely four minutes," she said. "No more. And finally, while it steeps, gently raise and lower the strainer occasionally for agitation."

I'm going to scream!

Ann droned on for four minutes about finger sandwiches and the best place for scones and real English clotted cream in Dallas. She went on to cover assorted pastries and appropriate topics of conversation. I spent that time fantasizing about sneaking away from Lauren's party early with Hank, and I reminded myself to work out a code with Julia to prevent walk-ins at the cabin.

"Once steeped, remove the infuser. Pour with the right hand, and use your left to hold the top in place." Ann poured tea with style—the steaming liquid rushed out as she lowered the pot toward the cup, and then she gently lifted it before the cup overflowed. She asked each of us how we preferred our tea, with a direct gaze, and paid careful attention to the answer. Cream was poured precisely the same way as the tea, and sugar was delivered in equal heaping spoonfuls.

She showed us how to hold the saucer and how to pick up the cup. We all took a sip. I grimaced.

"Miss McKnight, do you have something to add?"

"Just—I mean, it's *tea*. Nobody *really likes* tea. It tastes like bathwater." All the little girls cracked up, and Isabelle spilled some tea onto her saucer. "I feel pretty confident I'm never going to offer tea to anyone in my entire life—so why do I need to know how to make it?"

"Tea, or any beverage prepared for guests, is a reason to spend time in conversation with those you care about. It creates an intimate space, and your regard for details is a reflection of your regard for your guests. When you are a guest, then your attention is an indication of your regard for the host."

At 4:59 p.m. I bolted for the door.

"Thanks, Ann, great stuff."

"Miss McKnight?"

I paused at the door. "Yes?"

"Would you be so kind as to stay and help me clear up?"

Is she kidding?

"I am so sorry, Ann, but I can't—I have somewhere I need to be."

"Oh I know. You've spent the last hour making sure we all knew that. But I shouldn't have phrased it as a question. Stay and help me clear up."

Defeated, I put my purse down as the little girls filed out. I helped Ann stack plates and spoons and carry them all into the kitchen. When everything was on the counter beside the sink, I cocked my hip and gave Ann a truckload of attitude.

"Is that it?"

"They need to be washed."

"Isn't that what the dishwasher's for?" I looked at the dishwasher, empty and ready.

"This"—she indicated the plates and cups and saucers—"is two-hundred-year-old English bone china my mother left to me. It is hand washed, towel dried."

I huffed and ran water in the sink and looked around for a sponge while Ann took out a small towel from a drawer. When the water was hot I added soap to the sponge, and Ann, standing next to me, handed me a single cup. I took it and really felt it for the first time. It was as light and delicate as meringue. I held it to the light and could nearly see through it. The design was an Italian landscape, a vivid blue. I held it gingerly and washed it slowly, suddenly worried I might chip the edge or knock a handle off. I handed it back to Ann, clean, as carefully as you would a newborn baby.

"For some reason entirely unclear to me I suspect there is a fine young woman wandering around inside you," Ann said after she had dried the third cup, "and I find myself uncertain exactly how to unearth her."

"I'm sorry," I said. "I've got a lot on my plate this week."

"We all have times when we wish to be somewhere else, but showing impatience is rude, and rarely the wisest course. Neither is speaking every single thing we think." I had finished the cups and moved on to the saucers. "Being gracious means acting as if there is no place you'd rather be—even when that isn't true."

I rinsed the creamer and was working now on the teapot.

"You do realize that all those little girls look up to you?"

I stopped washing.

"Really?"

"Oh yes, you should have heard them talking about you before you arrived. You're just the kind of girl they all want to be—athletic but still feminine, able to play sports but also dress up and go to balls, make a debut. They watch you for clues, what to say, how to behave. I don't think petulance is the example you want to set—is it?"

"No. It isn't."

"I realize you don't like her, but pay attention to Lauren this weekend, how she behaves, how she carries herself. She can be very charming and gracious." Ann finished drying the creamer. "Though I'm not sure it comes naturally."

OMG! Did Ann just diss Lauren to me? I couldn't quite tell. Her face, calm and inscrutable, offered zero clues—no smile, no slight twinkle in her eyes or twitching of her nose—but I felt sure that was a dig.

"I will. And—thanks."

She said no more, and when all the cups and saucers and spoons and the teapot were clean and dried, resting on the counter, I gathered my bag. "Your mother's china is beautiful," I said.

"Thank you very much for not chipping any of it."

ഔe⌒

That evening my suitcase—packed, emptied and repacked, emptied again, exchanged for a larger one, and packed again—sat by the door like a dog expecting his walk. Tomorrow we were leaving for Lauren's "weekend," a full two days of hooting 'n' hollering that included a pheasant hunt, a cook-out, and her Denim to Diamonds gala. I finished oiling and cleaning my shotgun, locked it in its case, and set it by the door, and for no reason at all I rechecked the zippers and tightened the straps on my bag.

"What is wrong with you?" Julia asked.

"I don't know! He's hijacked my mind!" I exclaimed.

"Welcome to having a boyfriend," she said calmly.

"I've had a boyfriend before!"

"When?"

"Fred, junior year," I answered.

"Fred was not a *real* boyfriend."

This was true. I hadn't thought about Fred as much in the several months we dated as I had about Hank in the five days since we had made out on my couch.

"So are we settled on the code?" I asked. "I don't wanna walk in on you and Zach getting busy."

"Yes. A red heart emoji means you're sexiled."

"Great."

I stood my bag up against the door, checked that the handle was securely in place.

Wa-OO-gah!

Can I stop by?

It was nine o'clock and Hank wanted to "stop by." I thought I might faint.

Sure! I replied, and told Julia that Hank was on his way.

Not knowing how far away he was, I fretted over whether I should change clothes.

"They're cute, right?" I asked, indicating my pajamas.

"You look great," she assured me.

"They're not frumpy?" I asked, a puddle of worry. Julia gave me her *I pity you* look.

"This is normal," she told me.

"It doesn't feel normal! I Googled him!"

"What'd you find?"

"Nothing! There were a zillion Henry Waterhouses—the only famous one was a sea captain. I did find him on LinkedIn—he works in real estate, in an office building on Central Expressway."

"He might not be far away then," Julia said.

I ran for the bathroom and put on some lip plumper, then went to the window and peered down into the parking lot. There was an empty space across from our door, but I didn't see his car yet. I ran to my bedroom, rifled through my closet, sorted and discarded alternate choices like a gambler parsing odds, but couldn't find anything better to wear. When he knocked I was actually considering removing my pajama bottoms and going with just the shirt, but looking in the mirror I couldn't decide whether this would look sexy or as if I had simply lost my pants.

It would have to do. I hustled into the living room and "lounged" on the couch, pretending to read a very large history of the Roman Empire. Julia went to the door, and just as she turned the knob I realized the book was upside down.

"Hi, Hank," Julia said. I silently said, "One Mississippi," and then looked over.

"Hey," he said, to both of us.

"Hi," I said, then wondered if I had shouted it.

"Sorry to come by so late—"

"That's okay," I said too quickly.

"I was wondering if we could talk." It was clear he meant the two of us, alone.

"Of course," Julia said, nodding, and she went into her bedroom and closed the door.

"Want something to drink?" I asked.

"No, thanks." He came and sat next to me on the couch. "Listen . . ." he started. "There's just no good way to say this." He put his hand on my thigh and it caused a physical burning sensation. "I can't go."

"Oh. You mean, like, you can't go to . . ."

"This weekend. A work thing has come up—it has to be done by Monday and I am just so, so sorry."

"That's okay." The words rushed in to fill the crushing void inside me.

"I feel terrible, I tried everything to get out of it, but I'm low man on the totem pole, it's an emergency, and it's important for my job."

"I understand."

"So . . . I wanted to tell you in person and not just call or text, because I *really* want to go, I was really looking forward to it." He was so kind, so freaking handsome, so sincere, and so goddamn close, it almost made me feel better.

"I understand, really," I said. And nearly meant it. "I appreciate you telling me in person." He moved toward me and pulled me to him, bent his face toward mine. Tears had begun to well, and I wished with all my heart I could keep them from running down my cheeks. Against my will, I snuffled.

"I'll make it up to you—promise." Just the smell of him was making me crazy. He kissed me and I kissed him back, hard. I pressed into his strength, folded into his arms. I almost asked him to stay, but before I could, his shoulders slumped a little, and he broke the kiss, looked down at me.

"I gotta go—my flight for Austin leaves at six."

"Okay." I said. *Not okay.* But what could I do?

Seconds later he was gone, and only my bag remained by the door, taunting me. Julia's door opened and seeing her made the tears finally flow. I whimpered and she came and hugged me. I cried and told her what he said.

"It was really sweet of him to come by," she said, hugging me.

"I know!" And that made the tears flow even harder.

⌒e⌒

"I'm not going," I said the next morning, swirling my oatmeal around the bowl.

"You have to," Julia said.

"I'll say I'm sick. I went to Abby's party with a black eye and a head injury—they'll believe it's serious if I don't go."

Julia drank her coffee and I ignored my breakfast. Let down didn't express it. I felt . . . empty. Woebegone and sorry for myself and on the verge of a tantrum. I considered chucking my oatmeal on the floor, like a two-year-old.

"I know how you feel," she said, "but—"

"Nobody knows how I feel!" This boyfriend thing brought on a lot of shouting. "I'll be a train wreck, and everyone will know, and it will be, oh God, it will be horrible."

For something like the twelfth time since Hank had left, hot tears scalded my cheeks. I had nearly emptied a box of Kleenex.

"Megan—you have to go."

"Dad's not going." I sounded like a petulant teenager.

"I know. It worries me. Do you know anything new?"

"Just that it's weird and bad."

Julia sighed.

She was right, of course. I had to go. So I dried my tears, again, and loaded my bag and she drove and I sat, feet on the dash, head against the passenger window, in a funk of epic proportions. All my plans lay in ruins, and I was so determined not to have a good time, I packed my history textbook and planned on staying in the cabin and working on my term paper, alone.

⚬ℯ⚬

"So we're agreed it's either Enchanted Forest or Venetian Masquerade?" Julia asked as we skirted downtown.

"I guess."

"I'll tell Mom. Let's talk about our charity because we need to decide that too."

"If you want."

"How about breast cancer?"

"Obvious."

"How about the SPCA?"

"Ashley's doing that."

"Which Ashley?"

"Does it matter? And Lauren's doing Scottish Rite Children's Hospital—sick kids. So expected and above reproach. It's like, why don't we do 'no clubbing baby seals.'"

Julia let me vent without responding.

"Well, Megan, what would *you like to do*?" she asked.

"How about the Texas State Historical Society?"

"It's not very—sexy."

"Why does it have to be sexy? That's what I hate about this whole thing—like it's not really about what matters, it's all about the props. Sad little kittens in cages, kids in wheelchairs. Please!" I took a breath. "Besides, I think we'd do really well with this. Texans are proud and we could pick a building or a park, raise money to preserve it." I saluted Julia and called out, *"For Texas!"*

This sounded lame even to me. But Julia was the peacemaker, always avoiding conflict and confrontation, so she pretended to think about it and when enough time had passed, responded.

"Okay, we'll look into the historical society, but keep

thinking of options. We have to sell a lot of tables."

We curled onto I-35 and headed north, past American Airlines Center. The traffic was light and ten minutes later we were beyond Northwest Highway. Still an hour to go.

"Zach says Lauren thinks Andrew is going to propose over the weekend," Julia said.

"I thought they were already engaged," I replied. I knew she was just distracting me with gossip, but I didn't have anything better to do.

"People just think that. The Battles and the Gages are old friends. I think their dads went to Exeter together."

"He must be older, right?"

"Yeah, a few years I think. They started going out after Zach and Andrew started their business."

"Why does she think it's going to be this weekend?"

"His mom is coming down on a private jet. And the whole Denim to Diamonds thing was Lauren's mom's idea." She held up her ring finger. "Get it—*diamonds*?"

"Subtle as a semi," I said.

I couldn't explain why but this conversation made me feel worse, about the weekend and my own situation with Hank canceling at the last minute, and I retreated into my shell for the rest of the car ride. Julia tried several times to nudge me out of it, but my terse, one-word answers made it clear I wouldn't be budged. Finally, just a mile from the main gate, she pulled over, put the car in park, and looked at me.

"You know, he wanted to come, he sounded really sorry, but he had to work," Julia said. We were sitting on the shoulder of a two-lane blacktop north of Denton in a little town called Pilot Point. This was horse country, all clapboard fences and rolling grass.

"It's not that," I said churlishly.

"Just because it's Lauren's party doesn't mean it won't be fun. Abby will be there, and you always have fun with her."

"I guess . . ."

"Well, I really appreciate you coming for me—I need you here."

"I know."

"I'm sure he's going to call you next week."

"I know."

"Well, what is it then?" She was exasperated. "I've tried this whole ride to cheer you up, and give you space . . ."

I wanted somehow to express what this weekend had meant to me, how I had planned for it, hoped for it the whole week. I wanted to explain to Julia just how much I had been looking forward to it—to giving in to *romance*.

"I, I . . ."

"What?" she asked, coaxing. "You can tell me—anything."

"I, oh God . . ."

"What is it?"

"I *shaved*!" My eyes dipped toward my lap. "You know— down *there*."

She looked at me and I looked at her. Suddenly we both fell over laughing

"Oh, Megan . . ."

"Not like the whole thing, just a—you know—*a landing strip.*"

This started us all over again, and it was a full minute before she came up for air. She gazed at me lovingly, and I was grateful I had someone I could share absolutely everything with.

"Now that's commitment."

Julia drove on, and then, as we crested the final hill, we saw them—a flock of paparazzi camped in front of the gatehouse. A few lifted their heads at the sound of a car, but a blue Subaru didn't spur them to action. They had bigger prey in their sights.

"Oh, he's heinous."

Sixteen

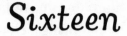

*In Which Megan Sees How the Other Half
of the One Percent Lives*

"WHEN YOU TWO GET HITCHED, I GET THIS PLACE!"
I said, leaning over to look down into the kitchen.

"It's yours," Zach answered from below. Julia sat on a
stool at the kitchen counter while Zach rummaged in the
cupboards. I liked him more and more. He wore his obscene
wealth as casually as anyone I had ever met. And he was
cute, and funny, and clearly crazy for my sister.

We had driven from the guardhouse up a road framed
by white fencing six feet high, beyond which were meadows and meadows of knee-high grass so deliciously green
it might have been wheatgrass. The fit and majestic horses
grazing on it certainly seemed to like it. When we had
gone far enough without seeing any building that I thought
a gas station might appear, we saw the main house, with
the barn adjacent. It was a tossup which was more palatial,

but in the end I went with the barn. We passed through the port cochere, and Zach met us on the other side.

He drove a good-sized Gator with six seats and room for the bags, the kind a hunting party might use. He was his usual carefree self, and he was impishly pleased to see Julia, like a little boy expecting Santa on Christmas Eve, peeking through the curtains when we pulled up. He tossed in our bags, then swung in behind the wheel.

"Hop in and I'll take you down to the cabin."

We loaded in and he took off, gunning the peppy engine down a paved path behind the house, large enough for bikes and such but too small for a car. We passed a helipad, then the lagoon he called a pool, then we zipped in and out of a forest of Texas live oaks and cedars, Zach expertly managing the twists and turns. It was clear he enjoyed driving the thing, and had come this way before.

We emerged to see the guest cabins—if you can call a three-thousand-square-foot, three-bedroom, three-bath wooden structure a "cabin." Perched on a hillside, they offered shade and comfort and a good deal of privacy.

Downstairs was a central living room, with a leather sectional couch facing a wood-burning fireplace. Neatly stacked wood, fireplace gloves, tongs, and a poker were nearby. Zach went around opening doors, as if he wasn't quite sure what he would find. He pointed out the powder room and a closet, and made his way to the well-stocked kitchen, where he opened the fridge and informed us there was wine, beer, water, sparkling water, strawberries, blueberries, Greek yogurt, and milk, and to let him know if we needed anything else.

I went upstairs to check out the bedrooms, which was when I decided that, should they try for a life together, I would very much appreciate the run of one of the cabins.

"Seriously nice digs," I said, coming down the stairs. He was leaning on the counter, and had poured Julia a glass of wine, and opened a beer for himself. "Thanks for letting us stay."

"No problemo," he said, still staring at Julia. "Hey, I was wondering—you wanna go for a ride? There's a great trail that goes out and around the lake."

"Sure," Julia said.

"You wanna come?" he asked me. I knew Julia wanted alone time with him, and I had no desire to be the third wheel.

"No thanks. I've got to get some work done on my term paper. You guys go—I'm gonna stay here and read."

"Give me a few minutes to change?" Julia asked.

"Whistle if you need help," he offered.

She blushed and waved before disappearing upstairs. I poured myself some sparkling water and sat down next to Zach.

"You should go up to the pool," Zach said. "It's quiet, the water's heated . . . there's towels and everything up there, and you'll find water and whatever in the fridge in the cabana."

"It won't be too crowded?" I asked. "I hate to mingle with the riffraff."

"Nah," he said. "Off season."

I laughed. I would have been hot for him too, if not for Julia. *This thing is gonna be good for her,* I thought. *He's Tyler's total opposite.*

Julia came down rocking hip-hugging, worn Wranglers, a green button-down shirt, and brown leather Nocona boots the color of toffee, just scuffed enough to prove they'd been used for more than traipsing around a honky-tonk. And her raffia hat was a work of art—I should know, since it was mine, and I'd spent years getting the creases just right, the brim curved just so. As she sauntered down the stairs, the net effect was one smoking-hot country girl. Zach noticed.

"Nice hat," he said.

"Thanks." She smiled at him and then glanced at me, and I kept quiet. Hey, if my hat helped land this place, she was welcome to the credit.

"I'll have her back before dinner," Zach said, and held the door for her. I nodded and they left. I watched them from the window walking toward the barn. Fall was a lovely time to ride in North Texas—the sun slanted more from the side rather than beaming down directly overhead, any heat would be broken up and scattered by the trees, and along the lake there was sure to be a breeze. Zach had probably ordered a breeze, come to think of it. He could afford it.

Now alone, I considered my options. Here? Or the pool? No-brainer.

I changed into a yellow bikini, then added a long blue SMU Soccer T-shirt and my flip-flops. I carried my book up the path to the pool, aka the lagoon, found some towels, and settled in to read the history of the Roman Empire in hopes of sparking an idea for my overdue term paper. I hadn't finished the first paragraph when I heard voices, then the jangle of the gate latch.

Lauren Battle appeared, and behind her Andrew Gage. So much for an afternoon alone by the pool. Lauren walked toward me, but when Andrew saw me, he froze. He stared at me, and I stared back—he clearly expected to have the place to himself. *What a jerk*, I thought, remembering him ducking the photographers he had called.

"Is this reserved?" I asked icily.

"No, of course not," he said, and came over. Lauren set her bag on the table.

"Hi, Megan."

"Hello, Lauren." I checked her finger, but no new ring. He was probably saving it for the big night with the big crowd, for maximum effect.

"Where's Julia?" she asked.

"Out riding with Zach."

"So *romantic*," Lauren said, her voice as sweet as treacle. "And when does Hank arrive?" I felt Andrew grimace at his name. She must have known they didn't like each other, but she asked all the same, right in front of him.

"Last-minute work thing. He couldn't make it."

"Oh no! So sad. Who's your date then?"

"I'm not sure—Ann said she would get back to me."

"Well, I'm sure she can find *someone.*"

Lauren removed her cover, revealing a teeny white bikini in perfect contrast to her long, blemish-free legs and arms. She tossed the cover aside, primped her hair, and gave me and Andrew time to appreciate the goods. I had to give her credit: she was hot and she knew how to make the most of what she had.

I shrugged down into my T-shirt and thought about the body underneath. Lean, muscular arms, reddish brown to the bicep, then beluga white to the neck, with another ring there. My legs were scarred and mannish, and I trembled at the thought of being compared to Lauren, especially under the intense scrutiny of Andrew Gage. In one move Lauren had shown me who was who, and what was what. Swimming was no longer part of my afternoon plans.

Satisfied that she had been polite, Lauren lay back on a deck chair and turned her face toward the weak November sun, determined to leech what radiation remained.

I had closed my book over my hand and waited as Andrew settled, thinking of how Ann would want me to do my bit in the idle chitchat department. But he never looked over. He took out an expensive fountain pen and stationery and without a word began to write a letter, by hand. *Well, I guess I'll just read my book then!* They were both so easy to dislike—Lauren the overnice rich bitch and Andrew the Proud, silent and aloof. They certainly deserved each other, and would no doubt spawn cold but perfectly formed children.

I struggled with my book for at least ten minutes. My eyes read the words, but my brain would not comprehend their meaning. I was distracted by my own discomfort, Lauren's insouciance, and most of all the annoying scratch of Andrew's sharp pen on linen paper. I focused yet again on my book.

"You like history?" Andrew's question startled me, and I realized the scratching had stopped, and he was looking at me.

"It is my major." I held up the book. "This is a story you'd like—it's all about pride before the fall."

He laughed off my playful dig.

"Have you read *Decline and Fall of the Roman Empire*?"

"Gibbon? Are you nuts? It's, what, six volumes and, like, five thousand pages?"

"Seven volumes, at least originally."

"Even worse."

He paused as he thought about it, looking off as if back in time somewhere.

"*In the second century after Christ the empire of Rome comprehended the fairest part of the earth, and the most civilized of mankind.*" Now he looked at me. "*The frontiers of the monarchy were guarded by ancient renown and disciplined valor, and the gentle but powerful influence of laws and manners had subdued the provinces.*"

"You memorized it?"

"Just the very beginning. My dad read it to me—it was his favorite."

He smiled shyly and I thought briefly that Andrew Gage was, well, nerdy and bookish and sentimental—in a good way.

"It's catchy," I said. "But this is gonna have to do for now."

"I get it."

He went back to his letter, and I went back to ignoring my book. Lauren eventually sighed and turned over. I imagined her as a grilled cheese sandwich, turning to brown the other side.

"No Wi-Fi out here?" I asked a few minutes later. He raised his eyes. I nodded at the pen and paper.

"I have no idea."

"Technophobe then?" I asked, and he laughed, the first genuine laugh I'd ever heard from him.

"No, not at all." He considered the pen poised in his hand, the paper in front of him. "But real letter writing, by hand, there's something special about it. I love the feel of the paper, folding it, sealing it, finding a stamp, and actually putting it in the mailbox. I like to think of it on its way, and someone receiving it, opening the envelope. It's visceral, so different from an email. It's also becoming a lost art, and I'm determined not to lose it."

"Who are you writing to?"

"My sister Georgie."

For the second time that afternoon he caught me off guard, and I tried to wrap my head around Andrew Gage.

He held my gaze, no doubt expecting some wry comment. In a rare occurrence none came and we continued to look at each other unblinking, as two fish might.

"I'm bored," Lauren said suddenly. Her declaration broke the spell, and seemed more a comment on our conversation rather than a statement about how she felt. She stood up in that itty-bitty bikini and stretched languidly this way and that. It had the desired effect. Andrew looked at her. She clearly enjoyed the attention, the way his eyes moved up and down and all around her body. "Come swimming."

"I want to finish this," he said, pointing to his half-written letter.

"Later." She beckoned with her eyes, and her hips and lips. Watching her act, I figured he was about to crater. What guy wouldn't?

"You go." His tone was firm, and she, predictably, pouted. When this too produced no result, she looked at me.

"Megan? Swimming?"

"Not right now," I said, still determined not to have my body compared to hers in anything resembling daylight.

"Eeerghhh." She slinked off and when she got to the steps of the pool she paused dramatically, then daintily dipped in one toe, swirling it like a straw in a daiquiri. "Oh it's perfect." She glanced now at Andrew seductively. "You're positively sure?" She posed by the steps awash in golden sunlight—this had to get him. After all, he had a pulse.

"You go," he said, and I felt her slump in disappointment. As if to further slam the door on the discussion, Andrew slid the very dark sunglasses from his head onto his face. I had gone back to my book to cover any notion I had a dog in this fight, but I watched furtively as she went down the steps and slid into the water with nary a ripple. She swam slowly and carefully, her neck extended and her head well above the water, to keep her hair dry. Galling as it was, Lauren swam as regally, and effortlessly, as a swan.

I was torn. I had zero interest in my book, and the thought of swimming around in this gorgeous pool was pretty tempting. However, this required I remove my T-shirt. But why let this guy and his snotty opinion keep me from doing what I wanted?

"Changed my mind," I said, standing and taking off my T-shirt.

Rather than enter via the steps, I went to the diving board, bounced high off the end, and flew up into the air. I tucked and grabbed my knees to my chest.

"Cannonball!" I hit the water with a giant splash.

The shock of the water temperature was less than I expected, and I surfaced feeling clean and alive. I dove again and swam hard along the bottom, reached the other end, and came up beside Lauren, now sitting on the steps.

She leaned back and rested her elbows on the pool's edge.

"Come join us!" she called to Andrew.

"No thanks."

"But why?" she pleaded.

"Two reasons. First, maybe you two have something private to talk about."

"But we don't," Lauren insisted, turning to me. "Do we?"

"Nope."

"What's the second reason?" she asked. He gazed toward us through his sunglasses.

"You both know how good you look," he said finally. "And I can see you better from here."

Lauren pretended shock but was secretly pleased at his compliment. I was perplexed. *Both? Why include me—out of charity?* I waited to see if there was more. But Andrew went back to scribbling.

"Let's tease him," Lauren said.

"Okay," I said.

"But how?" she wondered.

"He's your boyfriend."

"I know, but he's just so—so perfect."

"Nobody's perfect," I said. Now Andrew looked up, and I measured him from the steps. "Everybody's got flaws," I said, "and I think his is . . . arrogance."

Andrew thought this over.

"Possibly," he conceded. "And you . . . you think you know everything about everybody." He leaned toward me, and I saw a sliver of his eyes over his dark glasses. "But you don't."

Seventeen

In Which Megan Bags Her Limit

IN THEIR QUEST TO OUTDO EVERYONE ELSE AT debutanting, the Battles flew Bobby Flay down to cook for their Denim to Diamonds ball. The centerpiece was barbecued quail. Individual birds by the hundreds would be hand-rubbed with spices, stuffed with tiny fresh jalapeños, wrapped in bacon slabs, and slathered in butter, then roasted over an open pit that would have done nicely for an auto-da-fé. Just before serving, the tender birds would be bathed in a burgundy wine sauce reputed to be irresistible due to a secret ingredient.

Not content to make do with store-bought quail, the Battles had arranged for their guests to kill two birds with one stone, so to speak. That morning buses would take willing early risers to a fancy shooting ranch nearby, where they could pepper away at live quail flushed by dogs and their handlers.

At 4:28 in the a.m. I stuck my nose out of the fabulous Battle cabin. It was still dark outside and chilly. Back inside

I put on a heavy roll-neck sweater over an Under Armor base layer, jeans, boots, and a faded purple Elmer Fudd hat trimmed with rabbit fur—my hunting hat and good-luck charm. I grabbed my barn jacket and my shotgun case and left quietly, trying not to wake Julia, then walked along the path to the barn.

"How do?" an older man asked, tipping his hat as I joined the line for breakfast. He was a red-faced, well-fed sort with a grandfatherly smile.

"Great, thanks. You?"

"Fine," he replied.

"Smells good," I said. And it did.

"Real good," he said, sniffing the air.

Up ahead buffet tables were spread out on the drive with warming tables. Choices included breakfast burritos, huckleberry pancakes, biscuits and gravy, bacon, hash browns, and Bulletproof coffee. The Battles weren't skimping on the predawn breakfast.

Standing off to one side chowing down on a burrito, I surveyed the crowd and quickly realized I was the only one there sporting a womb. This was Texas and I knew lots of women who hunted, so I could only guess the other ladies found beds more tempting than the chilly morning air.

⌇

"Megan, have a seat," Zach said graciously, and moved to one side of the bus. I squeezed in between him and Andrew, who stiffened noticeably.

"Thanks," I said.

"Hi, Megan," Andrew said simply.

"Andrew." He looked out the bus window. Zach noticed my gun case.

"You brought your own gun?" he asked cheerfully. *Is he ever in a bad mood?*

"Present from my dad for my thirteenth birthday."

"Sweet," Zach said. "Does Julia have one?"

"No, she got diamond earrings."

He laughed. "So you really hunt?"

I nodded. "Mostly with my dad. We have a lease down in the valley, and when I was a kid we'd go down there, camp for the weekend."

"Deer?" Zach asked.

"Mainly, but also ducks, quail, anything that fit in the freezer. It was just nice to get one-on-one time." I felt kinda bad talking about quality time with my dad in front of Andrew. "Really I just love to shoot," I said.

"Well, I'm a terrible shot," Zach said, "but I have to be here. Should be fun, though."

Andrew continued looking out the window. I knew he was from New York. Had he ever hunted with his dad? Could he shoot? He seemed like the type that would hire someone to shoot his birds for him. As if he had heard my thoughts he glanced my way, but I looked toward Zach, unwilling to give Andrew the satisfaction of knowing that I had any thoughts about him, unkind or otherwise.

Cooper Creek Ranch was a first-class operation. Hosts

greeted everyone, and a gaggle of handlers in orange vests stood off to one side holding back dogs, mostly pointers and spaniels that knew the drill and were eager to get going.

We stood in a rough line on a bluff overlooking wetlands where the doomed birds still slept. Far to their right the dogs and men were about to start forward, and when they did the birds would flush up right in front of us. It was like skeet shooting, but with live targets.

"You should be down here, Miss," one of the hosts said, and led me to the front and low-right position. Ostensibly he did this out of politeness, as it would allow me first crack at any birds coming up, but from his manner and the shuffling and murmuring among the men, I knew this courtesy also spoke to some fear about my ability with a loaded gun. When I started blasting away, the smart money clearly wanted to be well behind me.

I felt someone arrive on my left, a few yards away, and just *knew* it was Andrew—I could feel his presence, that intensity that hovered wherever he went.

"If you're trying to intimidate me," I said without looking over, "it won't work. My courage rises when someone challenges me."

"I'm not trying to intimidate you—I'm here for tips," he replied.

My reply was lost in the whistles blaring below. The dogs surged ahead, barking, and I braced my gun against my shoulder and squinted down the sight, aiming low. As the dogs bounded into the marsh, I heard rather than saw the *whoosh* of a bird heading skyward.

Then I saw them: two quail rising in tandem, just feet apart. Without hesitation I fired and took the higher one first, just at shoulder level. An instant to re-sight and pump and my second shot came nearly on top of the first. If you weren't paying attention you might have thought it was an echo, but the result told the story—two clean kills in less than a second.

As the party had barely registered that there were birds to shoot, it was with some surprise that they realized I had taken both. Another flew up, and I let go another thunderous roar from the Remington. A quick downward flutter. The gun didn't move a lot in my hands, and after this display all the men now felt very comfortable standing pretty much anywhere but where the birds were.

"I guess you do shoot a little bit," Andrew said behind me. I smiled, already feeling better.

Now the dogs, all loose below us, moved in farther, and birds were coming up quickly in bunches. I took a pause and let them go, and the group along the bluff banged away. Within fifteen minutes I had bagged my limit, with only a single miss. Andrew too had bagged a good number of birds, and we were resting when Zach came up.

"Take mine," Zach said. I raised my eyebrows.

"Seriously?"

"Please—I can't hit them, and it'll make me look good

with my dad, and Julia. Plus, we need all we can get for dinner tonight."

"I got your back," I said, smiling. "You want half?" I offered Andrew.

"No, that's okay," he said. I shrugged and reloaded.

A quail flashed on my right and I followed it for a half second, finger on the trigger, then fired—down it went. More birds flushed below, and I caught another. It was downright noisy out there, but Bobby Flay would not be short for dinner.

⌒℮⌒

Flay and his toasted birds turned out to be supporting players in an evening so full of stars that astronomers looking north from Dallas might well have assumed a new galaxy had formed. The Battles drew some heavy water and the turnout was huge—250 tables of 6 sold for Scottish Rite Children's Hospital, and close to 1,500 people milled around their "barn."

Denim to Diamonds is a Texas thing. It means the most expensive and flashiest jeans and shirts and hats, the most exotic cowboy boots—ostrich, caiman, python, shark, lizard, and stingray. Lauren's boots were M. L. Leddy's, handmade in Houston from *farm-raised* alligator (wild alligators sported scuffs and scars) —and rumor had it they'd cost twelve thousand dollars.

Our hats were custom. Julia's and my handmade beaver Stetsons came from a tiny store in Jackson Hole where

McKnights had shopped for close on a century, and Mom wore a red Kate Spade ordered from New York. My shirt was black silk embroidered with yellow stitching and roses—Margot had found it in a vintage store, then tailored it to fit snug. Julia wore a starched pure-white Anne Fontaine cut in a severe hourglass, and Mom went with a hand-sewn Ariat in coral.

Then there were the diamonds. Size mattered, so there were massive diamond earrings, chunky rings, glittering necklaces, and ice-cube-sized pendants. There were also diamond-studded hatbands, tennis bracelets, and Texas-shaped brooches. Rather than knock over Harry Winston's in Highland Park Village, Mom went into the safe-deposit box for the family stuff. Julia wore matching diamond and sapphire earrings with a choker passed down from Mom's grandmother. I went with a diamond hatband and matching cuff links originally made for my great-grandfather to wear at his wedding. Yes, he wore a tux, but he matched it with black crocodile boots and a black Stetson. Mom wore one-carat round studs, her sweet-sixteen birthday present, and a diamond and emerald brooch. The whole affair was the kind of ostentatious dude-ranch display my dad loathed, and frankly, I was glad he wasn't here to see it.

The celebrity quotient was high. There were politicians, football players, and country stars, but the undisputed North Star that evening, the brightest light in the night sky, was Andrew's mother, Penelope Dandridge Gage—Penny to her friends. She had flown down from New York on the family jet, dragging along a Hollywood power couple and a talk-show host. She wore solid black jeans and a black suede shirt, but rather than cowboy boots chose Ferragamo ballet flats. And of course she brought Mitzy, her dog, who was the hit of the party, even when she peed right by their table.

I only saw her from a distance. Zach said she had a ferocious temper, and admitted to being scared of her. She wasn't tall but somehow towered over the entire room. Lauren never left her side, and introduced her to everybody who stopped by, a line that went clear to Fort Worth. Watching her I thought of the Pope conferring blessings and forgiveness on his audience.

Without Hank there I felt somewhat detached from it all. My date, Stephen Cromwell, a Beta from the University of Texas, was perfectly nice, amiable, and benign. We ate together and danced once, and then he went in search of his girlfriend, at my urging. With so much star wattage it was easy to fade into the background, and from my perch I saw Julia canoodling with Zach. According to Julia their ride had been romantic and then some, and it looked like that might continue later. Zach clearly adored her and I could tell that she was quietly falling for him too.

By ten the place was hopping, and hundreds of couples scooted around the dance floor, an acre or so of parquet laid down for the occasion. Abby drew the short straw for this party, with Hunter careening her around out there like a mad dervish. Ashley One danced with her very handsome date, a young heart surgeon named Dr. Chavez, and Sydney danced mainly with her father. Andrew danced first with Lauren, then his mother, and Mrs. Gage did her best to find the unusual two-step rhythm. Her effort drew applause—even Mitzy barked her approval—and she offered a small bow when the song ended.

At midnight we all went outside for the fireworks. Years before, my parents had taken us to Washington, D.C., for the Fourth of July, where our nation had generously provided a fireworks display worthy of the occasion. Soaring rockets and whizzing streamers and giant starbursts exploded for a solid twenty minutes, with flares and embers arcing over the Washington Monument and the reflecting pools. The Battles must have hired the same company. The scope and length of the majestic fireworks that night served, like a symphony's crescendo, as an emphatic reminder that in the race for biggest and most expensive deb ball, the gold medal was already taken.

Under the glow, Andrew stood next to Lauren. She looked put out, not sporting a new ring as far as I could see. She'd probably figured his proposal would happen before the fireworks, but clearly it hadn't. I supposed it could still be pending, but Andrew didn't look like a guy about to propose to the love of his life—he looked more like a cat in a carrier. He caught me looking his way and this time I didn't look away. Neither did he.

In the crush afterward I lost sight of both Julia and Mom. Getting up at four thirty to go shooting was catching up to me, and I was walking to the cabin and bed when my phone went *Wa-OO-gah*. A text from Julia: a single red heart emoji. At least one of us was having fun!

In need of a place to kill time, I found myself in the Battles' actual stable. Horses made good company, in my opinion, as they kept their thoughts to themselves. Inside I found the light switch and looked around. It was a stable, but not like any the horses I knew lived in—the cement floor gleamed and looked clean enough to eat off. But I could smell their scent, and when I walked back, noses poked out from stalls, eager for a rub and some attention. I wished I had a carrot or a sugar cube, but lacking any treats, I offered my hand to a sleek, gorgeous thoroughbred. He snuffled my palm, and I rubbed his nose softly. He rolled his head to the side and eyed me shyly. I closed my eyes and inhaled a rich animal bouquet with hints of tack and hay.

"Megan." It couldn't be. I turned.

"Are you following me?" I asked Andrew Gage, a bit testy.

"No. Of course not. Lauren isn't feeling great and I wasn't tired and I, I—like horses." So freaking awkward. "But if I'm disturbing you, then—"

"No. It's okay. You like horses?" I asked.

"Love them."

"Me too." He reached out his hand, let the horse snuffle it. "We have a barn," he said. "I've always liked going there."

"Full of Triple Crown winners no doubt?"

"There are no Triple Crown winners in our barn," he

stated, all mock outrage. "Maybe a Kentucky Derby or two. One took the Belmont, I think, but I am positive that none of them ever won the Triple Crown." I laughed—this was that same charming guy who parked my bike. *Where had he gone?* "Actually, we don't have racehorses," he continued. "Don't get me wrong, they're nice, but they're just for riding."

"And fox hunting?" I didn't phrase it as a question on purpose, but threw it at him like a dart. It landed, but not where I expected.

"I have actually been fox hunting—once," he said. "But secretly I rooted for the fox."

I laughed again.

"Is that really the way you think of me? Triple Crown winners and fox hunting?"

"In my defense you did come down here in a private jet."

He laughed. "That's really my mother's world. Not that I haven't benefited from it, but it's not what interests me."

"What interests you?"

"Building things, fixing things."

"Is that what you do?"

He nodded. "Zach and I, we take on older buildings, rehabilitate them, make them useful again. Factories, houses, malls—you'd be amazed what's been abandoned, thrown away. But there's always a way to rethink it, repurpose it."

This felt a million miles from an arrogant prick ducking photographers he'd summoned, and I worked to reconcile all the many pieces of Andrew Gage.

"What's it like living under all that scrutiny?"

"Strangely . . . normal. I mean, it's been there my whole life, and now it's just a part of my life. People see what they want to see, believe what they want to believe. It doesn't make it real. I've made my peace with it, in a way. But I don't court it."

"That's not what I heard."

"Really. What did you hear?" His eyes narrowed slightly, and from his tone I knew I'd hit bone. For a moment it thrilled me, made me feel like I had something on him. Then I imagined saying the words and quickly wished I had not opened this door.

"Nothing," I said. But he would not be dissuaded.

"Now you have to tell me."

"Just that—someone told me that your publicist calls them, the photographers, tells them where you'll be, and then you act all surprised."

This sounded truly awful and I wished again that I had never gone down this road.

"And do you believe that?" he asked mildly.

"I don't know." It was like stepping in a cow patty—it smells, it sticks to you, and it's nigh impossible to rub it off completely.

"That would make me—*anyone* who did something like that—a dick of epic proportions. Who told you that?"

"Nobody."

"*Nobody* told you?" When he said it back to me, it sounded petty, and stupid.

I squared my shoulders, set my head.

"Hank told me. He said he knew from when you were friends."

"Ahh." He let the sound dangle, and it irked me. "My friend Hank. And now *your* friend Hank." I hated the way he said it—his voice was cutting, cruel, full of judgment.

"We're more than friends," I said brazenly.

"Really?" This he hadn't known.

"Really."

"Hank Waterhouse is a lot better at making friends than keeping them."

"What does that mean?"

"It means just what I said—be careful."

"I'll be *friends* with whoever I damn well want to be friends with!"

He took his time answering, and I wondered how he had made me so mad so quickly. But he remained calm and steady.

"That is, of course, your prerogative," he said.

Oh, he was so haughty, so incredibly pompous, and in that moment I despised him more than ever. Without another word, I stomped out into the night.

Eighteen

In Which Megan Learns How It All Went Down

"IT'S AN UGLY STORY," HANK SAID, "BUT IF YOU REALLY want to know I'll tell you."

"I do," I said.

We were at Cafe Pacific for a makeup lunch, his way of saying sorry for missing the weekend. Filled with the usual lunch crowd of businessmen and trophy wives, the room hummed, but in a way all the hubbub made our small corner table more private.

"I'm from out west of Amarillo, a little catbox of a town called Dalhart. My family, well, it wasn't real good. My dad left early and my mom . . . struggled—different jobs, different guys. As a kid I actually liked going to school, stayed after when I could. I went to the library a lot, lost myself in books. It was a defense, I guess, against what was going on—with her, at home."

I nearly cried right there. He was so open, so vulnerable, and his voice so raw with unfiltered pain. I reached across the table and took his hand. I squeezed it once and he squeezed back.

"We really didn't have anything, but I had school and I ended up doing pretty well—good grades and high test scores. On a lark, and with a push from my guidance counselor, I applied to Harvard. And got in."

"Seriously?" He nodded. "How could you afford it?"

"If you don't have it they just waive it. Anyway, as you can imagine, it's a long way from Dalhart to Cambridge. And freshman year, Andrew Gage was my roommate. Everybody coming in had to spend their first two years in the dorms—it was a way of leveling things, I guess. Probably somebody in the housing department had a sense of humor, and they were like, "Hey, I know, let's put this poor shitkicker with the billionaire's kid.""

He half laughed, as did I, but it was the kind of laugh you swallow.

"I can't really explain why, but we became friends. We clicked. I don't know how he felt about it, but for me, it was—cool. Exciting. I mean, I didn't ever know that world really existed, and suddenly I was in it. Parties and credit cards and attention—even then they were hunting him for photographs—reporters asking him where he went, who he was dating. I was like a groupie with the band, you know?"

I nodded, with no idea where this was headed. But now that he was talking, I wasn't going to stop him. He took a measured sip of his beer. The waiter arrived, put down our plates, but we ignored them.

"By Thanksgiving he knew my story, knew I didn't have the dough to go home for a couple of days. I was planning to stay in the dorm and get some extra work hours in, but he invited me home with him. I thought he just felt sorry for me, but he insisted that wasn't it. So I said yeah, why not?"

"That must have been so wild—Thanksgiving at the Gages. It's like something out of a movie."

"Crazy doesn't begin to describe it. We flew on a private jet from Boston, and when we landed, there was this guy, a bodyguard, waiting with a black Escalade, all tinted windows. He called Andrew 'Mr. Gage' and me 'Mr. Waterhouse.' They have a freaking compound on Martha's Vineyard—heated indoor pool, tennis courts, the house is the size of . . . I really can't even describe it. I met his mom, and his dad was still alive, and it was just—yeah, crazy. They were so nice to me, really. I got along great with his dad. He was impressed that I had gotten myself to Harvard, told me again and again that it would be there my whole life, that education. There must have been eighty people there for Thanksgiving dinner—some celebrities, their neighbors, I can't even remember who all was there. They had about six turkeys, champagne. His dad did this big toast at the beginning, when we sat down, and he singled me out, told everyone how grateful he was that I was there with them, how proud they were to share their table . . ."

His voice drifted off here as he savored the bittersweet memory.

"Crazy stuff," I said quietly. He nodded, could tell I understood.

"Crazy stuff," he agreed. "And that first weekend, I also met his sister, Georgina."

Suddenly I had this awful feeling—just the way he said her name. He looked over at me, and begged me with his eyes and his heart and his cracked voice to know how hard it was to tell me the rest.

"She was seventeen then. But precocious. She dressed, you know—grown-up. And she hung around with us, around Andrew. She was into everything he was into. If he liked a band, she liked them too. If he liked a movie—you get it. So we met and that was all—she was his little sister, still in high school. It was just a couple of days, and then back to school, but somehow that trip, it made a difference. Maybe it was seeing me with his dad, I don't know. But our friendship . . . deepened, and they invited me for Christmas. At spring break his dad talked about us starting a business together. You gotta remember, I was barely six months out of West Texas, and here I was, listening to one of the most important guys in the country talk about me and his son, maybe all of us working together. It was . . . surreal.

"Then, out of nowhere his dad died in October. Everyone was . . . shocked. I went to the funeral, and afterward his mom, Mrs. Gage, talked again about us going into business, that we should do it for his dad. I'd be lying if I didn't say I felt like—yeah, like I was on my way. So the next year,

Christmas, we're at his house in New York City. They call it an apartment, but trust me when I tell you it's a house. It's the penthouse of the Dakota, six bedrooms on two floors. Late one night, really late—there's a knock on my door and I open it and it's Georgina. And she's—she wasn't wearing . . . much."

"Oh God no," I said. Yet I knew, deep in my bones, it was true. Hank had his head down like a prisoner condemned. I was still holding his hand, and now I squeezed it hard, telling him I was strong enough to hear it.

"I asked her what she wanted, what she was doing there. She told me she loved me. God, this sounds so stupid, but she said she was madly in love with me—always had been, and she wanted to . . . she *offered* me things. You know? I was shocked, and I told her no. I told her I didn't think of her that way, that I was flattered, but no—it wasn't going to happen. I told her to go back to her room and we'd forget the whole thing."

"But she didn't go." I could see her there, the younger sister, pining away for her brother's handsome older friend. He shook his head.

"No. She didn't go." He looked at me and I could see all the way inside him, could see the water at the bottom of his well. "She flipped out. Went insane. She screamed at me, and started . . . clawing at me. I know this sounds wild, but she was—I had never seen anybody like that, had never seen anyone change like that, so suddenly. She was screaming at me, calling me everything you can imagine. I asked her to be quiet, I put my hands out to calm her, and she bit me, she scratched at me, and she wouldn't quit screaming. Her mom, when she came to see what was happening, I started to tell her, but Georgina let loose, told her I had been flirting with her, leading her on, trying to get her to come to my room. I protested, but she—Georgina—she swore to her mom I was lying. I was . . . paralyzed. Finally, Mrs. Gage told me to go, and I did. I shouldn't have—I should have stayed, but it was their house, it was her daughter, and I felt sure that there was something really wrong with her—maybe she was . . . unbalanced? But that her mom knew and just wanted me to go so she would calm down. So . . . I went, straight back to school. I took a train that night, and the next day I called Andrew, but he didn't answer. I still didn't think anything was really wrong, just that they needed to settle her down, get things straight."

"That must have been horrible."

"It was. But the worst part was I couldn't defend myself, couldn't prove that she was lying. And I never got that chance. After Christmas break, Andrew never came back to the dorm. Some guys got his stuff and he moved into the city and I never really talked to him again. I waited for him on campus, tried to explain several times—but he brushed me away, wouldn't hear my side. And then, at the end of the year, mysteriously I received a summons from the board of review. I was no longer welcome at Harvard."

"You're kidding."

"I wish. Because as bad as it was—and it was bad—I wanted to stay, finish school. Even if Andrew and I weren't friends anymore."

"But they can't do that, just take it away, unless you did something to deserve it. Were you failing? Did they tell you why?"

"They said it was 'within our purview to review each and every student annually, and make any decisions we see fit accordingly.'" I could tell he had remembered the words verbatim, that even now they were bitter as burnt toast.

"And that was it. I knew Mrs. Gage was on the board of the university, and I knew she did it, but what could I do? So I went back to Texas, and that's when I enrolled at A&M."

"Did you ever see her again? Georgina? Talk to her?"

He shook his head.

"Never."

"You must be so angry with her."

"No," he said quietly. "I'm not. I mean, I wish it had turned out differently, or I used to want it that way. But now, I feel sorry for her. I think she is damaged, and I just hope she gets the help she needs. Money definitely can't buy you happiness, that's for sure."

"Oh my God," I said. "What cowards to not let you defend yourself, not just . . . oh, that makes me so angry."

"Not being believed was the worst part. I thought Andrew really knew me, knew where I was coming from, that my word—that's all I have. I would never risk that. If I ever did something I'd own up to it. But she's his sister. I guess I understand."

We were still holding hands. My palm was sweaty, and so was his, but it didn't seem to matter. I squeezed his hand again, smiled at him.

"I warned you—it ain't pretty," he said.

"No, but I'm glad I know. Thanks for telling me."

We sat in silence for a moment, and then he motioned for the waiter to bring the check. I looked down. Our lunch was cold and long forgotten, and neither of us was hungry anymore anyway.

"I'll take you home," he said. I nodded.

⚬ℯ⚬

The drive home was quiet and uncomfortable. When we arrived, Hank opened my car door and walked me up. With the key in the door I turned, feeling like I had to say something. I just had no idea what. We looked at each other.

He spoke first.

"Hey, I'm not dumb. I know how all this sounds and that it probably . . . changes things. But you asked and I couldn't not tell you the truth. I really like you. I've had a really great time with you these last few weeks but . . . you know, no hard feelings. I get it."

He gave me a peck on the cheek, turned, and walked away.

"Hank, no." He stopped and turned back. "I'm shocked, for sure. It's horrible but . . . but I don't want to end things between us."

"You don't?"

"No. I feel awful for you."

"Don't feel bad for me." He walked back to stand right in front of me. "Lesson learned. A&M gave me plenty—it was a great education and the Corps was all about honesty, and process. Seriously, I wouldn't trade what I have now for all the Gages have. Plus . . . I met you."

I smiled at him. He reached out and pulled me into a hug. I felt warm and safe and comfortable in his arms.

Nineteen

In Which Megan Enjoys a Brief Respite from the Madness

WITH NOTHING BUT THE TRUTH BETWEEN US NOW, Hank and I were closer than ever. Our intimacy reached a new level, if you know what I mean, and it turned out he was good for my game. I scored goals in seven consecutive matches, a stretch in which we qualified for the AAC tourney in mid-November. I had made it through two deb balls and three more deportment classes without incident. Ann nearly smiled at me at Sydney's classic Black and White Ball, and I was relieved to know that no matter how sucky our party, it would have to be better than Ashley Two's disastrous Arabian Nights, a party so over-the-top even Lauren looked pained to be there—the ginormous blow-up rubber Moroccan tent and imported belly dancers were the good parts. Julia and Zach were a sizzling, delicious thing. I approved and he practically lived at our place.

Best of all, Hank's "drawings" of the Aberdeen turned out to be full-blown plans, gorgeous renderings that, if carried out, meant the Aberdeen's future would be ranching houses, not cattle—very big houses, on massive lots, with a greenbelt, a central barn and arena, and riding trails for horses. Hank was so proud he showed them to his boss, who said he had a buyer for something like this.

"I don't know how I could do any better than this," Dad said. The plans were spread out on the kitchen table in front of us.

"Angus, are you serious about this?" Mom asked.

"Yeah, I am. I know this is what you want. They're not offering oil and gas money, but it's enough."

"It's not about the money," Mom said. "It's never been about the money. It's about *us*. It's about the next thirty years of our life together. I'm scared that if we don't sell, we don't have a life together. You will work yourself to death, and I will become old and bitter."

"That's what's been bothering you?" Dad asked.

"Yes. We both know you're eventually going to sell the ranch, but your waiting till the very end, until you can't work anymore, feels like you're choosing the ranch over me. But I don't want you to do it if you're going to resent me."

"I'm not gonna resent you. I would never resent you. I've known for a long time I was the last McKnight that was gonna ranch cattle, but it's hard for my old cowboy brain to let go."

"I know," Mom said tenderly.

"I understand, honey," Dad said. "It's been a long, tough ride, but we've raised our girls, and I don't want to spend the rest of our marriage struggling for survival. I want to enjoy it with you."

"That's what I want," Mom said. "I want to enjoy it."

"I love you, Lucy."

Mom gurgled like our creeks in spring but finally managed to choke out "I love you too."

Julia and I had been holding our breath, not wanting to break the magic moment we had just witnessed.

"Are you girls okay with this?" Dad asked.

"Yeah." Julia and I nodded.

"It means something for you too," Dad continued. "Trusts will be set up, and you'll have a pretty good start on life."

ꞩ℮ꞷ

On Friday, November 17, I attended my graduation from Young Ladies' Etiquette & Decorum in a ceremony back in the good old Bordeaux Room at the Crescent Hotel. Ann played "Pomp and Circumstance" and the girls and I all walked in slowly and carefully. Everyone dressed up, and many of the girls' parents stood in the back filming the ceremony.

"You have all accomplished so much in these past weeks." Ann spoke from a small podium while we sat ramrod straight in our chairs, hands in laps and ankles crossed. "You are transitioning from little girls and becoming young ladies—some of you later than others."

Several of the parents laughed. But the jab wasn't mean

or cruel—it came off as playful, and I wondered for the first time, *Is it possible Ann likes me?* After all, you only tease people you like.

"Of course today is not a destination, but the first steps on a lifelong journey. But I feel supremely confident that all of you now possess the skills and poise to handle whatever is thrown your way. It is a distinct milestone, and in recognition of your achievement, I want each of you to come up and receive a certificate of merit."

Parents stood again, phones poised to capture the moment.

"Carli Amber Johannson." Carli stood and walked up. Ann held out her certificate, and they posed for a picture. Hannah, Isabelle, Jayla, and Paige all went up.

"Megan Lucille McKnight." I stood and went up, feeling strangely grown-up. Ann and I shook hands, and she handed me my certificate. My name was written in a lovely, thick calligraphy, no doubt another of Ann's talents. We stood side by side smiling, and Carli's mom took our picture.

Afterward we posed for a group picture, drank pink lemonade, and ate cake.

I opened my purse, brought out a stack of cards, and handed one to each girl.

"I just want you all to know how much I've enjoyed these past six weeks," I told them. "It's something I will never forget, so I brought you a little something." They tore them open. Inside each was a handwritten note and two tickets. "The tickets are for next Wednesday's game. It's the first in our big tournament, and I was hoping you could all come a little early so I could give you a tour of the locker room."

"Oh my God, thank you!" Hannah said. And then to her mom, "We can go, right?" Her mom nodded. There were fist bumps and high fives. The parents looked on approvingly, as did Ann.

"What a lovely gesture," Ann said a few moments later. She had found me alone as the girls and their parents were packing up.

"I have one for you too." I pulled out one last card from my purse and handed it to her.

"May I open it?"

"Please." She carefully opened the envelope and read the note, then smiled.

"I took your advice about not saying *everything* I think," I said, giving her a quick smile.

"It's perfect—very much appreciated," she said. She held up the ticket from her envelope.

"About that," I said, gesturing toward the ticket. "It would have been rude *not* to invite you, but it's going to be crowded, and I doubt you're a soccer fan. Seriously, you don't have to come."

Ann examined the ticket—the date, the teams, the time—then looked at me very directly.

"One of my students has graciously invited me to an important event in her life, and you think I wouldn't attend?" She tilted her head and gave me just the slightest smirk. "Megan, you should know by now: that's not the way I roll."

The old lady was growing on me. It felt like she was try-ing to show me a way to be a smartass in society and get away with it. You had to be a ninja, not a clown in the WWE.

⚬℮〜

All the girls and Ann arrived early Wednesday and I took them out onto the field. Hannah and Jayla and Isabelle were wearing SMU soccer jerseys and ran up and down the pitch. Each of them scored a goal, and Jayla even did a sliding goal celebration. I passed a ball to Ann and she attempted to kick it back, but it squirted off her foot. To be fair, she was wear-ing pumps. I gave her credit for trying.

When I showed them through the locker room, they went around peeking inside the lockers, running their fin-gers along the jerseys, trying on shin guards, and marveling at the long metal studs on the cleats. Ann hung back, but she looked proud. We took tons of selfies and assorted pic-tures, and they went to their seats while I got dressed with the team.

We were playing UConn, a team we had beaten in the regular season. Both teams showed nerves early, but I scored a goal just after halftime. Leading 1–0 late, on the verge of moving on in the tournament, we let in two quick goals during the last ten minutes. We fought hard for the equal-izer, hoping for extra time, but the clock ran out. Abruptly, my soccer season was over.

Afterward, stunned at how sudden and final it all was, I accepted hugs from the girls and from Ann. When they left

I couldn't muster the anger to kick over chairs and Gatorade, and I didn't really think it would make me feel better. Instead, I stood in the center circle for a few minutes, feeling the joy and privilege of playing in such a beautiful stadium. I went into the locker room and found Cat, angry and crying.

"Hey," I said. "We had a great season."

"So?" she replied.

"It's just not all bad—and we still have another year."

She glared at me.

"*You're* offering *me* lessons in sportsmanship."

"I'm not—"

"Is that something they teach *debutantes?*"

"Where'd that come from?" I asked, hurt.

"Reality. Friends call each other, friends hang out. You've been completely unavailable. All you care about is your stupid society thing!"

"That is totally unfair! You know my mom forced me to do it—"

"I know, poor little rich girl. You're so right. I can't imagine how hard all this must be for you." She grabbed her stuff and stormed out.

"Cat!" I called. But she was gone. I felt blindsided by our fight, angry enough now to kick over chairs, but I knew she was right—I hadn't been a friend to Cat this season. I sat down.

Coach Nash came in and pulled over a chair.

"Hey," she said. "You showed a lot this year, Megan. Twelve goals in twenty games is impressive in any league."

"Thanks."

"I've also never seen a player grow so much in one year. You're becoming the kind of player, and leader, I always imagined you could be."

"Really?" I asked. She nodded.

"It's night and day, from where you were in August to now." She paused. "I know you went to the Under 20s last year and it didn't work out, and they're not much for second chances. But I'm gonna call the coach for the Under 23s and tell him he'd be crazy not to take another look."

"Are you kidding me?"

"You've earned it."

She gave me a squeeze on the shoulder and left. Alone, I sat by my locker, unlaced my cleats, removed my socks and shinguards, and examined my legs. They were a mess, a mix of scars and scrapes and bruises. I sighed. My season was over, my best friend hated me, but Coach Nash had held out a ray of hope for the national team.

Failing at the Under 20s had been the biggest disappointment of my life. But the truth is, I wasn't ready then and I thought that door was closed forever. I felt ready now, and if they ever brought me back, I'd kick that door down.

ഒരു

Lying in Hank's bed the next afternoon I thought over the day before. Soccer was really over for the season. I felt sad and a little empty, but not heartbroken like last year, when I'd bawled for a week. Don't get me wrong, I wasn't happy about losing, but it felt normal for there to be beginnings and endings. Maybe Ann was right: I wasn't a kid anymore, but on my way to becoming a woman.

"I thought you might be thirsty," Hank said, breaking my reverie. He walked in buck naked and handed me a glass of cold white wine.

"Mmmm. Thanks."

He leaned down and kissed me.

My phone rang. I paused mid-kiss.

"Let it go," he growled. It rang a second time.

"Just let me see who it is."

"Okay." He grudgingly allowed me out from under him, and I grabbed my phone. It was Julia, and I answered it just before it went to voice mail.

"Julia?"

"Oh thank God you picked up!" The second I heard her voice I knew there was trouble. "Megan, you won't believe what's happened."

"Okay, Julia, slow down, I'm here. Where are you?"

"I'm—I'm in jail."

Twenty

In Which Megan Pays a Visit to the Hoosegow

It took me seven minutes to reach the Highland Park Police station at the corner of Drexel and Euclid. I knew exactly where it was and how to get there because Uncle Dan and Aunt Camille lived a few houses up on Euclid. As kids, Abby, Julia, and I played at Prather Park, across the street from the low-slung building, and we had often seen the crew-cut officers in their cruisers coming and going. They always gave a friendly, welcoming wave, and we waved back—sure they were there just to keep us safe.

I pulled into visitors' parking, jumped out, and ran in. Behind the bulletproof glass at the front desk was a stone-faced cop. He looked neither friendly nor welcoming, and I realized none of us were kids anymore.

"Yep?" he asked in a slurry twang.

"I'd like to see Julia McKnight please."

"You are?"

"Megan McKnight—her sister."

"ID?" He banged the metal drawer open, and I placed my driver's license in it. He wrenched it back, and it crashed open on his end. A meaty hand lifted it out, and he peered at it, tilting his head to one side as he read. He glanced at me, and I gave him my brave, confident smile, though inside I quaked. He put the ID back in the drawer and slammed it open. I put it in my wallet.

"Wait over there." He nodded at some plastic chairs by the wall. I sat, for an agonizing twelve minutes.

The side door opened.

"McKnight?" another cop asked, although I was the only one waiting. He held the door and it clanged shut and locked behind me. Then I passed through a metal detector, my purse was X-rayed, and he led me through another self-locking steel door into a corridor. He held the door again to a small interview room, and I went in and sat. When it opened again, Julia came in, and she rushed into my arms, sobbing.

"Ten minutes," the cop said, and closed the door.

I held her and let her cry for a good thirty seconds, then pushed her back far enough to have a look at her. She had no cuts or bruises, no injuries I could see.

"Julia, I'm sorry to push, but we don't have much time. You have to tell me what happened."

"Okay." She nodded and wiped her eyes. She inhaled through her nose, and let out a big exhale.

"I, I—you know I've been texting with Tyler for about a month. Just checking in, little stuff about parties, school, asking about his leg. It was normal and friendly. Then today he asked if he could see me. I told him no, I didn't think that was a good idea. But he . . . begged, coffee, somewhere public. Just being friends again, you know? When I said fine, he thanked me, like ten times, and we agreed on the Starbucks in the Village. He picked me up and we—"

"Why didn't you just meet him?"

"You had the car!" she cried. Of course. Since I had been seeing Hank, I had been using the car more. I felt a deep stab of guilt knowing what I'd been up to all afternoon.

"When I got in, I knew right away something was wrong. He was . . . I don't know . . . nervous, edgy. I thought it was just because we hadn't seen each other in a long time."

Julia, so trusting, always assumed the best of people. I closed my eyes to hear the rest.

"He was driving toward the Village, and he asked me straight out, 'So who's Zach?' I told him that was none of his business, that I was there just to find out how he was doing, and then he started yelling, 'How do you think I'm doing? Huh? Huh?' I told him to turn around and take me home. I told him he was scaring me. That made him really mad, and he started driving faster and faster, screaming at me, 'How about this? Is this scaring you?' Megan, it was crazy. He was going like seventy miles an hour. He ran a red light, just missed a car coming the other way, and there was a cop there."

"Thank God."

"No—Tyler wouldn't stop. The cop came after us and I

was screaming for him to stop but he zoomed around this car and into the intersection at Mockingbird and Prestwick. There were cars in both lanes and nowhere to go. . . . I thought he was gonna plow into them, but he slammed the brakes and we spun sideways and somehow ended up on the other side of the road. The cops were there immediately, right on top of us, and Tyler got out with a gun—"

"What?!"

"He had it in the car. He pointed it at the cops, and they had their guns out, screaming at him. And then he pointed the gun at himself. Right at his head. I thought he was going to do it. The cops were shouting for him to put the gun down, and I saw his finger squeeze, but . . . he dropped it and just fell to his knees, The cops whammed him to the ground, and pointed their guns at me. I had to get out with my hands up."

"Oh, Julia."

"I tried to explain but they just pushed me against the car, and handcuffed me. They read me my rights. They fingerprinted me. And took my mug shot and . . . and . . . Megan, what am I going to do?"

⚬ℯ⚬

I sat on the steps outside. Waiting. The door opened and Uncle Dan came out, with Julia behind him. I ran and hugged her. She was pretty much beyond tears by now. It was after eight o'clock, and she had been in jail more than four hours. She hung on me for a moment. Then I hugged Uncle Dan—hard.

"Thank you. Thank you so much."

"It's okay. I'm glad you called." I let go and realized I was crying.

"Girls, this isn't over." He looked at Julia. "They found boxes of Mexican steroids and two more guns in the trunk. Tyler is facing some very serious charges. Assault with a deadly weapon, felony drug possession, evading arrest—and because you were in the car . . ."

"I'm going to prison," she said.

"Julia, look at me—you are not going to prison," Uncle Dan said. "You are going to cooperate in this investigation, and we will get them to understand that you had nothing to do with this, that you were just in the wrong place at the wrong time. But we have to take things in the right order. And the wheels of justice turn slowly. I've posted bail—"

"Thank you," I said.

"You're welcome. Now go home. Get some rest. Go to school tomorrow, go about your normal life." He turned to face Julia, held her by the shoulders. "But do not, under any circumstances, have any contact with Tyler. No calls, no texts, nothing. Do you understand?"

She nodded.

"Are you going to tell Mom and Dad?"

He thought about this for a long moment.

"You are over eighteen and I am your lawyer, so I am not

going to say anything to anyone unless you want me to."

"Would you tell them for me?" Julia asked, her voice barely a whisper.

"Yes."

"I just feel like you could explain it better, that it would come better from you."

"I'll call them right now—but you're going to call them as well, right?"

She nodded again.

"We're gonna fix this, but it's gonna be tough at first. I need you to be strong."

"Okay," Julia said.

"I love you both. Now stay calm and I'll be in touch soon."

After he was gone, Julia rubbed her wrists.

"Sore?" I asked.

"A little. I just want to go home."

"Julia, I'm so sorry, but that is gonna have to wait. We need to go see Ann Foster. Right now."

She raised her head. She hadn't thought about this at all.

"Are you delusional?" she asked. "Besides, maybe she won't find out."

"Julia, picture the headline: 'Star SMU Football Player and Debutante Arrested with Guns and Drugs After High-Speed Chase.'"

"That sounds horrible," she said.

I nodded. "We need to get out in front of this—fast."

⟋ℯᴓ

"I must say, you McKnights do keep things interesting," Ann said.

Julia and I sat in Ann's living room, knees together, feet crossed, in dark dresses and simple but formal shoes. We had taken an extra five minutes to pull our hair and makeup together, to soften the blow of landing on her doorstep with our sordid tale. Surprised to see us, she invited us in, and clearly hadn't heard.

Once seated I dove in and told her exactly what happened, from the beginning. I wanted her to have context, to understand how long they had known each other, how this could have happened. She sat erect and attentive, and didn't miss a detail.

"And this is the entire . . . episode? You haven't left out *anything*?"

"Not a thing," I said, and Julia nodded solemnly.

"You did the right thing coming here," Ann said.

"I didn't want to, but Megan insisted," Julia said.

"Can you help us?" I asked.

"I'll do what I can," she said, and rose to get her phone, "but I really can't promise—"

Her phone interrupted. She studied the number.

"Excuse me," she said to us, and took the call. "Hello? Yes, she's right here, actually. Yes, in my living room." She listened for a moment, and then turned on the TV.

Tyler had made *SportsCenter*. A young reporter recapped from the parking lot, and then police video cut in—Tyler's car racing along Mockingbird, narrowly missing a car at the intersection. The officer's voice provided color commentary over the squawk box, and then Tyler braking, sliding, and skidding to a stop. Now the police were out, guns drawn, barking orders. First Tyler emerged, with the gun. He pointed it at the cops. Then himself. And then, yikes, Julia, hands held high. An officer immediately turned her toward the car, locked on handcuffs.

Now the reporter had video of the haul from Tyler's trunk—steroids, two more automatics, needles, extra ammunition. The police suspected he had been dealing steroids to other players as well as taking them himself. Back to the anchors, who weighed in from the studio—"the scourge of privilege," "wasted talent," blah, blah, blah.

"Yes, I'm watching it now," Ann said. She walked away, into another room.

"I'm toast," Julia said glumly. I felt so bad for her, and terrified. Seeing the video brought home just how much danger she'd been in, and it made me livid with Tyler. How could he do this to her?

Julia's phone beeped. She looked at it, rolled her eyes, and then showed it to me. It was a Facebook post on Julia's feed—*Orange Is the New Black!* Not funny, I thought, but realized this was just the beginning of the tea and scorn.

Ann returned, her call ended. Whatever hope I had felt vanished now.

"Julia, that was the president of the Bluebonnet Club. I'm sorry . . ." she started, and Julia choked back a sob. "I have sympathy for your situation. There truly are times when people are simply in the wrong place at the wrong time, and I believe this is one of those instances—but there are very clear rules."

"I understand." Julia was calm. I was fuming.

"He wanted to bar you immediately, but I argued that implies you are guilty without a trial, and he relented. However, the best I can do is allow you to withdraw voluntarily."

"No!" I nearly screamed it.

"Megan," Julia said, "let her finish."

"If you withdraw this does not preclude you from coming back another year, or from future events, when this is resolved. But realistically you must focus on your legal situation now, and that must take precedent."

"But it's so unfair! She didn't do anything!"

"Megan, stop!" Julia cried. "I put myself in that car, and she's right, I need to focus on this now."

"If she goes, I go!"

Ann stayed silent.

"You can't do that, Megan," Julia insisted. "You have to stay in—for Mom, and Dad."

"But I can't do this without you!"

"Yes you can." She turned back to Ann.

"Thank you, Ann—I appreciate what you've done."

"You're welcome," Ann replied.

"Now what do I have to do to withdraw?"

Ann showed her to her desk, and gave her a pen and paper. We watched as Julia wrote a brief note to the Bluebonnet

Club, requesting that she be allowed to withdraw for "personal reasons" from the current debutante season. She signed it stoically.

Ann gave us each a hug at the door. Outside, alone on the front steps, Julia looked at me.

"You think Uncle Dan has told Mom and Dad by now?" Julia asked.

"If he hasn't, she's dead in front of the TV."

I put my arm around her as we walked toward the car. She stopped after she had opened the door, looked across the roof at me.

"I need to call Zach."

Twenty-One

In Which Megan Steps Through the Looking Glass

ZACH DIDN'T ANSWER JULIA'S CALL AND SHE LEFT A brief message for him to call her. Her phone pinged as she hung up. Then again. And again and again and again and again. Instagram and Facebook were exploding with the news and pictures taken at the scene. Some of it was concern from friends, but most was cruel, personal stuff, and Julia was in tears for the third time that day when I grabbed her phone, shut it off, and tossed it in the backseat.

But that was just the start. A few minutes later we turned onto our block and saw two satellite news trucks stationed in the parking lot of our apartment building. Reporters armed with cameras and microphones lay in wait. It looked like a hostage situation.

"What the hell?" Julia asked, incredulous. Things were decidedly bigger than either of us had realized, and desperate measures were required.

"Duck," I told her, and she bent her head under the dashboard. I cruised by the horde, glanced over innocently, and breathed a sigh of relief as we passed by without anyone recognizing me or seeing Julia. Three blocks later I pulled over to have a think.

Julia's empire of brains and beauty was smoldering rubble now, torched by Tyler's 'roid-fueled break with reality. Unfortunately, Mom often made situations like this about her—how she felt, the impact it had on her. *Not what's needed at the moment.*

The Aberdeen offered the only shelter from a media storm. I hoped we got through the gates before some intrepid reporter thought of it.

"We're going to the ranch," I said, and Julia, in shock, just nodded.

It was blissfully quiet, bucolic really, when we arrived. Just the usual grass bent by the wind and a few hundred cattle grazing.

Mom ran out crying and hugged Julia as hard as she could.

"Thank God you're safe," she said. "It could have been so much worse."

She bundled her inside, made chamomile tea, and quickly tucked her into bed upstairs. In a short time Julia, exhausted, was asleep. I wondered if Mom had crushed half a Xanax into the tea to make sure she slept soon and long.

Downstairs Dad told me Uncle Dan had called, and he and Mom had watched the news.

"I'll kill that sumbitch," he said. It was probably best for

Tyler he remained in jail—he was safer with the inmates than with Dad.

When Mom came down, the three of us sat in the den in silence. It felt like a tornado's aftermath, when the contents of lives lie strewn about for scavengers to sift through and TV cameras to document.

"Well, I'll call the florist and the country club in the morning," Mom said finally, her tone and manner all resignation. "And, you know, I haven't put down the deposit with the caterers—I was going to do that tomorrow—so that's good. And your idea about the Texas State Historical Society has not panned out—we've barely sold half the tables."

I looked over.

"What are we talking about?" I asked.

Mom offered me a look equal parts pity and compassion, as if I were the slow child.

"We have to cancel our party."

"But I'm still in this thing," I said.

"Megan—no. This is a huge scandal. You can't go on alone. Not without Julia."

"Mom, I am not a quitter."

"It's not *quitting*," she said. "It's reality. You have to know when to throw in the towel. And if I remember correctly, you didn't want to make your debut in the first place. I would think you'd be relieved to be let off."

She was offering me the exit door—*just step through it, Megan, for God's sake!* But for some bizarre reason, I didn't want that door anymore.

"If we quit, if we fold up our tent," I said, "it says we're ashamed of Julia, that she's guilty. And she is not guilty—she did nothing wrong. She's the victim here. Tyler split her head open, threatened her, and nearly killed her." I took a breath. "We need to cowboy up here. Would Old Angus quit? Not a chance. And Dad, you've always told me that challenges define us. I think there's a way we can turn this into a positive."

"I don't see how," Mom said.

"We change our charity." Mom and Dad looked at me, waiting for me to explain. I was making this up as I went along, but I had the germ of a big idea. "We need to find a charity that addresses violence against women. What we do now shows people who we are and shapes how they are going to think about this."

I wasn't precisely sure who was saying this, or where exactly she lived in my body, but I liked this new me. From the look on his face, Dad liked her too.

"She's right," Dad said, looking first at Mom, then me. Mom remained unconvinced.

"Megan, this has only just started. People will dine out on this for months . . ."

"Let 'em," I said. "I want to talk about it! People should know the truth and not just the rumors, and if we're not out there talking about it, then rumors are all there will be." I remembered Ann's words to me the night of Abby's party. "We can't control what other people say, but we can absolutely control what we do."

"What do you think?" Dad asked Mom. In the end it

would be her decision. There were still parties to attend, and a huge party to pull off. Even if I was game, I couldn't do it alone, and Dad wasn't going to choose a menu or keep track of a guest list. Mom looked like she'd swallowed a bad oyster—but she choked it down, then looked at me.

"Are you *sure?*" she asked.

"I am more sure about this than I've been about anything since I started this whole ordeal."

"Okay, then," Mom said. "Let's cowboy up."

⚬ℓ⌒

Blind loyalty is my best quality, so standing up for Julia when she had been wronged came naturally, and I accepted the job with relish.

The first event post-arrest was Ashley in Wonderland, Ashley One's party three days later.

"Megan," Margot said in her familiar accent, "please—just try it on." We were in my bedroom at the ranch, and she held the gown out for me to see, the sleeveless sheath bodice the color of Himalayan salt. The bodice dropped all the way to midthigh before flowing out in Chantilly lace a half shade lighter. The lace had been embroidered with tiny delicate bows.

"When we started this I told you I had two absolutes: no bows and nothing pink. Now correct me if I'm wrong, but that is a pink gown with hundreds of bows."

"Trust me," she cooed, holding the gown a few inches higher and shaking it lightly, as if I were a bull she hoped to entice. This dress contravened my entire style maxim, but I figured the quicker I humored her, the quicker I'd be into whatever backup dress she had waiting in the wings. I stepped into the gown, and she zipped the back and arranged the shoulders, smoothing the lace while I huffed and rolled my eyes.

"Now look," she said, and she turned me to the Martha Washington mirror.

"Margot, this dress is—*awesome!*" She beamed. My bare shoulders and arms looked fantastic and the portrait neckline reinforced with a push-up bra did yeoman work for my cleavage. The long, tight silhouette gave the appearance of length and added a sexy heart-shape to my butt. I thought of pink as drab, but under the light, when the bodice material stretched, it shimmered in a thousand directions like broken glass. The lace was dreamy, and the endless bows made it wonderfully romantic and playful.

She fixed my hair in a single side braid, and though I could have worn sneakers and nobody would have been the wiser, she produced teeny white satin pumps that lifted and tilted me slightly forward. When I walked, the front of the dress skimmed the ground and it looked like I was ice-skating. I walked around and around my bedroom faster and faster while we both shrieked. *I will own Ashley in Wonderland in this thing!*

The party was held at Ashley's parents' gargantuan mansion on Armstrong Boulevard in the heart of Highland Park. At Christmastime these few blocks attracted thousands of gawking tourists every night. They drove along at a crawl to moon over the lights and decorations, all on an amusement-park scale. As it was not yet Thanksgiving, the other houses were not lit, but when Hank and I turned the corner we caught the glow up ahead.

"Thank you so much for being here with me tonight—it means a lot," I said as we neared the curb.

"You're welcome," he said simply, and squeezed my hand.

We stepped out and looked up the walkway but couldn't see the front door. Fog rolled across the lawn and right up to a mega-stadium Jumbotron-sized mirror that obscured the entire front of the house. Two guards, dressed as playing cards, stood in front of this thing, staring straight ahead. We approached and they stepped aside ceremoniously and stamped the ends of their spears on the ground.

We looked at the mirror in front of us. We could see our reflections in it, but it couldn't be glass—could it? Hank and I smiled nervously at each other. We looked to the guards for instructions, but they remained stoic. Our image shimmied ever so slightly, and finally Hank reached out and put his hand *through* the mirror. It wobbled and his hand disappeared. He drew it back and we realized it was an illusion, projected somehow. He held my hand as, still nervous, I stepped right through it, and sure enough found myself at the steps leading to the front door. Hank stepped through and we smiled in wonder.

"Cool," Hank said, genuinely impressed.

"Very," I agreed.

We climbed the steps and instead of the front door entered an oversized rabbit hole. The curved entrance glowed in crimson neon, and we walked down the wooden path inside a tunnel decorated with overgrown wisteria, boxwood, and moss. At the end we pushed through a screen of tall wispy grass and found ourselves in the house proper—in the main entrance, but blocked now by the Queen of Hearts, a fierce woman twelve feet tall in a scarlet heart-shaped dress. We barely reached the midpoint of her dress, and I realized that she must've been standing on stilts under the huge skirt. The bodice of her dress and head were normal size, but so far above us we craned our necks to see her garishly made-up face framed in bright red curly hair. She eyed us suspiciously.

"Good evening," she said in a booming voice.

"Good evening, Your, Your Majesty," I said, bowing slightly.

"Who are you, then?" she asked menacingly.

"Megan McKnight, ma'am."

"What about him?"

"Hank Waterhouse, ma'am."

She considered us for a moment.

"Off with her head!" she replied in that same booming voice, pointing at me. Then she exploded in a shriek of laughter.

We moved on as Sydney and her date arrived behind us. We heard the Queen of Hearts query them and shout "Off with her head!" as we entered the living room, passing by two more playing card guards. Soaring columns and brick castle walls framed this room, which was filled with giant mushrooms and paper flowers. We joined the receiving line and chatted with the older couple in front of us about the unexpected and fun entrance. While we worked our way toward Ashley, set on an enormous throne in a blue ball gown, everyone jabbered away, amazed at the scope and sheer inventiveness. Once again I dreaded my own party. All the parties except Ashley Two's had been pretty spectacular, and I sighed, knowing mine would rival Arabian Nights for the lamest.

"Oh, Megan, how great to see you." Our turn arrived and we stepped forward.

"Thanks so much, Ashley, and congratulations—this is truly magical."

"Thank you."

She introduced us to her parents, and I introduced myself and Hank.

"I apologize for my mother's absence," I said, turning back to Ashley. "As well as Julia's. They would have loved to have been here, and asked me to pass on their regrets."

"I completely understand," Ashley said. "I just want you to know how much I feel for her and for your whole family. I just can't stop thinking about Julia and what she must be going through. If there's anything I can do—anything at all to help her or your family—please don't hesitate to ask."

She spoke so earnestly I nearly cried. *I was so wrong about you, Ashley—you're much more than a basic blonde.*

"That is incredibly sweet and generous of you," I said.

"I mean it," Ashley said firmly. "And I'm so glad you came. Please, enjoy yourselves."

"Thank you," I said, and really meant it.

"We will," Hank said.

"Okay, through the first wicket," I whispered to Hank as we moved on. "Just hope everyone is that nice."

We went through more curtains and out into the backyard. The entire space had been tented and temperature controlled, so the November evening was a balmy seventy degrees. Tables of all different sizes covered the lawn. The settings were teacups and saucers and small plates of every dimension and color. The wooden chairs were all different shapes and sizes, some small enough for a child, and the centerpieces were unique to each table. Many were clocks or timepieces, but one table featured a hookah and another a croquet set. The pool had been covered with a checkerboard dance floor, purposely warped and uneven, which made standing difficult, and dancing for those brave enough an adventure. Costumed characters from the books formed the band—the March Hare played the trumpet, the Cheshire Cat the violin, Tweedledum the piano, and Tweedledee the drums.

"This is unreal," I said as we looked around.

We got a drink and walked around, still admiring the detail, and while I could feel a current of whispers and stares as guests noticed me, I simply ignored it. The few times someone asked directly about Julia, I offered a line about "taking strength and perspective from my ancestors, who conquered the prairie." It was a genius answer—like opening up a can of Texas whoopass, and one older man who heard me say it patted my shoulder and said, "Damn straight."

I did have one errand to run that night, and when I saw Lauren chatting with Ashley Two, I went over and waited patiently while she finished a wonderfully exciting story about just where she found the tortoiseshell combs for her hair.

"Hi, Lauren," I said.

"Megan! Oh, I'm just so shocked—shocked and sad about Julia. How is she?" Her voice dripped ersatz sympathy. Ashley Two stood by, hoping for gory details.

"She's well, thanks for asking."

"I just can't believe it. My mother told me she's the first girl kicked out in more than fifty years!"

"Actually she withdrew voluntarily," I said.

"Well . . . was she really *arrested*?" Internally I seethed, but I just nodded calmly. I was determined not to give her the satisfaction of seeing me lose it.

"She was trying to help an old friend who was clearly disturbed, and she had no idea how bad off he was and just got caught up in a scary and horrible situation. But it's all going to come out okay."

"I'm just glad she's all right."

"Me too."

"Hi," Hank said, stepping into our little group. "I don't

think we've been introduced, but I'm Hank Waterhouse." Lauren had no choice but to shake his hand.

"So nice to finally meet you," she said in the same fakey tone. "I've heard so much about you." Lauren looked at him like he was her gardener, and I felt my spine stiffen and my fist clench.

"I'm sorry I missed your party," Hank said evenly.

"Not as sorry as Megan," Ashley Two said, giggling. "She was so *prepared*. Weren't you, Megan? *Prepared?*" Ashley Two giggled again and bumped Lauren as if to say, "Remember?"

"Well, I heard it was great," Hank said evenly, ignoring the jibe.

"So listen, have you seen Zach?" I asked Lauren now, my voice a tad edgy.

"Of course—he's my brother."

"Lately, I mean? As in, is he here?"

"Here? No, he's in New York. Didn't you know?"

"New York? No, I, Julia hasn't spoken to him since . . . that day. She called him right away, texted . . ."

"*Really?*" she asked, and then chewed slowly on this savory morsel, enjoying the obvious pain and duress his silence had caused.

"Really," I said.

"Well, it was all rush-rush. He and Andrew have this very important deal, and they had to go. Still, I'm surprised he didn't call her." She paused now, as if considering whether to say more. "I probably shouldn't tell you this, but Zach"—and here she leaned in conspiratorially—"Zach puts a lot of faith in Andrew's judgment."

"So you're telling me that Zach hasn't called Julia because Andrew told him not to, and took him to New York?"

Lauren shrugged. "You can see the awful position I'm in," she purred. "You know Andrew and I are, well—and Zach is my brother. Honestly, I'm mad for Julia and if there was *anything* I could do to help . . ."

"I'm sure."

"Give her my best?" Lauren said, overdoing the sad smile.

"Of course."

"That bitch," I seethed, once twenty feet away. "That whole business thing, it's total B.S. Andrew took Zach away on purpose."

"That's his M.O.," Hank said. "He just cuts people off, and I can see him telling Zach what to do."

"It's just what he did to you," I said. "What a dick—off with his head!" Hank could only nod in agreement.

Abby came over and gave me a real hug.

"How are you?"

"Good. Okay, mad."

"About what?" Abby asked.

"Ashley Two and Lauren and their fake sympathy over Julia getting the boot. They're *oh so sad* about it."

"Ignore them."

"I'm trying, but it's hard. Zach is ghosting Julia."

"You're kidding."

"I wish I was. Not a word since her arrest—no calls, no texts, nada."

"I'm sorry she can't go to New York with us," Abby said.

"Why can't she go?"

"Dad told me she can't leave the state of Texas while she's under indictment."

"Is there no end to the bad news?" I asked.

I took a sip of my drink. Abby left and I thought about our New York trip. The truth was, I'd completely forgotten about it with everything that was going on. Aunt Camille had planned it months ago—she, Mom, Abby, Julia, and I were supposed to spend Thanksgiving weekend there. It was a girls' trip to see shows and shop for debut gowns. Without Julia, and probably without Mom, it didn't sound like much fun, but this dark cloud had a silver lining.

I'm going to New York City next week and that's where Zach is.

Twenty-Two

In Which Megan Hatches Plan B

I STOOD LOOKING OUT MY WINDOW HIGH UP IN THE Plaza Hotel. Outside snow fell in heavy white flakes as dense as leaves, and the people bustling along Fifth Avenue looked as though their hats and shoulders had been frosted. Five inches already, and the forecast said snow until morning, maybe a foot in all. I wiped away steam and peered down. I could see the corner of Bergdorf's, and closer a band of Peruvian pipers on the small square of cement adjacent to the hotel entrance. I put my ear to the window and could just hear them—trilling whistles above and deeper tones below, the latter so plaintive they could have been blown through a conch shell.

So far, the trip had been as advertised. My suite was fabulous—an upper-floor corner with a full living room, a monstrous bedroom, and a bathroom larger than a good many Manhattan apartments. Last night I had luxuriated in sixty gallons of hot water infused with lavender and Japanese bath salts. The food was delicious, the shopping successful. Abby and I had both chosen to adapt Vera Wang wedding dresses, and all the fittings were done. We saw the Christmas tree lit in Rockefeller Center and went to *Wicked* at the Gershwin. We took in the Museum of Natural History, MoMA, and an Andrew Wyeth exhibition at the Whitney, my new favorite museum.

Was I happy? Not by a long shot.

"The answer is no." The night before I'd left, Julia had been emphatic.

"But why not? It's the perfect opportunity."

"I won't chase him, Megan."

"I'm not asking you to chase him—I'm asking you to let *me* chase him for you!"

She crossed her arms and set her chin down and to the left. This was "resolve," which she only adopted in serious situations.

"I called him. I texted him. He did not reply."

I paused over my open suitcase.

"But if he just heard your side of the story."

"He's done with me, and I don't blame him—I'm radioactive."

Her calm and logical reply didn't fool me. I knew she cared about Zach, that his complete silence added insult to what was already a painful injury. But she never gave in, and I left for New York with Abby and Aunt Camille. Mom canceled to focus on Julia's troubles and our Venetian Masquerade party, which had ballooned so big I cheekily suggested it would be cheaper just to fly everyone to Venice. *They already have the canals and the gondolas!* She told me to decide on a charity "yesterday" because I had a hundred and fifty tables to sell.

Each day in New York I thought about calling Zach. I was in New York City, for God's sake, and so was he! I had to corner him, explain the situation. Everywhere we went I searched the throngs for him, hoping against all reason I would bump into him by chance. *Good luck with that, Megan—there's only twelve million people here.*

I even pondered trying to "bump into him" not so accidentally. I Googled the Gage Group for their address. It was down on Wall Street, quite a distance from Central Park, and it seemed unlikely I could convince Julia I'd been in the area for any other reason. But tomorrow was my last day, and opportunity was slipping away.

In the window I had unconsciously doodled a large question mark in the steam. *What is my question?* I wondered. *How to get around Julia, of course.* She had forbidden me to contact Zach. Okay. But she had not forbidden me to contact Andrew Gage. It wasn't quite as good, but the idea of explaining her situation to him while giving him a piece of my mind was a close second. It would have to do.

∘⌣∘

The next morning I pleaded exhaustion, and Aunt Camille took pity on me. She told me to rest, go to the spa, and they would check in later. I yawned for added measure, but as soon as they left I quickly showered and dressed. Bundled up in a cashmere Burberry trench and looking every bit the young lady of consequence, I went downstairs, where the doorman whistled up a cab and instructed the driver to take me to 14 South William Street. Driving downtown, I imagined the building where Andrew Gage would house his offices. It would be one of the soaring phallic skyscrapers I could see in the distance—a giant dick, just like him.

But South William Street, while in the shadow of Wall Street's behemoths, turned out to be a spindly interior street of low-level, historic-looking buildings. And number 14 was a church. As I approached the door, I wondered if I had the address wrong, and checked my phone. There was no sign, just the plaque with the number 14 and a plain wooden door with a wrought-iron handle. No gate, no heavy security, no elevators, no hustle, and zero bustle. Puzzled, and still thinking I must have gotten it wrong, I nevertheless climbed the three stone steps and tried the right door. It was locked. I looked about for a buzzer, an intercom, but found only the original bell pull. Feeling faintly ridiculous, I yanked it, heard it ring inside. While pondering just what I should say to the elderly priest sure to open the door, I was surprised to hear a voice instead.

"Gage Group, how may I help you?"

I could see no speakers, nor any wire—nothing electronic anywhere on the door or in the framing. But going on the assumption that if they could speak to me I could speak to them . . .

"Um, hi. I'm here to see Andrew Gage, please."

"Who's calling?"

"Megan McKnight."

A pause, and the door buzzed, though I still couldn't see how, but when I pushed, it swung open, whisper silent. I entered, and it swung closed.

I passed through the vestibule and into the space beyond. Once a rather intimate church, built in the classic cruciform, it was now an offbeat, one-of-a-kind office building that delicately straddled the past and the present. Much of the original church remained—the stone floor, the central corridor, columns, two spiral staircases, and the vaulted ceiling with frescoes.

But in the nave the pews had been removed, and offices framed with antique paneling—three on each side—lined both sides of the central walkway. Ancient stained-glass windows with religious motifs were set into the walls, and the bright office lights within set off prism bursts of light and color all down the central corridor. In a warm touch, worn padded pews, obviously scavenged, were placed here and there as benches. Staircases to my right and left led to the choir, home to more offices with the same paneling and more stained-glass windows. These upper offices glowed like fish tanks at night.

Two more offices lived in the north and south transepts, but across the altar a stone wall had been built. The tumbled bricks, pinkish and weathered, matched the building's exterior. *Looks like they framed a courtyard at one time,* I thought.

Set in the wall and barring the way to the apse and the vestry beyond were two very old doors—how old I couldn't tell, but very old, even ancient.

I thought back to my conversation with Andrew in the barn. What had he said? "You wouldn't believe what gets thrown away." *Was this church abandoned?* I wondered.

The door to the south transept office opened, and a young African American woman came toward me. She wore jeans and a crisp white linen shirt—very business casual.

"I'm Gracie," she said, extending her hand. "Andrew's assistant. I apologize, but he isn't here just now."

"Oh, um—is Zach here?"

"No, I'm sorry," Gracie said, shaking her head. "He's taking care of some business upstate today. I did leave Andrew a message, and he should call back in a few minutes. Would you care to wait?"

"Sure," I said.

"Please, sit." She indicated a pew. "Would you care for a coffee?"

"Um, sure. Just milk."

"Regular coffee or would you prefer a cappuccino, or a latte?" What was she gonna do, make a Starbucks run?

"Don't trouble yourself, please."

"It's no trouble," she replied, and she meant it.

I thought of the cold and slush outside, the brisk wind off the Hudson that blew so hard it made the buildings tremble.

"A latte would be fantastic."

She nodded and left. I sat on the pew. It was comfy.

When she returned she handed me a latte in an Illy ceramic cup and saucer with two tiny sugar cubes and a platinum demitasse spoon. As I stirred I wondered why she had called Andrew and where had she gotten this perfect latte anyway—had she made it, or was there an Italian coffee shop tucked back there in the vestry with the robes and chalices?

"Thank you so much."

"You're very welcome." She sat beside me. "Are you visiting from Dallas then?"

"I am. How did you know?"

"I recognized your name—and your accent." She smiled, a lovely smile full of warmth—the most genuine one I'd received since arriving in New York, I realized. "Can I show you around while we wait for him to return?"

"Sure." I carried my coffee, took a sip. It tasted even more delicious than it smelled.

"The building is Dutch," she said, gesturing up and around, "and dates to the mid-sixteen hundreds. It was a neighborhood church for centuries, but eventually fell vacant, and then into a bit of a shambles."

We stood now in the central aisle, and she pointed up to the domed cupola.

"The dome and roof partially caved in, and it became a roost for pigeons and squatters, and eventually the city condemned it. It was sold to a hotel developer who planned to tear it down. A few people, scholars mainly, protested—they said it was of real historic significance. But the developer had friends at City Hall, and the demolition was scheduled when Andrew brought a last-minute injunction."

We had climbed the steps now, and walked along past the upstairs offices and stopped in a small alcove. Inlaid in the curved wall was a mosaic, thousands and thousands of tiny gold tiles arranged to show a humble Christ on a donkey, his disciples trailing behind him. Without thinking I reached a hand out, and nearly touched it before drawing back. As a very small girl I had once, innocently, touched a lily in a Monet at a museum, horrifying my mother and leading to a lesson I could never forget.

"That is—it's just . . ."

"Right?" Gracie said. "This was a wonderful surprise. It had been plastered over at some point—all of them were." She pointed to these upper alcoves, each with a finely detailed tile mosaic.

"Plastered over?" I was shocked. *What moron would plaster over centuries-old gold mosaics?*

"Andrew brought in experts from Holland who attested to its heritage, and with some work on the political side he forced an about-face—the building was designated a historical landmark, and Andrew agreed to buy the developer out. He was ridiculed in the press—you know, he was an idealistic but foolish young guy with too much money and too little experience—but he was determined to save the building. He found a contractor in Missoula who specialized in old Western buildings, and he reinforced the existing walls with a skeleton of timber and steel. Each layer was carefully scraped back by hand, in case something was behind it. Much of the stained glass you see was found in the basement windows, blacked out with spray paint. Materials came from Pennsylvania, Tennessee, Latvia—he found the front doors in a village in Argentina. He had a vision for what it could be."

"It's remarkable." And I meant it. It was a masterpiece—easily the most unusual, most beautiful office building I'd ever seen.

She led me downstairs, along the central corridor past the transverse and up the steps to the stone wall and those ancient doors. *This would be Andrew's office, the inner sanctum, home to the high priest of business.* Gracie opened the door. It was surprisingly spare—formal, for sure, but in the best way. Stacks of papers, a set of blueprints on the desk, a green Moleskine calendar book, a jar of pens, and some knickknacks. The chair behind the desk was an old leather high-back on swivels; it was senatorial, but lived in, well used.

"His father's," Gracie said, indicating the chair. I put my hand on it, and could sense the history embedded in the creased leather the way you can holding a rare first edition. It felt . . . authentic.

"Would you excuse me for a moment?" Gracie asked. I nodded and she went out. Left alone, I sat in the chair. His dad had been extraordinarily rich, politically connected, wielded real power in the real world. This was in every way a big chair to fill. *I bet it's hard for him to sit here.*

When Gracie returned I was standing.

"I tried him again but he's terrible about answering his phone."

"That's okay. I was taking a chance that I would run into him."

"He's supposed to be at his mother's later. Would you like to try him there?"

Surprised by her offer, I stumbled over my answer.

"Sure. I guess."

"I'll call a car."

And before I could refuse, she was gone. Minutes later I stepped into the backseat of a town car.

"The Dakota, please," Gracie told the driver.

"Great to meet you, Gracie! And thanks!"

"You too, Megan. I texted him that you were on your way—hopefully he'll see it."

I glanced back through the rear window. Hugging her arms around her chest to ward off the cold, she smiled and waved. I waved back.

Twenty-Three

In Which Megan Braves the Yukon in Pumps

AS I STOOD BENEATH THE DAUNTING FAÇADE, THE
Dakota glared down with palpable malice.

Enormous, a Teutonic fortress a hundred yards square,
it bristled with gables, turrets, dormers, balconies, and span-
drels. The walls at the base were so thick that if the enraged
villagers brought nothing but axes and a battering ram,
they'd still be at it a month later. On the way, curious about
where Mrs. Gage lived, I had Googled it. Built in the 1880s,
its name derived from its location—far north and west of
civilization at the time. It had been a landmark of the Upper
West Side for a century, and was a favorite of the glitterati. I
wasn't surprised that she chose it.

I tightened the belt on my trench coat, squared my shoulders, and marched to the front door, held open by a doorman. It shut behind me with a thud. Inside the light was
dim, and the stone floors and walls felt cold and indifferent.

"Megan McKnight for Andrew Gage, please," I told the

bald and muscle-bound man at the security desk.

He looked me over long enough for me to know he knew Andrew's type, which I was not, then reached for the phone. I turned away and dawdled, heard him speak something unintelligible in a low voice. A pause, and then he said, "Very good," and the phone hit the cradle.

"Ms. McKnight?"

"Yes," I said, turning ever so casually.

"This way please." I entered the elevator. He inserted a card key, and pressed the number ten—the penthouse.

"Thank you." The brief incline of his head was the last thing I saw before the doors shut and the car whooshed skyward. I sighed in relief—I'd bluffed my way into Buckingham Palace and was now moments from surprising the capricious queen.

What will I say to her? You're here for Julia; you'll know what to say.

The elevator doors opened and I stepped out, expecting to land in a hallway. Instead I found myself in the Gages' foyer. They didn't live in some tacky apartment with a number—they lived on the *entire* top floor!

Directly opposite, a Van Gogh of violets in a vase hung on the wall. I took two steps forward for a better look and I could see globby swirls of paint curling off the canvas. *Um, that's not a print.*

I took a breath. In my world the Battles were rich, but they'd have to liquidate the oil business, pawn the houses and the ranch and the horses and the family silver to go halfsies on that painting. And that didn't include the wall to hang it on.

"Megan?" That couldn't be Andrew's mom—there was no way she sounded that young.

A girl about my age raced down the hall toward me. In Levi's and a white T-shirt, she was too shabbily dressed to be the help, but who was she? The answer would have to wait until after she released me from an enthusiastic hug.

"I'm so glad to finally meet you!" Her eyes were bright and full of enthusiasm. I still had no idea who she was.

"Me too," I said automatically. Finally, she realized my conundrum.

"Georgie. Georgie Gage." This was Georgie the sultry psychopath? She must be absolutely deranged, because standing there she seemed like the most normal girl I had ever seen. *Maybe more sociopath than psychopath*, I thought.

"Of course. So . . . nice to meet you." *Don't set her off.*

"Come in, please, over here." She led me down the hallway and into an open room. I followed her and stopped again—and gawked. Across the room, floor-to-ceiling windows created a living tableau of Central Park and the city beyond: the rolling hills of the park, all white; the zoo buildings; and there in the distance, the Plaza.

"Sit down. Let me take your coat."

"Um . . ." I shrugged out of my coat while still looking out the window. Georgie paid it no mind. *The Sistine Chapel probably gets old if you work at the Vatican every day.*

"Have we met?" I asked cautiously.

"No, but I feel like we have. I've heard so much about you."

"Really? How?"

"From Andrew. He wrote me all about you—that you had the most amazing black eye at the first party, that you play soccer and ride horses and can shoot a shotgun and you lived on a cattle ranch—just everything!"

"Oh," I managed, still confused. "So . . . interesting. Well, that's actually why I'm here. I wanted to see him. I went to his office, and they sent me here."

"He's on his way. You can wait with me!"

"I'm afraid that won't be possible."

Mrs. Gage stood in the doorway. Her presence, her voice, the shock of seeing her, lifted me to my feet. From afar at Lauren's party I'd thought her attractive. Up close in the daylight she presented a much sterner, more formidable, and frankly frightening face. Her features were all slightly too pronounced, and I realized she had been under the knife and needle several times. Her folded arms told me she brooked no nonsense and I'd better get to the point.

"Mrs. Gage, hello. I'm Megan McKnight." I walked toward her. "I'm sorry to drop by unexpectedly, but my sister, Julia, and I—"

"I know all about you and your sister and the whole sordid affair, and you have some nerve showing up here. Perhaps in *Texas* these things are done, but not here—not with my son and his friends."

Apparently, Mrs. Gage subscribed to the notion that if a fight is inescapable, it's best to throw the first punch. I gathered myself.

"With all due respect, Mrs. Gage, you don't know what happened or anything about my sister, Julia. She is the kindest, most compassionate person I know, and—"

"That's a matter of opinion," she said tartly.

"Mom!" Georgie broke in, but Mrs. Gage silenced her with a look, then turned back to me. "Now, unless there was something else . . ."

This was not a question but an invitation to leave. I was pissed—at her, at Andrew by proxy, at the whole bunch of them. They were such snobs, and it was so incredibly unfair to Julia. But I held it together, imagined Ann standing in front of me: what would I say to her?

"Could you please tell Andrew I stopped by? I would very much like to speak with him."

"Of course," she said. I scribbled my number on a piece of paper and handed it to her. She held it like a gob of toxic waste.

"Really nice to meet you," I said. She crinkled her mouth in reply.

Waiting for the elevator I fumed about Andrew and his mother. The doors opened, I entered and pushed L. Just as the door began to close, Georgie slid in.

"I am so, so sorry," she said. "I'll for sure tell Andrew you stopped by."

"Thanks. I just want a chance to explain things to him."

"Where are you staying?"

"The Plaza, but we're going back to Dallas tomorrow."

She grabbed my phone and entered a number, pushed call. She handed it back, pulled her phone from her back pocket and made sure it rang.

"Call me if you're back in New York."

"I will."

In the lobby I stepped out, the doors closed, and she was gone.

∽

I spent fifteen minutes in ankle-deep slush trying to hail a cab going downtown, then gave it up as hopeless and decided to walk back to the hotel. It couldn't be more than a mile, I reckoned—I'd seen the Plaza from the Gages' living room window. So I pulled my coat tight, turned up the collar, crossed Central Park West, and entered the park at Seventy-Second Street past Strawberry Fields. I took the first path south, directly into the wind, and immediately found myself making feeble progress.

My flimsy, sodden shoes slipped and sank in the snowy slush, and within a few hundred yards my feet were numb below the ankle. I leaned into the buffeting, hostile wind, but each two steps forward were accompanied by at least one sideways, or a stumble, if not an outright step backward. My eyes watered and my cheeks stung, and several times thick dollops of snow blew down on my uncovered head, soaking my hair and freezing my scalp. I bucked myself up by cursing Andrew Gage and remembering the staunch hero-ism of historic American marches in terrible conditions, like the ragtag Continental Army inching toward Valley Forge.

Twenty minutes later, when I made the turn east, I was hobbled and shivering incessantly. I coaxed each step with a fantasy of indulgence I told myself was only minutes away—a hot soak in the tub, room service, dry socks, and a plush Plaza robe. Washington's poor army again came to mind, and with horror I recalled they left bloody tracks and more than a few toes behind them in the wilds of Pennsylvania that December. Did I face a similar fate?

Emerging from the park at the corner of Fifth Avenue, I practically sobbed. A mere hundred yards to go. I winced and moaned and snuffled my way across Fifty-Ninth Street, and my lip trembled as I gingerly climbed the final ten steps. I'd made it. I closed my eyes and turned my face skyward to thank God for my salvation, and nearly fell into the arms of the doorman. He didn't recognize me from this morning, but he tipped his hat as I passed. I could smell the warmth from the lobby as I entered the revolving door.

Halfway around I saw Andrew Gage coming out through the same door.

Our eyes met and our heads turned and we followed each other all the way around. It was like *Minuet Performed with Revolving Door*. Realizing that neither of us had stopped, we went around again, and this time I exited in the lobby, and he went outside. The third time, he stepped out in the lobby and I went all the way around, finally landing beside him.

"Megan!"

"Andrew! I've been looking for you all day!" On a different day this might have seemed funny—I had been up and down Manhattan in a blizzard looking for this guy all day, and found him in my hotel lobby. But at this point, I was exasperated and on the verge of tears.

"I know—I'm so sorry."

"What are you doing here?"

"Looking for you! When you were at the office, I was up in the Bronx. Then I was on my way to my mom's, but the traffic, with the snow, it was terrible, and by the time I got there I had just missed you. But Georgie told me you were staying here, so I came down, and I've been waiting. What took you so long?"

"I couldn't get a cab. So I walked."

He looked me over. My hair had caked in long brown icicles. My eyes streamed, my nose glowed cherry red, and my coat, sheathed in ice, crackled when I unbuttoned it like the frozen sails of a clipper ship in the Antarctic. I was pretty sure my shoes were about to crack open, and when they did my raw bleeding feet would ruin the hotel's very expensive carpet.

"Are you . . . okay?" he asked carefully.

"NO! I AM NOT OKAY!" Was I shouting? I couldn't hear very well because my ears were frozen, but my voice sounded really loud. "I am cold and wet and I look like roadkill!"

The douche bag laughed.

"You're the best-looking roadkill I've ever seen."

"Are you *fucking* with me?" I asked. "Because I am *so* not in the mood to be fucked with. Your mother just fucked with me and the weather has fucked with me and—"

"I'm really sorry about my mother—Georgie told me what happened. She just acted that way because she feels threatened by you."

Mrs. Gage, threatened by me? My hearing is *messed up.*

Our last exchange caused a few people in the lobby to look our way.

"You better start making some sense, buddy," I said, staring hard at him.

He shuffled around, and I wondered what he'd say next. Based on the past two minutes, it was sure to be a doozy.

"Look, ever since I . . . parked your bike," he said, "I haven't been able to stop thinking about you. And then at that first party, you showed up with that black eye and so much attitude, and I thought—"

"I was a lesbian!"

"I apologized for that!" *True.* "You gotta understand, everything in my life, from day one, it's just so . . . *expected.* And nothing about you—nothing you do, nothing you say— is expected. I have no idea what you are going to say or do next and I *love that.* Then at the pool you knew who Gibbon was, and you were right, I did follow you to the barn that night—I had to see you. And then today, you were looking for me, and I thought that's great, so I came looking for you, and here you are. And I guess I was wondering if, maybe if you . . . change clothes—if you want to have dinner with me, because I'd really like to get to know you better."

"Are you demented?"

"You seem upset," he said.

"I AM!"

"Why?" he asked innocently.

"Because after my sister was arrested and slandered, you convinced Zach to ghost her, to never even give her a chance to explain, and that's just so, so typical of you—nobody is allowed any faults or flaws, and any whiff of scandal makes them a pariah. Do you have any idea how much misery you've caused her? She was inconsolable—she cried herself to sleep for weeks because she couldn't reach him, couldn't tell him what happened. All because of you. And don't bother denying it, because Lauren told me all about it."

If the first salvos had attracted glances, this one drew a small gathering, and at least two of the onlookers recognized Andrew and took out their cell phones and started snapping pictures. Andrew glanced their way, realized what this meant. He turned back to me.

"When Zach found out about Julia," he said, his voice much calmer than mine, "he *asked* me what to do, because he's my best friend. We talked it all out—the guy, the . . . circumstances. I said I think there's a good chance she's still in love with this guy. They'd been together a long time—much longer than she had known Zach."

"But that's not true! She's not in love with Tyler—and she's crazy about Zach!"

"That's not the way it looked," he said. "She was with him that day; they clearly had a . . . history. I said this guy Tyler seems unstable, dangerous, so let things cool off, get some distance. He agreed, so I suggested he come back to New York, give her some space to figure things out."

"But why not call her? He could have explained this to her. It's exactly what you did to Hank at Harvard."

His gaze narrowed at the mention of Hank.

"First, Zach's decision to come to New York, and how or when he did or did not contact Julia—that's on him. I only told him I thought it wise to take a step back. And if he asked me again today, I'd tell him the same thing. He's my friend, and I told him what I thought was right, and prudent." Now his gaze grew, if possible, even more measured. "And as for *Hank*—whatever he told you, it's something less than the truth."

The way he said *Hank*, so dismissive, so pompous—it sent me over the edge.

"He told me exactly what happened. Let's hear your version."

"I'm sorry, I can't."

"Well, guess what, Andrew Gage. I believe him. It fits. Neatly. You iced him out then, and you told your friend to do the same thing to Julia."

"I had no idea you thought this way about me."

At least twenty people had now gathered, including

staff from the hotel, uncertain what to do. After all, this was Andrew Gage. Dozens of pictures had been snapped. Andrew paid them no heed but looked at me with anger.

"I'm sorry I took up your time," was all he said.

"Well, you're not forgiven!" I shouted at his back.

He went through the revolving door one last time, lit in a blaze of camera flashes, then strode down the steps, hands shoved in his jacket pockets, and into the night. The cameras now turned toward me, and I ducked and ran for the elevator as the hotel staff kept the curious from following. Once inside, with the doors firmly closed, I shook.

What the hell just happened?

⤳ℯ↶

In the shower I stood under a waterfall of piping-hot water until I felt warm inside. I washed my hair and scrubbed myself and wrapped up in the ten-pound hotel robe. I curled up in a chair and ran through everything I had said to him about Julia and Hank. I had skewered him with the truth, but somehow it didn't feel like victory. I studiously ignored the fact that Andrew Gage had just stood in a crowded hotel lobby and confessed his *feelings* for me. I couldn't even go there yet.

When Aunt Camille and Abby returned I met them in the lobby restaurant for a quick bite. They asked about my day and I lied and told them I'd stayed in my room and watched old movies on TV. I picked at my fish and chips and then went back to my room, got under the covers, and turned out the light. But my mind hummed and I couldn't get comfortable, no matter how many different ways I arranged the pillows.

I finally drifted off, but I slept badly and woke grumpy the next morning. I dressed in jeans and a sweatshirt and a ball cap for the ride to the airport, and once in the sleek Suburban, slouched in my seat and stared out the window. Yesterday's lovely white snow had turned to a thick and dingy stew overnight. Traffic poked along and the people, faceless under dark hats and mufflers and giant coats, tramped through the grimy slop.

This whole city is just a giant catbox, I thought. I closed my eyes and leaned my head against the window.

Ding!

Abby's phone chimed and she read her message.

"Oh my God! Great, great news—all the charges have been dropped."

Aunt Camille and I looked over.

"Really?" I asked, sitting up.

"Hunter says the hearing went just as they hoped," she said, still reading through the message. "Julia is fully cleared. Nothing more to do and nothing on her record."

"That is just fantastic," Aunt Camille said.

"He said Dad was great!" Abby added, smiling at her mother.

"Wow, that's amazing!" I said.

"And he's meeting us at the airport!"

"Why did you get the news from that ass instead of straight from Uncle Dan?"

Abby looked like I had slapped her, and Aunt Camille bristled.

"For your information, Megan, Hunter's been a huge help to Dad on Julia's case. He gathered the police reports and delivered filings and helped in a hundred different ways."

"Why?" I asked.

"Because he's sweet and he likes me. He was at the hearing this morning because I asked him to be—I wanted to know as soon as there was news."

"Oh," I said in reply.

"We've spent loads of time together the past month and . . . he's genuinely nice to me and I really like him too."

"I'm so sorry. I had no idea," I managed.

"You might have if you'd bothered to ask," Abby retorted. "I know you've got a lot on your mind, with Julia and everything, but we've just spent the past week together and you never even once asked about my life."

"I'm so sorry."

"It's okay," Abby replied, softening. "But really, consider every once in a while that you might not be right about absolutely everything."

I shut my mouth for the rest of the ride to the airport. If I had driven Abby—sweet, bubbly, easygoing Abby—to this outburst, my self-absorption had reached epic levels.

Her comment about not being right about everything cut to the bone too. Was that really how people saw me—as the Hermione Granger know-it-all? I floundered between angst over my jerky behavior to her and the joy I felt about the charges against Julia being dropped.

We checked our bags and passed through security, then wandered up the concourse toward our gate. We grabbed coffees, and Abby peeled off to the bathroom while Aunt Camille and I passed a news kiosk. Right there, in a rack, was the New York *Daily News*. The big headline involved Wall Street, but right below that was a picture of Andrew Gage, in the lobby of the Plaza Hotel, dressed exactly as I had seen him last night, with the headline "Mystery Brunette Snubs Prince Charming."

"I think I'll grab some magazines for the flight," Aunt Camille said, turning into the kiosk. I grabbed her shoulder abruptly and spun her around, away from the papers.

"No, no, no, no, no. You go sit down, Aunt Camille, and I'll buy you whatever magazines you want."

"Well, that's very thoughtful of you, Megan."

"Not at all," I said, moving her toward the gate. "You've done so much for me this week, and I feel horrible about what I said—really, go sit down over there." *Way, way over there.*

We found her a seat by the gate and I returned to buy her a *People* and a *New York Times* and "anything else that looks interesting." But first I grabbed the *Daily News*.

Andrew's picture had been cropped from his waist to his head. He was staring at someone, his exquisite features hot with anger.

Under his picture was one of me—or at least my turned shoulder and the fall of my hair. Somehow, praise Jesus, they'd missed my face. I opened the paper and skimmed the article, a breathless account of our fight in the hotel lobby. But no mention of my name. I was "an unknown young woman," according to the "hotel source." There was another pic of him leaving, hands thrust in his pockets, and much speculation about just *who* had the audacity to spurn Andrew Gage, and what this meant for his current relationship with "stunning Dallas socialite Lauren Battle." Her tiny picture graced the very bottom left-hand corner.

I looked again at Andrew's picture and noticed something I hadn't seen in person—hurt. I thought about all he'd said before I drilled him. He'd been thinking about me for months, ever since we met over my bike. And he wrote to Georgie about me, and Gracie knew who I was, and his mom was threatened by me.

I had been reading him wrong this whole time.

Twenty-Four

In Which Megan Questions Her Judgment

"Y'ALL KNOW I'M NOT MUCH ON SPEECHES, BUT I DID want to take a moment tonight and say that, well, this is big and I'm just glad I get to share it with you," Dad said, holding a glass of red wine in his hand.

It was Friday night, the day before our party, and Mom and Dad had convened a family dinner to celebrate the sale of the ranch. The contracts were signed, the ink was dry. What had begun as a conversation several months ago at the Nasher had become a reality. My parents had graciously invited Hank to join us.

"Lucy . . ." he continued, turning toward Mom, "I couldn't have done it without you, wouldn't have wanted to."

Mom smiled up at him.

"Girls, the Aberdeen cattle business, and probably the McKnight name, will end, but it will always be part of you. You are the descendants of a great family, a family that came from far away with very little and built something that lasted a hundred and fifty years. Never forget where you came from, what you stand for, and know that you are capable of great things."

"We won't," I said as Julia nodded.

"And Hank"—and here Dad turned to the lone guest—"I'm glad you're here with us tonight . . ."

While the flight back from New York had felt like the hours after a loss in the big game, the two weeks home had been nothing short of a national championship. Not only had the sale of the Aberdeen been finalized with a very large stash of cash in escrow, but Hank told us that all of the twenty-five oversized lots already had a deposit—the development had sold out overnight. For the first time in their adult lives my parents were about to be debt-free. They bobbed like corks in the sea, relaxed and smiling in a way I could not recall. You really don't know the weight of your burden until you set it down.

And Mom was planning the party of her life. With cost no longer a concern, the venue had grown from a hotel dining room to Turtle Creek Country Club. The quartet became a chamber orchestra, Veuve Clicquot stepped in for its lesser California cousin, the menu expanded, and the florist ordered thousands more flowers. This sudden growth of the McKnight party was due mainly to the "release the hounds" on the budget, but my success selling tables now kept pace. I had found a charity called Refuge, and made ending violence against women our cause. The ladies *loved it*, and by working the phone and the parties we soared to a hundred tables of six, and then a hundred and forty.

So everything had turned awesome—the ranch had sold in minutes and my parents' marriage was saved; our party was assured success, and now I sat at our ranch listening to my dad thank my attentive, smart, and handsome boyfriend for making it all possible. I should have been euphoric.

I was not.

I had a knot in my stomach the size of a hockey puck. For two weeks I had tried to ignore it, dissolve it, or digest it. But it remained. Something big was bugging me. And that something was not Andrew Gage. It was his sister, Georgie.

I really liked Hank, and I could never believe he would lie to me. But when I met Georgie Gage in New York, she seemed lovely, someone I would totally be friends with—and nothing like the manipulative lunatic Hank made her out to be. Which meant *I had to be wrong about one of them*—and that bugged me, big-time. But which one was it?

"To Hank Waterhouse—thanks a million. Make that several million!" Dad raised his glass, and everybody joined him. We smiled and laughed, and Hank grinned sheepishly. We clinked glasses, and still there was that hockey puck.

"Speech, speech, speech," Mom clamored, and tapped her fork on the glass. Julia and I laughed and Hank finally stood.

"Well, I can only say that this is all because of Megan." Hank turned to me, with love in his eyes. "I knew from the first moment I saw your picture that I was on to something good. And to be here, to be part of this, well, none of it would have happened without her."

∽

"Morning, gorgeous," Hank said the next day, and gave me a kiss. We were naked under the sheets, warm and cozy and relaxed. "Coffee?"

"Does the Pope wear a funny hat?"

He smiled at my lame joke and went to the kitchen. I admired his bare ass all the way out the door and thought once again about what Hank had said last night—just about the sweetest thing anybody had ever said about me.

From the first moment I saw your picture . . .

I froze.

When Hank and I met on the veranda, he asked me if I was a deb or family. I remembered answering "both." And he didn't know my name; we'd introduced ourselves. But if he'd seen my picture, it had to have been in the announcement—with my name right underneath it.

Had Hank come looking for me that night?

"Where you going?" Hank stood in the doorway, still completely naked, holding two coffee cups.

I had already slid on my jeans and was tying my shoes.

"I forgot—final fitting this morning. My mom just texted to remind me."

"No coffee?" he asked, holding out a cup.

"I'll stop for something," I said, and went into the living room.

"See you tonight?"

"Of course," I said, and left, head down.

I walked down to my car, got in, and started it up. Afraid he might be watching me through the window, I drove out, went another block, turned, and pulled over on a quiet street, under a large elm tree. I was shaking.

Megan, calm down, you're being paranoid. There must be a perfectly reasonable explanation for what Hank said. Only I couldn't think of one. And I couldn't ask him directly.

But there was one person I could ask. It would be weird, but the nagging dread wasn't going away until I sorted this out.

"Hi—Georgie? It's Megan McKnight."

"Oh my God! Hi!"

"You got a minute?" I asked.

"Of course. How are you?"

"Good—okay."

"Did you know you were in the paper here?"

"Yeah, that was weird."

"Any fallout in Texas?"

"Not yet, not that I know about. What about there?"

"Mom freaked out, and so did Lauren."

Well, forewarned is forearmed.

"We were talking about my sister, Julia, and things just got out of hand. I don't know why they imagined it was some lovers' spat . . ."

"Uh-huh," Georgie said, unconvinced.

I knew she didn't buy my story, but I didn't call her to

discuss that. I girded myself to ask the hard question.

"Listen, Georgie, the reason I called—well, I feel pretty sure you don't know this, but—I've been, been dating Hank Waterhouse . . . for a few months." Awkward, agonizing silence. Uneasy, I tried to fill it. "I do know there's some . . . history between Andrew and Hank, and that it . . . maybe it involves you . . . and something's happened now and I'm, I'm beginning to think that maybe I don't know the whole truth. So I was hoping you'd be willing to, um, tell me your . . . side of the story?"

Another agonizing pause, and then she sighed.

"Sorry. That was the last thing I expected you to say. Of course Andrew would never have told me that you were dating Hank," Georgie said finally. She took a breath.

"I really hate to pry," I said.

"No, that's okay. I'll tell you. I met him at Thanksgiving his freshman year at Harvard—he was Andrew's roommate, and he came to our house on Martha's Vineyard. I was sixteen."

"Yep," I said, mentally ticking off the first box.

"I fell in love with him in about five minutes," Georgie said. "Everyone did. None of us had ever met anybody that handsome, that charming, that well-spoken and funny and just—he was perfect. But I fell in love with him, you know, romantically. And that first weekend, when he went back to Boston, he had my phone number."

"Go on."

"So the next day, Monday morning, he texted me. All it

said was *I have this problem.* And I was surprised, so I texted him back *What's wrong?* And the he texted me. *I can't stop—*"

"*Thinking about you*," we said in unison. Her words—those *exact* words—pinned me to the seat of the car.

"And I just . . . melted. For the next month we texted constantly, and sometimes he called late at night. And then he spent Christmas break with us. We slept together the first night, and every night after that. I snuck over to his room and he would be waiting, and it was the most exciting week of my life. First of all, the sex was amazing . . ."

This all sounded *so* familiar, and I braced against the impact of her story.

"But more than that, I had a secret, a passionate secret love, and it—he—just took over my life. I'm not proud of it, I should have known better, but I couldn't stop it, and he didn't want me to. He told me right from the start he loved me, that I was so mature, so beautiful—it was like I was drunk all the time. And after that, when he went back to school, it was just madness. I snuck up to Boston and we stayed in a hotel a couple of weekends. He told Andrew he was doing community service. And that next summer he was at our house, working in Martha's Vineyard, and it continued. And the next fall, and then, just before Christmas their sophomore year, I went up to Boston. We stayed in a hotel and—look, we were having sex all the time."

"I understand." That was an understatement. I was

sweaty and pale, and my stomach lurched around inside my body.

"A couple of weeks later there was this party, a bunch of guys from Harvard, and Hank was showing some other guys this—he was showing them a video he made, of that night. I didn't know anything about it—he used his laptop to film it, I guess . . . and—"

"You don't have to tell me this, Georgie."

"I want to. I need to," she said emphatically. "I had no idea you were dating this guy, and he's a bad guy, so you need to know this."

"Okay," I said.

"So they were watching . . . the video, and he was bragging about it, telling them how he was nailing America's heiress, and saying disgusting things about me, what I would do for him. Anyway, word got back to Andrew."

"Oh God," I whispered.

"Yeah. Andrew wanted to kill him." *I bet.* "But he also was worried about me, about how this could affect me—not just the video, but if I was in love, how hurt I would be. Without telling me about it, he flew home and told my mom."

"Holy shit."

"You don't even know. She asked me point-blank if I was involved with Hank—sexually. She could read it on my face, and I couldn't deny it—I was so in love with him. Then . . . then she told me what she knew. I was horrified. He couldn't have done that, wouldn't do that to me. Film us? And then show it around at school? It wasn't the guy I knew—or thought I knew. It was . . . gruesome. She asked me about the video, and I told her the truth, that I didn't know anything about it. I had texted him, sure, and even sent him a few pics, but nothing with my face in it. I had read about that stuff, and my family—well, you know. I swore to her I had no knowledge. She could tell I was crushed."

"Oh my God—you were, what, seventeen? Did they charge him? Was he arrested?"

"No—"

"But, but he filmed you without your knowledge—and your age—it had to be statutory rape at the very least."

"You have to understand about our family. My mom—charges meant a case in court, with publicity, bad publicity—lots of it. And this was all going on before I was even out of high school. She thought it would derail me, permanently."

"What did she do?"

"They—Mom and Andrew—went to see him."

"Seriously?" I tried to imagine this scene in my mind.

"Seriously. They went to Boston and she asked Hank to meet her for lunch at her hotel. She told him it was business, and when he got there she and Andrew confronted him with our attorney. Hank tried to laugh it off as a prank, but after the lawyer explained to him the criminal offenses and the average jail time he could expect, he got very quiet."

"I can't believe this." But I did. I believed every word.

"Me either. I wasn't capable of it. I thought the whole

world had landed on me—I couldn't get out of bed. But Andrew and Mom, they were determined to finish it."

"So they charged him?"

"No. Remember, Mom was desperate to avoid a scandal—so they . . . they offered him a deal."

"A deal?"

"He could sell them his laptop, or they would prosecute."

"I don't get it."

"It was the lawyer's idea. If they bought his laptop, they wouldn't have paid him off, exactly—they were buying something from him. Something tangible."

"How much did they offer?"

"Two hundred and fifty thousand."

"Wow." A quarter of a million bucks for a laptop?

"I know," Georgie said.

"And he had to sign a paper stipulating that there were no copies, anywhere, no downloads, nothing. And finally, that he would leave Harvard voluntarily and never return, and never contact anyone in our family ever again."

"What did he do?"

"He handed it over. And she wrote him a check."

"And he took it and went to Texas and enrolled at A&M, joined the Corps. That sly bastard." *Paid for his education. Probably paid for that car. And the suits.*

"Yeah."

Telling me took a lot out of her. She was sniffling.

"I am so, so sorry, Georgie. But thanks for telling me this."

"I'm glad I did."

There had always been something too good to be true about Hank, something too perfect. But there was still one thing I didn't understand.

"Georgie—why didn't Andrew tell me any of this?"

"Oh, he would never tell anyone this. He's loyal and honest, maybe to a fault. He sees this as my private thing, only for me to tell. Look, if he has a flaw it's that he's a little . . . socially awkward. He has trouble talking to people, getting to know them. But he's one of the good guys."

"I am such an idiot," I said. Though I wasn't sure exactly how, I knew Hank had played me, since the beginning. And Andrew had tried to warn me—how many times? Three at least. But I was too smart for that, so stubbornly, immovably certain of my judgment.

"Megan," Georgie said. "Has he done something *bad* to you?"

"I'm not sure. But I've got a bad feeling."

"Trust that feeling, please," she said. "Trust that feeling."

Twenty-Five

In Which Megan Attends a Ball Packing Live Ammo

IN THE HOURS SINCE I'D SPOKEN WITH GEORGIE, I'D FELT like I was holding a grenade with the pin pulled. I'd held it during the three hours while Margot piled up my towering wig and sewed me into my gown. I'd held it during the limo ride with my family. Sure, I wanted to throw it, dispose of it safely, or at least pass it off to someone. But who? Mom? She was hosting a party for nine hundred. Julia? She was preparing for an evening of well-meaning but intrusive questions about the case and Tyler. Dad? He had just made the deal of a lifetime and was exultant. Why would I do that to him? Cat would have been perfect, but we hadn't spoken since the blowup in the locker room. No, I had no choice but to hold on to it. It left me anxious and sweaty, worried I would drop it and it would go off during the party.

I felt sure Hank had targeted me somehow. But why? I wasn't the hottest deb. I wasn't the richest. I doubted he had filmed us having sex, as that held no prospect for real scandal—who would be interested? No, it had to be the land deal—but I couldn't see anything nefarious about it. We had brought him into it, he had done the drawings on spec—so what was the catch? Knowing I would see him at my party made me sick to my stomach. What would I say? Would he sense something wrong? At least he wasn't my date. Mom and Aunt Camille had made an early pact for Abby's brother Simon to escort Julia to Abby's party, and me to ours.

Fortunately, all my pent-up anxiety about our party being a dud evaporated with my first glimpse of Mom's Venetian Masquerade. The entry plaza at Turtle Creek Country Club had been transformed into St. Mark's Square, circa 1760. Lit by torches and fiery lamps, it was shadowy and mysterious, a fantastical world that was part street fair, part magic show, with jugglers, an organ grinder with a live monkey, contortionists, fire breathers, and weird and grotesque performers of every stripe and color all braying in Italian at the startled guests. As they moved through the crowd to the heavy doors, pickpockets fleeced guests, then amazed them with returned jewels, watches and wallets, tsk-tsking their victims with a shake of their fingers and a warning to "beware."

Inside the Georgian ballroom a seedy chamber orchestra played mischievous period music. Tumbled stone walls framed the whole balcony, and lavish pink frescoes—of fat, naked angels blowing trumpets—adorned the vaulted ceiling. The lighting here was courtesy of a huge real candle chandelier hung from the ceiling. Hundreds of flickering lights reflected off huge turning and twisting masks suspended from the ceiling.

Outside, guests descended from the veranda and walked along a misty cobbled street to a boat dock, where three long gondolas bobbed in Turtle Creek. From there they set out in parties of two and four and six, snuggled under fur blankets, while gondoliers sang love songs and rowed them out into the dark green water, a perfect match for the Venetian Lagoon. They crossed under the arched stone bridge—made over to resemble its Italian cousin—to the eighteenth green, and when they turned back they saw the moon hanging. It wasn't the real moon, but it looked like it.

From the moment you arrived it was like being whisked back three hundred and fifty years. So what if Mom had gone over budget? We'd sold the ranch and would soon sell the cows. It was enough to erase our debt and provide a comfortable retirement.

Of course everyone wore extravagant costumes, and this was Margot's finest hour. Inspired by Titian's portraits, she dressed us as a ducal family. Dad was in a rich orange marmalade coat over a woven brown shirt, with breeches and high boots and a small black hat and mask. Mom and Julia both got high period wigs and thick, dramatic makeup. Margot dressed Mom in a full-sleeved blue velvet gown with a high ivory linen front. Her lorgnette mask on a stick mirrored her dress and sported a single blue feather. Julia and I were the innocent daughters. For Julia she chose a heavy burgundy brocade with a sky-blue shawl, and for me a plain emerald silk encrusted with thousands upon thousands of pale yellow glass beads. Both gowns were off the shoulder, with a tight bodice over a wide skirt. Julia's mask, which covered her eyes and nose, was burgundy and gold, and a single burgundy rose perched on one side. Mine, a little wider, was gold lace filigree in the shape of a butterfly. All of our fabrics were bold and luminous, and standing side by side in the receiving line we shone.

In the end the head count breached nine hundred, so Simon and Julia and Mom and Dad and I spent two hours greeting guests, who all wore masks too—some small and easy to see through, others larger and more elaborate. Some guests had full head masks; often I didn't recognize them until they removed them, usually with a shriek of "Guess who?" My aunt Camille and uncle Dan wore gorgeous owl- and eagle-head masks. Sydney, escorted by Hunter, went simple with a small lorgnette, while Hunter chose the expected and lame Phantom of the Opera mask. Ann Foster flew solo, in a classic and simple midnight blue gown and a pearl mask. Ashley Two and Stephen Cromwell arrived, and then Abby and her date—Abby wore a feathered Carnival mask, and her date went the full commedia dell'arte jester.

Even more fun than seeing the other debs, though, was the sight of our ranch staff and my soccer team all gussied up. Silvio and his wife came dressed as rustic European cattle herders, and Cat and her sister and her parents came too, as Spanish royalty. We comped them, of course, as they had to spring for the costumes, and I could tell the extravagance of the party shocked them.

"I didn't think you'd come. But I'm glad you did," I said to Cat. It was a little uncomfortable, but there wasn't time to clear the air. More couples passed, and when I next looked up a wolf and cat waited.

"Surprise!" Ashley One said, tipping up the kitty cat mask with whiskers. "I brought something for you." She motioned to the wolf beside her, who I knew to be Hank.

He lifted his mask.

"You. Look. Amazing," Hank said, smiling widely.

"Thank you." I kept my voice even, hoped it wouldn't betray me.

He leaned in for a kiss on the cheek.

"Meet me in the woods later," he growled. Knowing what he'd done to Georgie, it made my skin crawl. I wanted to run to the bathroom and scrub my cheek. I chuckled instead.

"Have fun." They moved on, and he fawned over Mom, glad-handed Dad. I wondered how I would avoid him for the entire evening.

Couple after couple after couple passed—I thought it would never end. When it dwindled to the stragglers, Lauren and her date finally arrived. She wore a turquoise silk gown and a matching jeweled eye mask with a peacock feather headdress. She carried a peacock feather fan.

"So excited to be here," Lauren said mildly. She offered a hand. We greeted each other with the bare necessities, but I could tell she wanted to peck my eyes out. Neither of us mentioned the article or pictures in the *Daily News*.

I steeled myself to greet Andrew, but when Lauren's date lifted his Guy Fawkes mask I was shocked to see Zach. Julia's head snapped in his direction. Neither of us had seen him since her arrest.

"Zach. Hi," I said. He cut his eyes to Julia.

"I hope it's okay that I came," he said nervously. He hung his head sheepishly.

"For Christ's sake, Zach," Lauren said. "*Of course* it's okay you came." She stomped off, dragging him along in tow.

There was an obligatory dance with Simon, and one with Dad. From across the room I saw Hank looking around, trying to find me. I did not want to be found, but it's hard to disappear at your own party, so I just kept moving. Cat found me at the bar.

"Hey," she said.

"Hey."

"Your party is really amazing."

"Thanks. But you know, it's not really my party. It's my *mom's* party." Just then a performer with a torch took a swig from a bottle and spewed fire into the air.

"I mean, look at this. This isn't me."

"Definitely not," she agreed. "Listen, I'm really sorry for what I said. I know this is a big deal to your mom—my mom was a maniac before my quinceañera."

"Thanks. I'm never getting married," I said. "And you were right. I've completely taken our friendship for granted, and I'm sorry. Is there anything I can do to make it up to you?"

"Give me a hug?" she asked.

I gave her a long hug.

"I have to confess something really horrible," she said earnestly when we broke apart.

"What?"

"My mom has, like, four doggie bags in her purse."

I burst out laughing and we hung on to each other until we regained our composure.

The doors opened and teams of servers wheeled in the food: whole roasted pigs and guinea fowls and sea bass, gorgonzola-braced polenta, fig and arugula salad drenched in olive oil and fresh lemon juice. To drink, guests chose Prosecco, white Soave or red Valpolicella wine, or Peroni beer jacked from wooden barrels and served in frosty mugs with a thick stick of cinnamon. Desserts were handcrafted tiny fruit tarts, blackberry and raspberry, with dollops of crème fraîche, sprinkled over with raw cacao, and bricks of tiramisu with made-from-scratch ladyfingers drenched in espresso. With the desserts served it was time to address the guests, and I stepped to the microphone.

"Welcome and good evening, everyone. Thank you so much for coming. First, I have to thank my mom. This is the craziest party, and I am just so overwhelmed by everything she pulled together." The crowd clapped and whistled in appreciation, and Mom took a small bow. "If it had been up to me, we'd have had a kegger at the soccer stadium." That got a huge laugh. "But it's unlikely we could have convinced you nice people to pony up five hundred a person for a red Solo cup and Dickie's Barbeque, no matter how good it is." More laughter. "And I want to thank my dad for, well, for just being my dad. I love you so much." Lots of "awwws" here. "I also want to thank my sister, Julia, for loving me no matter what and for being the one person who understands me completely—which is not an easy job." Julia smiled and waved.

"But most of all I'd like to thank her for inspiring tonight's event, which is held in honor of Refuge, a safe house and counseling center for women who have survived domestic violence. I must admit I didn't know that much about Refuge or this issue a month ago, but finding out who they are and what they do, and being a small part of that, has changed my life forever. I want to say thank you now to each and every one of you, for reaching deep and making a significant commitment to helping women in need. It is my great honor to announce that we have raised more than four hundred and sixty thousand dollars!" The crowd broke into massive cheers, but I wasn't done, and waited for them to quiet down. "I am proud to have helped raise that much money, but honestly, I think I can do more. Between us, Julia and I have a grand total of fifty-six designer gowns and cocktail dresses that have been worn exactly once. So we've asked our stylist, Margot, to arrange a dress auction, and we are donating our Season wardrobe to raise additional funds for a new Refuge Safe House. I'd like to challenge the other 2016

Bluebonnet Debutantes to do the same. Basically, I'm asking you for the dress off your back—after the party, of course."

Abby was the first to stand, sticking her hand in the air. "I'm in! They're all yours!"

Then Sydney and Ashley One were up, shouting, "Me too!"

I hadn't expected to get answers on the spot, but the crowd was in a fever. Sydney's mom stood up, Mom and Aunt Camille too, and after that it was a blur. Lauren and Ashley Two eventually stood, but you could tell it pained them. Within a few minutes we had more dresses pledged than I could count, and our small idea had blossomed into a huge new donation source.

"Thank you so much," I said when the crowd quieted. "Now I'd like to introduce Maggie Copeland, the executive director of Refuge, who is going to say a few words while I go work on renting a warehouse. Maggie?" I gestured toward our table, and Maggie Copeland stood up. She was in her midforties, and it turned out she was a close friend of Aunt Camille's. I handed her the microphone and stepped away to give her the stage.

Standing ten feet away as Maggie spoke enthusiastically about how they planned to use the funds raised, I smiled, but felt sure I would crack open and crumple to the floor. I scanned the room. Mom, Dad, and Julia sat with Aunt Camille and Uncle Dan at one table, all blissfully unaware of my predicament. In the back I noticed a man by himself. He wore an elaborate, gorgeous horse mask and he must have come in late because I would have remembered that amazing mask. Hank and Ashley were at a table of six, with two couples I didn't recognize. Hank's wolf mask lay on the table, and he winked at me. I crinkled a smile. So far I'd kept it together, but I wasn't sure I'd be able to if we spent much time alone. I just had to hang on until the party was over.

Maggie finished speaking and I took back the microphone.

"Thank you, Maggie, and thank all of you again—for making a difference!"

I walked through the tables now, saying hello, asking about the food, making sure everyone was happy. Parched, I went to the bar, where I found myself beside Ann Foster. I ordered a Pellegrino over ice with extra lime.

"That was very impressive, Megan," Ann said. "The way you turned Julia's situation around, what you've done with it. I can't imagine a better outcome. You should be very proud of yourself."

"Thank you. Raising all this money, helping these women, I feel . . . useful, almost grown-up—in a way I've never felt before."

"I told you this was more than parties and dates." She looked over at Hank. "Although I've heard the dating is going well for you too."

Then it hit me. Ann Foster approved all the escorts.

"Ann—how did Hank Waterhouse end up as an escort this year?"

"Hank? He was recommended by a Bluebonnet member—Sam Lanham."

"Sam Lanham—the president of XT Energy?"

She seemed surprised I knew who he was. She gestured to Hank sitting at a table with several men behind masks. One had gray hair. "Yes. That's him with Hank now. He's recommended many escorts over the years and it's always worked out well."

My whole body tensed.

"Megan, is something wrong?"

"Yes," I said through clenched teeth. "Something is very, very wrong. Would you excuse me please?"

I straightened my wig and marched across the room to Hank's table. He was in the middle of a story, charming Sam Lanham and the other guests. When I slammed my fist on the table, the dishes rattled.

"You sorry piece of shit! How dare you sit here at my party, the guest of my family, and pretend!"

Hank, as rattled as the dishes, gawked at me. Ann Foster had trailed me, wondering what was up. She leaned in.

"Megan?" she asked. I leaned down toward Hank.

"XT Energy! Ring a bell?"

Now I looked at the other men at the table. Besides Sam, the other two were beefy ex-football players—the kind who gravitated to the energy business with its high-dollar deals and dick-swinging bravado.

Hank looked around at the full room of people having a lovely time. He stood and took my arm. "Let's talk about this outside," he whispered.

"Why? So you can lie to me some more?"

"Megan, do you really want to do this here?" People were looking our way.

"Why not?" Dad was now headed over, with Mom hot behind him. She looked mortified. Wait till she heard the rest. Aunt Camille and Uncle Dan stood up, concern on their faces.

"What on earth?" Mom asked. "I'm so sorry," she said to Hank and the men sitting with him. Ann just watched now that Mom had arrived.

"Don't apologize to him!" Every eye in the room was on us now.

"Megan!" Mom said.

"He doesn't work in real estate! He works for XT Energy!"

"Is that true, Hank?" Dad asked.

"I'm afraid it is," Hank admitted.

"I'm not sure I understand," Ann said, looking between Hank and Sam Lanham.

Hank stood and took a step to his right.

"I can explain."

Dad stepped across him, pinning him in.

"Is there a housing development or not?" I felt more than saw Mom's hand go over her mouth. "I'm waiting for an answer, Hank," Dad said, his voice now serious, and menacing. The room was silent.

"Sort of," Hank said quietly.

"But the drawings, the lots, the restrictions?" Dad asked.

"There's a clause," Hank said. "If all the lot holders

agree, they can change the covenants and restrictions."

"I own six," Sam said.

"Four," a younger guy said, smirking.

"I got one too," said the last guy.

By now Silvio, Uncle Dan, and Simon had come over. Even Hunter, bless his heart, was with them, ready to back Dad up.

"You told us it was for our protection. It had to be unanimous."

"It *is* unanimous," Hank said. "XT Energy, its employees and board members own all the lots. And they're agreed—they don't want to build houses."

"Oh my dear God," Mom said. There was nothing more to say.

"You dirty son of a bitch," Dad said. "You can forget about this deal."

The men at the table stood. Sam Lanham, the older man, took off his mask.

"It's too late, Angus," Sam said. "The papers are signed—you took the money."

Dad glared at him.

"I'll sue your ass," Dad said to Sam.

"You'll lose," Sam said. How could he be so calm? The Aberdeen, my ranch, my family's ranch, the ranch that had been in business for over a century, would be fracked, blown to bits and pieces, just like my party.

I looked at Hank.

"It was never me, was it? You did it all to get the ranch."

"I'm sorry, Megan—truly. It was just business."

"But why me? Why not Julia? She's way prettier."

He shrugged. "That's why. I thought you'd be . . . easier."

Dad grabbed him by the scruff, hoisted him, and reared back with his fist.

"Do it and I'll sue you!" Hank said, dangling there.

Dad paused. Looked around. Only about nine hundred witnesses, and Hank had done nothing illegal. Dad's eyes narrowed as he considered.

"Sue *me*, motherfucker!" I shouted as I delivered the haymaker Dad planned. I threw it from my shoes, with everything I had, and it caught Hank flush between the eyes. I felt the cartilage in his nose give way, and blood spurted out. My wig flew off from the jolt, and a searing pain shot from my hand through to my shoulder.

All hell broke loose as the oilmen came at Dad. Dad ducked a punch and nailed Sam in the face, then took a shot from a younger guy. Silvio, Uncle Dan, Simon, and even Hunter jumped into the fray. It was a classic saloon fight, right out of an old western. Men joined in on both sides, and chairs and tables flew. Some ladies ran for the exits while others pulled out phones to capture it on video. I clutched my bruised hand and watched.

⟨꙾⟩

The ballroom was near-empty. Those who remained were bruised and bloody with torn costumes and broken masks—friends and family. Ann had disappeared. Hank was long gone, probably to a hospital to have his nose reset. I soaked my hand in a wine bucket full of ice water. Dad held a towel full of ice against his cheek.

"I'm so sorry, Mom," I said. "I tried to wait."

"It's okay, honey," she said. She looked around, bereft.

"Lucy, you wanna dance?" Dad asked Mom.

"Angus, please."

"What the hell? The band's paid for. And I haven't danced with my wife yet."

"I'll dance with you," I said, and removed my hand, dried it with a napkin. "But let's change the mood."

I went over to the musicians, who had been waiting uncomfortably for some sign from us.

"Hey, you guys feel like cranking it up?" I asked. The band leader perked up.

"Sure."

"Do it. Something rowdy."

I went to the bar.

"You guys got any Tecate back there?"

The bartender popped a longneck and handed it to me. I squeezed a lime in it, took a good swallow. Then another.

"Ice a few more, would you?"

"Yes, ma'am."

I grabbed two more and a handful of limes, and headed back to the table as the band—a chamber orchestra— scratched out the first notes of "Up Against the Wall Redneck Mother." Perfect. I offered Dad my good hand and we went out onto the dance floor.

Simon and Julia joined us. And then, reluctantly, so did Mom, dancing with Hunter. For the next couple of hours we left the disaster behind. We drank beer and ate cold pig and laughed and danced and hugged and cried, and then laughed some more. Those who stayed still swear it turned out to be the party of the season, if not the decade.

Twenty-Six

In Which Megan Single-Handedly Takes on Big Oil

UNFORTUNATELY, TOMORROW WAS ANOTHER DAY, OR more accurately the next afternoon was another day, because I didn't get out of bed until two. After all the hoopla, an ER doctor at Parkland set my hand in a cast at 4 a.m. I had a boxer's fracture—a transverse fracture of the fifth metacarpal.

"Third one I've done tonight," he said to me. "But the first in a ball gown."

I found Mom and Dad and Julia hungover at the kitchen table, sipping coffee and facing the cold reality of our situation. XT Energy now owned the ranch, and planned to frack it. We were rich but had given up millions of dollars in the process. Hank Waterhouse had screwed us over—me literally—and done his company proud. *He's probably not in the crappy junior office anymore*, I thought, not cheering myself up.

I poured some coffee and sat.

"I can't believe I brought this on us."

"Megan," Dad said, "this ranch, and any deal for it, is my responsibility. Hank fooled all of us, me included."

"If I hadn't pushed so hard," Mom said. "I wanted it so bad—but not this." Dad reached for her hand. "Never like this."

"I know," Dad said.

The doorbell rang. Julia went to the door, and then came back to the kitchen, wide-eyed.

"Uh, Megan? Andrew Gage is here to see you."

"Here?"

"In the front hall."

Mom, Dad, and Julia all looked at me.

"I don't know why he's here." I left them.

I had said nothing about my run-in with Andrew at the Plaza, not even to Julia. What would I have said? *Hey, did I mention that Andrew Gage has secretly had the hots for me since the beginning of the deb season and tried to tell me that Hank was a bad guy but I ignored him?*

"Andrew."

"Sorry to just drop in, but I wanted to speak to you—in person."

"Sure. You want to sit down?" I motioned toward the living room.

"Um, how about a walk?" he asked.

"Any photographers out there?" I asked teasingly.

He laughed, shook his head.

"I didn't call them."

"Me neither," I said.

We went down the front steps. Walked across the driveway

toward the barn, then started out across a pasture, not headed anywhere really, just farther away from the house. It was a typical December afternoon, brisk but sunny, and we steadily increased our pace, tramping out well beyond the barns. Neither of us spoke, but it was a comfortable silence.

"That was some punch," he said, finally. I stopped.

"You were there?" He nodded. "The horse mask—that was you." He nodded again.

"Georgie called me after she got off the phone with you. When she said you thought Hank had done something bad to you, I . . . I had to come." His words made my stomach go flip-flop.

"You came to protect me?" I asked.

"Megan McKnight, you don't need anyone to protect you. But I was very . . . concerned."

For months I had slapped this guy down, but he still had my back. It was thrilling.

"Andrew—I'm so sorry. I didn't listen to you. You tried to warn me about Hank, and I ignored you. And all the things I said about you in New York? I was wrong."

He stared at me for a moment and then laughed, hard. Not what I had expected.

"What's so funny?"

"Not funny," he said. "Just . . . exasperating."

"What do you mean?"

"I came out here to apologize to you, and you beat me to it."

"Apologize—why?"

"For this whole situation. It's my fault, my family's fault."

I didn't understand. "We knew who Hank was, the kind of person he is—and we kept silent. Worse, we rewarded him, because we were afraid—of bad publicity, a scandal, some slight to our name. We were too . . . proud. We should have exposed him. Maybe if my dad had still been alive, we would have handled it better—but we didn't. We kicked the can down the road and it landed on you and your family. I'm so sorry."

The quality and sincerity of his apology surprised me.

"Wow. You're forgiven. Right here, right now."

"Thank you," he said.

We turned back toward the house. This guy was absolutely not who I thought he was. He was warm and sincere and thoughtful. I . . . liked him.

"I'm jealous, you know." We stood in the driveway. "I've wanted to hit Hank for a long time."

"What?" I asked, laughing. "You mean you didn't get any licks in after I softened him up for you?"

"No! I tried but I got tied up with some other asshole. But I gotta tell you, that's the most fun I've had since I was a kid. I never get to do that kind of stuff, because it gets reported."

"You just need to hang with my family more. My great-great-aunt fought in the Mexican Revolution!"

"You clearly get it from somewhere." He looked out over the grasslands. "It's so beautiful. It's a shame what they're planning."

I waved as he drove off and thought, *I really don't know him at all*.

ᖗᘿᕼ

I didn't go back inside after Andrew left. Instead I walked for a while, just around the Aberdeen, until I arrived at a metal equipment shed. Years ago, after Mom complained long enough and loud enough about me peppering the garage door with a soccer ball, Dad had painted a goal on the side of the shed for me to practice on. It was well away from the house and he figured no matter how hard I practiced, it wouldn't do any harm.

I found an old ball and started thumping it off the side of the shed. The goal lines were faded, but still there. This was my way of thinking. And the more I thought, the angrier I got. *We can't just give up the ranch and let it be destroyed!* After another half hour of kicking that ball against the shed, I had an idea.

What if we could somehow get the state of Texas to designate the Aberdeen as a historical landmark? The more important question was, would that prevent XT from drilling? I didn't know the answer, but I knew someone who did. And I realized even though he'd just left the ranch, I really wanted to hear his voice again.

"It depends," Andrew said. I reached him before he arrived back in Dallas, and we agreed to meet at the Starbucks in Highland Park Village. He understood immediately what

I was getting at. I was using a play from his playbook. He thought for a bit longer. "It's always murky. The stipulations likely won't prevent drilling outright, but the language in these things is usually ambiguous enough that we could threaten them with a lawsuit. That might be enough for them to reconsider."

"What should I do?"

"You need to ask your family if they're up for it," he said. "It's risky, and expensive, and there's no guarantee you'll win. You might use up all your resources and still lose. I've seen it happen."

"Look, this is in your wheelhouse and . . . I need some . . . help."

He paused. "From me?" he asked.

"Yes." I sighed. "From you. Would you please help me explain it to them?"

"Nothing would make me happier."

So for the second time that day Andrew Gage drove to the Aberdeen and we sat at the kitchen table and explained the plan to Mom and Dad.

"So first you get the landmark designation," Andrew said, recapping. "*Then* tell XT Energy you have it and—this is the important part—you tell them you'll return the money if they'll rip up the contract. And if they won't, you'll sue."

"Why do it that way?" Dad asked.

"If you go in guns blazing, they're more likely just to start shooting back. Give them a reasonable out."

Dad nodded and Andrew told them plainly this was a calculated gamble, but we had to be prepared to return to the financial Armageddon we'd just escaped—heavy debt, large bills, even larger now, and a dim future. But we'd have the Aberdeen back.

Andrew and I waited while Mom and Dad thought through all this. It had caught them by surprise, for sure. Dad, torn, looked over at Mom, gauging her appetite for a fight.

"You know what I say?" Mom sounded surprisingly chipper. We all turned to her and waited for her to continue. "I say McKnights have faced longer odds than these, and if we stick together we'll come through this too."

"But Lucy," Dad said, "what about the bills, the debt?"

"What about 'em?"

"Honey, you've been counting on this sale to get us out. For our future."

"Yeah, but I know something that I didn't know before. You care more about *us* than this land. So if you want to fight, I'll stand by you to the end. Besides, there's plenty of beef in the freezer—it'll be a long time before we starve."

"God, I love you, woman," he said, and they kissed, hard, and he pulled her closer, hugged her to his chest.

In that moment I understood the depth of their love, and I felt bad for all the times I'd judged my mother harshly. In our darkest moment she was standing taller than any of us.

"Girls?" Dad looked to me and Julia.

"I'm in," I said.

"Me too," Julia added.

"It won't be easy," Dad warned.

"Nothing worth it ever is," Mom answered.

♁

XT Energy occupied the top three floors of a glass and steel building just off Central Expressway near Northwest Highway—the same building Hank "worked" in. From the conference room you could see Northpark Mall, and in the distance downtown Dallas. I had driven by it many times, but never been in it until that afternoon.

For the past hour Uncle Dan had laid out our position to a silent and stoic Sam Lanham, four random suits, and a petulant Hank Waterhouse. Hank still had plaster across his nose, and two black eyes. Sam and his boys had skinned cheeks and cracked lips, as did Uncle Dan and Dad. I spent the meeting staring at Hank, who never met my eyes.

We had the historic site designation. Mom called her old flame Hardy, who pushed it through before the Christmas recess. It prohibited "material changes," and we were prepared to file a motion the moment anything larger than a pickup passed the gates. But, if they wanted to tear up the contract, we'd return the money.

"We'll be in touch," Sam said, and stood up. Uncle Dan began to gather papers, and Dad stood up, pushed his chair back. I sat at the gleaming conference table, stunned. *That's it?*

"Well?" I asked, once inside the elevator. Uncle Dan looked sanguine.

"Hard to say. The language is pretty clear, but they know as well as we do that lawsuits are never slam dunks."

We arrived in the parking garage.

"How long will they take to decide?" I asked.

Uncle Dan shrugged. "They're gonna think this through hard. They'll look for wiggle room, consult with their attorneys, try to figure out if we're really serious. There's the Christmas break. Ten days? A month is more likely."

"Ugh. And we just have to wait?"

"Afraid so," he answered.

∽

With our entire life in limbo, the weeks after our meeting at XT Energy were excruciating. Even Christmas didn't offer a distraction. Julia and I pleaded with Mom and Dad to forego gifts. We needed nothing, had already bought too much, and we could be pushed back into massive debt anytime the phone rang.

Relieved, my parents agreed, and we settled on a quiet Christmas at the ranch. We'd make a big breakfast and go for an afternoon ride, like we did when we were kids. We threw Mom one bone and let her buy us matching Christmas PJs, which was a family tradition. We opened them Christmas Eve. Mom went extra silly—red flannel footy pajamas with dancing snowmen and penguins. We put them on and had hot cocoa with mini marshmallows downstairs and then went up to bed early. Julia and I always slept in the same bed on Christmas Eve. When we were girls we stayed up too late giggling and talking, waiting and waiting for the hooves to clatter on the roof. Finally Dad would come up and tell us to go to sleep or Santa wouldn't come at all. That night we lay under her quilt face-to-face, inches apart, enjoying the familiar comfort, the shared memories of all those Christmases at the ranch.

"I'm so proud of you," Julia whispered. "You are so brave."

"I don't feel brave. I've been terrified the whole time."

"Being brave doesn't mean you're not scared. It's being scared and doing it anyway."

"I can't believe you won't be there next week with me," I said. "You should be. You should do it next year."

"Hey, if everything goes the way we hope it does, we won't be able to afford it next year."

"That's true."

"But I don't think I'd do it anyway," Julia said.

"Why? I thought you loved it."

"I did. But I think I got what I needed—even if I don't do the walk across the stage."

"I love you so much, Julia." I reached over and put my hand on hers, and squeezed.

"I love you too, Megan." She squeezed my hand back.

I held on to her hand, and in a few minutes her breathing

deepened and she slept. Long before any reindeer landed, I fell asleep too.

We padded downstairs the next morning and in lieu of gifts, Mom had put out a spread—huevos rancheros, chila quiles, bacon, biscuits, gravy, and a gallon of dark coffee. We stuffed ourselves with comfort food, then lolled on the couch.

"I did get you girls one small thing," Dad said.

"Dad! You promised—no gifts!" Julia said.

"They didn't cost nothing but time," he said. Okay, now we were intrigued. He handed us each a flat box, about a foot square. Weighty.

"That's a pretty heavy sweater," I joked.

Julia and I tore open the boxes, and inside each found a small sculpture he'd made from two large horseshoes welded into an *M*, with a smaller one welded perpendicular. Together they formed the letters *Mc*. Our first names were engraved in the upper-left crescent.

"You made these?" Julia asked.

He nodded. "I got to thinking after that sculpture show. Now I gotta admit they aren't art, but—"

"They're awesome," I said. We both hugged him. I thought about all the crap I'd wanted all those years, all the crap I'd received. This piece of scrap iron would be the one Christmas gift I would keep forever and pass down to my kids.

Later, Julia helped me practice the Texas Dip in the living room. When my knee hit the ground I always bumped noticeably, and even with a chair I couldn't get all the way down to the floor. Somehow my back leg just wouldn't get out of the way. I feared I had done too many squats, had run too much. My thigh muscles were just too big for such a graceful move.

"Again," Julia said. I bent forward, one hand on the chair. While I scooched and prodded my body down, the doorbell rang and a moment later Zach Battle appeared in the doorway, with Mom behind him.

"Hi, Julia—Megan, Merry Christmas," Zach said. He held a small box.

"Merry Christmas, Zach," I said.

"Merry Christmas," Julia said. Awkward silence followed.

"Would you like some breakfast?" Mom asked.

"No—thanks. Um, I was wondering if I could have a moment alone—with Julia."

"Absolutely," I said, and dragged Mom to the kitchen. We then snuck back to listen at the edge of the doorway.

"I brought you something," Zach said. He handed Julia the box.

She opened it and pulled out a small dancing elf who said "Sorry" over and over.

"First off, let's get one thing straight. I am a jackass."

"I agree," Julia said, stifling a smile.

"I am more than sorry. I wanted to give you some breathing space, to work things out, and I went to New York. And then before I knew it three days had passed, and I felt like a jerk, and I thought maybe you didn't want to talk to me, and then I waited so long I just got—paralyzed. Finally, Andrew called me and said, 'Stop being a coward and go see her.' I never, ever meant to hurt you and I really hope you can find your way to giving me another chance."

"I like you, Zach. And I appreciate the apology—it helps. And maybe we could have something. But not now. Not for a while. I need some time to work out my own stuff before I add a boyfriend back into the mix."

"I'll wait," Zach said.

"It might be a long while," Julia answered, grinning.

"That's okay," Zach said. "I've got time!"

Then she smiled. "I'll make you a good-faith gesture," she said.

Zach looked up, expectant—hopeful.

"I need a date for the Bluebonnet Ball this Saturday. How about we start the clock after that?"

"I'm your man."

Mom spontaneously hugged me.

As Julia waved to Zach, Dad came to the kitchen door. He looked thoughtful as he put his phone in his back pocket.

"What is it?" Mom asked.

"Sam Lanham called. We can have the Aberdeen back."

"You're joking," Mom said. But he wasn't. We really looked at each other then. Were we willing to give back the money and take back the ranch, with all the debt, and the work, and the cows, and the worry? *No-brainer*, I thought.

"Well, I say Merry Christmas!" I shouted. Dad hugged Mom, and then me, and Julia came in and made it four.

Zipped into my tight beaded bodice with yards of flowing tulle skirt, with tiny yellow roses woven in my hair, and my makeup model perfect, I struggled, working to get a long white glove over the cast on my broken right hand. I pulled. I pulled again. I stretched and pulled. But it would not go on.

"I can't do this!" I said.

"Leave it," Margot said casually.

"I have to wear gloves!" I cried. By this time, after more than two hours primping to get ready, with the limo waiting downstairs, I was a wreck. I just wanted it to be over.

"But your cast—it looks enough like a glove. I think it's emblematic of your struggle."

"I was planning for my Texas Dip to be emblematic of my struggle."

"Stop worrying about this dip. Who cares? What if you only go three quarters, or everyone can see you put down one knee—what happens? Prison?"

"Nothing."

"Will you be less of a woman?"

"No."

"Forget it, then. Do your best and be satisfied. Being a grown woman means embracing who you really are, your true self—flaws, mistakes, all of it. Look at me." Here she gestured to her hippie getup du jour—a calico blue-and-white flowered prairie dress that ended just below her knee. She wore creased combat boots with red laces, and I could see the hair on her legs. "Is it for everyone? No. But it is *me*—and it makes me happy. You be you."

Twenty-Seven

In Which Megan Does Her Version of the Texas Dip

THE FORMAL BLUEBONNET DEBUT BALL TOOK PLACE AT
eight o'clock on December 31 in the ballroom of the Mansion
on Turtle Creek. The themes were evergreen—tradition,
prestige, and wealth. The linen draping the tables was thick
enough for a tapestry. The heavy silver gleamed. The goblets
shone. The crystal sparkled. Each table featured a spare and
simple yellow rose centerpiece. Women wore classic, formal
gowns. Their husbands and dates wore white tie.

From the stage a walkway extended out into the tables,
and soon each of us would emerge, move across the stage
with our father as an escort, then leave him and walk to
the end of the catwalk. There we would pause, perform the
Texas Dip, acknowledge the guests on both sides, and when
we returned our debut journey would be over.

Backstage we waited in the greenroom like fighters before a title bout, the atmosphere tense and fueled with adrenaline. Sydney and Abby adjusted their elbow-length white

gloves. Ashley One smoothed a wrinkle from her gown, and Ashley Two checked her hair and makeup one last time in the mirror. I sat by myself, calm and reserved. My gown was perfect, my hair and makeup too. I looked down at the one elbow-length white silk glove on my left hand, and then at my right—from the fist to the elbow just my sparkling white plaster cast. I wiggled my fingers.

The one anxious person backstage was Ann Foster. She was on her phone trying to find out just why Lauren Battle had not yet arrived. It was very close to showtime, and no-body, not even Ashley Two, knew where she was. Ann had spoken to her mother, who said she had left hours before. Ann was now leaving Lauren a message.

"So please call me the instant you receive this message," Ann said. She ended the call.

"A no-show?" I asked hopefully. "Has that ever hap-pened before?"

"Never," Ann replied.

"Where is she?" Ann turned toward the words, spoken from the door. I knew that voice the second I heard it.

"I need to see Megan McKnight!" Mrs. Gage said.

Ann stepped in her way.

"I'm very sorry, Mrs. Gage, but this is completely inap-propriate. She's—"

"Do you not hear well?" Ann recoiled. I felt pretty sure nobody had ever asked Ann that before tonight. "I am not here to speak with you—I am here to speak with Megan McKnight."

She saw me and blew past Ann. Lauren Battle, in her gown and gloves, followed her in. She had been crying, and her makeup was a mess.

"Well? What do you have to say for yourself?" Mrs. Gage peered down at me.

"How about, 'I'm a dirty backstabbing boyfriend-stealing bitch'?" Lauren put in.

"I'll handle this," Mrs. Gage said to Lauren.

"Mrs. Gage, this is really not the time." Ann again stepped between us. "Now, I'm sorry, but you will have to leave. And Lauren, you need to clean up—we start in fifteen minutes."

"It's okay, Ann," I said, and stood up. "You help Lauren." I stepped past Ann till I was toe-to-toe with Mrs. Gage. We were in a similar weight class, she and I. "Now how may I help you?" I asked.

All the girls drew closer.

"Andrew has broken it off with Lauren, and there are rumors," Mrs. Gage said. "Not that I believe them, but there are rumors that he is seeing you."

"It seems to me, Mrs. Gage, that you coming all the way down here is more likely to support those rumors than dispel them."

Gotta hand it to the broad, she could take a punch. I hit her right in the face with that, and she didn't flinch. Word of her arrival had spread, and several mothers appeared now—Mom and Aunt Camille among them. They too moved closer.

"Cheeky girl. Do you know who I am?"

"Yeah," I said. "I know who you are."

"Then you know Gages sailed on the *Mayflower*. We have been governors, senators, and statesmen for hundreds of years. Andrew will join this line. He will be a very important man one day, and I can say categorically that *you* are not the girl for him."

"Does your son know you're here?" I asked.

"My son does not always know what's best for himself— or his family. But trust me when I say I do."

"And that includes paying off Hank Waterhouse and allowing him to prey on others?" Several girls gasped, and Ann narrowed her eyes at Mrs. Gage.

"Enough! Just tell me, in simple English—are you seeing my son?"

I rose to my full height and stared down Mrs. Gage, but remembered Ann's maxim: *You don't have to say everything you think.*

"No."

"Well, thank God for that!" Mrs. Gage said, and Lauren cried in relief. But rather than leave it at that, she bared her teeth at me again. "You are never to see him again. Do I make myself clear?"

"I beg your pardon, Mrs. Gage, but Andrew is my friend. He's helped my family and supported me, and I intend to do the same for him whenever he needs me to. Now please—leave."

The vein that ran from her temple bulged and pulsed. Her eyes dilated and her nostrils flared. I hoped she would keel over right in front of me.

"Mrs. Gage, you have insulted me in every possible way. But trust me that I will not only survive, I will endure. I am a native Texan. My great-great-grandfather faced down wolves and cougars alone on the prairie, and if he can survive that, I can certainly survive an invasion from a Yankee blowhard in a wool suit. Now if you will excuse me, I have a debut to make."

Mrs. Gage didn't move. Abby stepped to my left shoulder, in solidarity. Then Sydney moved to my right. Ashley One moved in beside Abby. A phalanx of Texas debutantes glared at Mrs. Gage.

"She said *leave*," Sydney said coldly.

Mrs. Gage stayed.

"You heard her—go on," Abby added, a distinct twang in her voice.

And then, with no cards left to play, Mrs. Gage huffed and walked out. I took a deep breath and looked at the faces around me.

"Geez—thanks, y'all," I said, and they whooped it up. I high-fived Abby and Sydney, and then, to my everlasting surprise, I high-fived Ann Foster. My mom and Aunt Camille all came in to give us a hug. Even Ashley Two threw me a look of admiration as she helped Lauren spackle her face.

"You're really not mad?" I asked Ann a moment later.

"Gracious no, Megan. I am proud, so proud of you." Tears formed in the corners of her eyes.

"You are?"

"Look at you now—everything you were and so much more." She hugged me hard, her face pressing into my dress. "Oh shit!" she said, jumping back, worried that she had smeared my dress. It was the first curse word she'd ever said around us, and we all cracked up.

"Megan, do you need a moment?" Mom asked softly. I took a breath.

"I do. Thanks, Mom." We looked to Ann—was that allowed?

"We begin in ten minutes. Be back in five," Ann said.

Mom and I walked arm in arm down a hallway and outside onto a back veranda. It was a quiet space surrounded by oak trees. I took several deep breaths, then turned to her.

"Thanks, Mom—for insisting I do this."

"You're welcome."

"You were absolutely right. I made unforgettable memories that I will cherish for the rest of my life." How would I ever forget Hank's face as I drove my fist into it? Or the five little tweens oohing and aaahing in the locker room? Or Ann—at that first tea, the first deportment class, our graduation, and tonight? I would never forget Margot, or the women at Refuge. I certainly wasn't going to forget Andrew Gage.

"I'm so glad. I just felt sure that one day you would need skills beyond . . . dribbling. Every young woman does." She hugged me, tight. "That's what you are, you know—a lovely and beautiful and strong young woman."

"A lot like you, I bet," I said.

"Too much like me," she agreed.

"I love you, Mom." I willed myself not to cry.

"I love you too. It's hard between mothers and daughters, isn't it?" she asked.

I nodded. "But we have the rest of our lives to work on it," I said.

"You take the time you need, honey. I'm going to find my seat."

She gave my shoulder a squeeze and blew me a kiss as she left. I walked to the edge of the low stone wall and looked out. Through the trees I could see the buildings of downtown Dallas, lit in white and green and red lights.

I heard the sound of footsteps running. When I turned toward them, Andrew Gage was standing there. He wore jeans and a T-shirt and sneakers. His hair was windblown. He had never looked better.

"Andrew? What are you doing here?"

He was slightly out of breath. "My mom's in Texas and I had to see you before she—"

"She was already here."

"Oh, God. Look—whatever she said, it's not true."

"She said you had broken up with Lauren."

His brow crinkled. "Oh. That's true."

"I'm glad." I smiled at him, and he smiled back. He came over to stand in front of me. He took my hand, and I felt the jolt of connection.

"Look, the last time I tried to say this, in New York, it didn't go very well," he said quietly.

"A lot's happened since then."

"I really think I've fallen in love with you, Megan. And if you don't feel the same way, I'll understand, but if there is even one chance you do . . . I have to know."

What answer could I give? Only the truth.

"I think about you every day," I told him.

He kissed me. Hard. And I kissed him back.

"The Eyes of Texas" began to play and Ann stuck her head out the door.

"Megan! We're starting." We broke our kiss, but he still held me.

"I have to go," I said. "Will you be here after?"

"I'm not going anywhere."

Backstage, the six of us waited in the wings, in alphabetical order, to make our entrance. I was next to last, with only Sydney behind me.

"Miss Ashley Harriet Abernathy!"

Ashley One emerged, took her dad's arm, and walked gracefully to the center of the stage. From there she walked steadily alone to the end of the catwalk and performed a very acceptable Texas Dip. Her legs folded slowly beneath her, and her head nearly touched the floor. Then she rose easily and walked back. Her dad brought her backstage.

"Way to go, Ashley," Abby whispered, and fist-bumped her, and all of us except Lauren stepped forward to congratulate her quietly. Ann gave her a long hug.

"Miss Lauren Eloise Battle!"

Lauren emerged to loud applause and took her father's arm. She walked quickly, but on the catwalk she teetered ever so slightly. At the edge she gathered herself, and then began her Texas Dip. She bowed and folded and let her head fall to the side, and the crowd clapped loudly. She stayed down and they clapped harder, showing appreciation for the depths of her bow. The clapping slowed when she failed to rise, and stopped altogether when she lifted her head and mouthed "help me!" to her father. He hustled out and with an assist she rose and made her way backstage. Hot tears poured down her face, and though Ashley Two reached toward her, Lauren dodged and ran out, ignoring all of us too. We shared a look. *So sad.*

"Miss Ashley Diann Kohlberg!"

Ashley Two gathered herself, went out, and dipped just fine.

"Miss Margaret Abigail Lucas!"

"Go, Abby!" I whispered up to her.

She beamed and went out to wild clapping. I would be next, and then Sydney. I still fretted over my Texas Dip. I knew I had never really dropped all the way down, and had never been able to really get my back leg out of the way. I was considering a radical new move when Sydney spoke to me for the first time since the Nasher luncheon.

"I never thought you'd keep it a secret," she said quietly. I knew instantly what she was talking about.

"Really, why?" I asked, glancing back. She looked thoughtful and earnest.

"Just—your sister was in this, and your cousin. Not that you'd be mean about it, but I was sure you'd tell them, and three people can't keep a secret. I spent the last four months just waiting for the shoe to drop, but you really never told anyone, did you?"

"Not a soul. I didn't think it was anybody's business."

"I never thought I'd make it this far," she said. "Once it came out I figured they'd dump me, or Lauren and Ashley would make it so hard on me I wouldn't be able to stay. I was so freaked out that a month ago I came out to my parents— just to prepare them for what was coming."

"Wow. And?"

"Best thing I ever did," she said. "Anyway, just wanted to say thanks—and good luck."

"You're welcome. You too."

Abby came back and gave me the big thumbs-up. We fist-bumped as she went to give Ann a hug. I smoothed my dress and wet my lips, stepped to the edge of the curtain.

"Miss Megan Lucille McKnight!"

I emerged into the hot, bright lights and heard the applause. I took Dad's arm and he led me slowly, majestically to the center of the stage. I nodded to him politely and started down the catwalk. It seemed very long and the crowd dim and far away. *You got this*, I thought, and two steps from the end I decided to try a version of the Texas Dip I had never practiced, and never heard any other deb talk about. Out there exposed alone under the lights, I was on a tightrope without a net.

I stopped and looked at the crowd, and began to bow. But instead of folding my right leg behind me, I simply let it stick straight out in front and did a pistol—a one-legged squat—on my left leg. I did them all the time in workouts, and with my wide skirt nobody could see which way my right leg was pointing. On only my left foot I lowered myself in one smooth and graceful and continuous motion all the way to the floor. The applause grew and my leg quivered slightly under the strain, but nobody could see it. I held my bow a full extra second. Just as the crowd thought I might be in trouble like Lauren, I flexed my left quad hard and squeezed my gluteus maximus tight and easily pushed myself back to standing. The crowd roared its approval at my devastatingly perfect Texas Dip. I smiled and waved in both directions, and scooted back to Dad, who led me backstage with a proud smile. I had arrived.

Afterward there were hugs, and Mom told a large crowd about my talk with Mrs. Gage, how I had invoked old Angus, then finished by saying, *"Now if you'll excuse me, I have a debut to make!"* Everyone died laughing and this remark enshrined me as a folk hero in Bluebonnet lore.

Zach and Julia congratulated me, and Julia held on to me fiercely.

"I am so proud of you!" Julia said.

The first dance was always dads and daughters. Out on the dance floor, Dad put one hand on my shoulder, the other on my waist, and we turned slowly to the music.

"Did you grow taller?" he asked.

"These are three-inch heels!"

"Where did you learn to walk in three-inch heels?"

"I've learned a lot of things in the past few months," I answered.

"Me too. Was it as bad as you thought?"

"No."

"Good, because I never, ever want to make you unhappy."

"You could never make me unhappy, Dad."

As the song ended, Andrew appeared beside Dad.

"May I?" Andrew asked formally. Dad nodded and gave way. Andrew held me and we began to dance.

"I've been thinking about something," I said a moment later.

"What?"

"Well, if I'm in Dallas, and you're in New York, how are we ever going to see each other—Skype?"

"Actually," he said, "I'll be spending a lot of time down here in the next year or so."

"Why's that?"

"I have a new venture. I'm developing a historic ranch in Texas."

I stopped dancing and put my hands on his shoulders.

"You're joking, right?"

"I told you I like to recycle historic things. I'm buying the Aberdeen."

"Shut the front door!" I said, and whacked him on the arm with my cast.

"Your dad showed me Hank's plans, and I thought, why not do it that way?"

I found my dad's face in the crowd, and he nodded. Andrew now put both hands around my waist, and pulled me toward him. It was . . . comfortable.

"But don't think I did it just because I like you, or out of charity. I'm gonna make some serious money on this." He noticed the worry on my face. "What's wrong?"

"It's just—look, I'm worried about my dad. What's he gonna do now, without a job?"

"Oh, he's got a job."

"I don't understand."

"That's the best part," Andrew said. "It's the one thing Hank missed. You wall off a chunk, keep part of the historic cattle ranch at the center of the whole thing, but scaled down—fewer horses, fewer cows, no expectation to make money. It makes the whole thing authentic, and you keep the historic designation. The development really will sell itself."

I had been horrible to this man. I had insulted him, been rude to him, humiliated him in the tabloids. He'd seen me at my worst, with all my defenses down, and he still liked me. *No, he said he loved me.* I knew I could be myself around him, and it gave me hope. I put my head on Andrew's shoulder and we began to dance again, and other couples joined in: Mom and Dad, Julia and Zach, Uncle Dan and Aunt Camille, Abby and Hunter, all the other moms and dads.

I saw them all, maybe for the first time, as they really were: complex, flawed, human, and beautiful. Mom could be manipulative and demanding and still have my best interests at heart. Margot could dress like a gnome and still have great taste in clothes. Andrew could be awkward and disgustingly rich and still be an amazing guy. I could be a tough jock and rock a ball gown.

I'd been so worried that making my debut would change me, but here I was, at the end of it all, and I was still me. Only better.